When [illegible]*ke*

When We Last Spoke

Marci Henna

Happiness grows at our own firesides
and is not to be picked in strangers' gardens.
—Douglas Jerrold

For my handsome husband, Louis,
my far better half—whose steadfast love
and encouragement have moved mountains and
whose deep intelligence, good nature, and genuine
concern for the welfare of others have made
all the difference.

And also in memory of my brother, Michael Gipson,
and father, Jules Gipson, who passed away during
the writing of this novel.

One

Ruby came to me for the first time last week, years after her death. Now it was December of 2002, and I was having a walleyed cleaning fit, starting with all four rooms in her and my grandfather Walt's yellow brick and gingerbread house. Well, it was my home now, but their claim upon the house felt almost as strong as it was upon me.

For the most part, I'd left the house exactly as I'd remembered from my childhood. Grandmother Ruby's kitchen was a virtual museum, a monument to the jillions of perfect pies and cakes that had been baked there. Even the old rotary phone remained, although the party line was long gone. It was the excess of useless items I wanted to unload, however. My whirlwind mission to rid the entire homestead of mangled drugstore eyeglasses, old canned goods that could kill on contact, and hole-infested 1940s vintage cotton stockings was my way of working through a bad case of nerves.

My only sibling was coming to visit for Christmas, and my anxiety was justified, according to the sorry state of our sisterhood.

It had taken me a solid month to talk one-on-one with Evangeline, and I had somewhat neglected my House of Cranbourne homemaking shop in town. I hadn't made quite as much orange-peel potpourri as usual, or as many lime westerner and rum cakes, which represent only a fraction of my products that make entertaining more delightful for the homemakers of Fireside.

I had managed, though, to write Saturday's copy for *Juliet's Fireside Variety Hour*, broadcast every Saturday afternoon on station KOFF. My involvement with the local Central Texas radio station represented my version of a marriage—it was how I spent my nights and weekends.

When I finally heard from my sister, I asked why she hadn't called me back right away. As usual, she plucked an excuse out of the air. Bless her pea-picking heart. She'd always been busy with her fruit trees, and you know how hectic that can be. You see, Evangeline was an Oregon State University plant geneticist who conducted research on the *Rosaceae* family of fruits, especially peach and plum trees, so that their disease resistance could be enhanced.

She'd grown up watching Texas fruit growers suffer each season due to various blights and had wanted to make a difference. Her work had received international recognition, but it could be done in Texas as well as Oregon. I thought she ought to come home and work in the Hill Country like she intended, and I couldn't help but wonder whether she'd stayed away because of me.

I had told Evangeline that we needed to pick out a headstone for Walt and Ruby. Now was as good a time as any. She ought to come on down to Fireside, and we'd spend the holidays together. It had been way too long.

Anything I had ever suggested to my sister met with bullheaded resistance. She'd sighed heavily and said no—that I ought to go ahead and decide for both of us because she just couldn't bear to do it.

I had shot right back—well, neither could I, so we ought to just do it together. We were sisters, weren't we?

There was dead silence for a minute or two, and finally she'd replied, "Oh, thunder, Juliet." She just couldn't totally commit about coming in case something hot came up with her current experiments.

That inability of hers to commit to anything other than genetics about drove me out on my tin roof. So I just let her have it as it came to me. I said something like *hell's bells,* I wouldn't want to come between her and her piddling peach and plum seedlings. I told her I knew she was boiling in that fast-paced, pressure-cooker, tree-watching industry. Didn't she realize that honoring the memory of Walt and Ruby was way more important than how a plant was growing?

I had hung up Ruby's black rotary phone and sulked, worrying Evangeline wouldn't come at all. A week later, however, I received a fax in my office of Evangeline's itinerary into Austin-Bergstrom International Airport.

After I had finished cleaning the house and was still on a roll, I went out back and tackled the storm cellar. That dank, concrete-walled room looked like a Pompeii grocery store—as if everything had been suddenly abandoned and left to ripen for over two thousand years.

Ruby's musty old cellar was shoulder deep in Ball jars of gaseous peach, watermelon rind, tomato, and fig preserves. The jars were buried up to their necks in mold and dust. Ruby once told me that jellies and jams lasted forever. That was what Walt told her, and he was always right about everything. It was the row of canned sauerkraut that was the chigger in my drawers, however. Let me just say that if one broken jar had combined with leaky, biliously ancient peach preserves, the gas explosion would have blown the ranch clear out of Maitlin County.

Eight years had stacked one atop the other since Ruby had gone on to heaven and motioned for Walt to follow. I'd have just as soon eaten a truckload of beets than clean out the cellar because the job unnerved me. For one thing, it was Ruby's hideout, and I was an intruder. For another, the cellar was known to attract all sorts of slithering creatures.

I shined my flashlight nervously around the damp earthen floor, checking for king snakes, rattlers, and lizards. I saw no reptiles, just a bin of cobweb-covered potato eyes, a pile of rotted newspapers, dead bugs, empty garden pails stuccoed with dormant dirt-dauber nests, and Ruby's transistor radio.

I leaned down to pick up the radio and instantly felt as if she were standing behind me. You might not think that all my checkers are on the board by telling you this, but *she was there.* I couldn't see her, but I could feel her just as if she were in the flesh.

When Itasca was at her worst, Ruby hid out in the washhouse or her cellar—both places her mother-in-law wouldn't set foot in if you'd paid her. She'd light a kerosene lantern, perch on top of an old milking stool, cruise the radio dial for Elvis's music, and read the *Saturday Evening Post.* Her cellar that she'd dug herself in the 1940s ranked just below her Thunderbird and Walt.

From then on, I knew Ruby was with me. When I went back into the house to cook dinner on her broad electric stove, she was there. When I climbed into her and Walt's old feather bed to sleep, she climbed in too.

In my forties, and living alone in their house like I did, I began to feel the presence of Walt as well as Ruby. They both gave me pearls of wisdom just when I needed them.

I could almost hear Ruby whispering to shut the gate so the Herefords wouldn't trample her hens-and-chicks cacti along the sidewalk. Walt reminded me to trip the windmill to fill up the cattle troughs. Even after death, they had not abandoned me.

You might wonder why in creation it took Ruby so long to come to me (heaven knew that wherever Ruby went, Walt was close behind). All I can say is that timing is everything, and Ruby had something on her mind. If I hadn't been in her cellar, touching her radio, I might not have been sure it was she.

One day when I moved Ruby's kitchen table across from the woodbox to mop, June of 1967 hit me like a two-by-four between the eyes. I'd found a picture of our father, James Nelson Cranbourne, that had fluttered from its resting place on a shelf to lodge underneath the table's base. While he'd resembled Walt for the most part, he had Ruby's green eyes and determined mouth. He wore his army fatigues and stood posed with his hat in his hands near his tent outside Khe Sanh during the Tet Offensive. I had meant to put the photo in my gigantic bright-red scrapbook, but it was just another project of mine I'd yet to finish.

Our father was an only child and Ruby and Walt's blue-ribbon boy. He'd earned part of his college education by showing and selling prizewinning steers at the Maitlin County livestock show each January in Fireside. After high school, he married our mother, Marguerite Milford, and enrolled at the University of Texas at Austin. I came along nine months and fourteen days after they married. Evangeline arrived during the same month I was housebroken. I'm sure it was a very happy month for all.

Next, our father earned a bachelor's degree in history and had planned to go on to graduate school and eventually earn his doctorate so he could teach on the university level. He'd sat out for a year or two so he could earn some money for all our sakes, but that turned out to be a terrible mistake.

Then, because he'd registered for the draft in Fireside, land of few eligible draftees, his number came up. Mama thought he could have gotten out of it if he hadn't been so darned conscientious about being a patriotic American. He'd had to go straightaway to old Vietnam and fly Huey helicopters for the army. In my opinion, he should have gone to the Yukon or Ontario instead.

Our mama sang and danced like nobody's business. She won the Miss Talented Texas title by tap-dancing and singing to "Dixie." That was in 1957 before the Civil Rights movement got a good toehold. She went on from there to perform as Gretel in *Hansel and Gretel* in New York. Then, although she was three years older than Dad, she gave up all her fame to settle down and raise children when they married. She would have been happier, I suppose, if she'd held out to be in *Hello Dolly* or a James Bond girl.

She left us all for good when our father went off to Vietnam, saying it was a good time as any to get her career back on track. We waited every afternoon in our grandparents' front yard for her to come home. Eventually, parcels began to arrive in the mail from our mama. This delighted us and gave us something to hope for, but that is another story.

When we arrived to live with Walt and Ruby permanently during August of 1967, the words *sock it to me* and *flower power* were all over the airwaves. But their meaning escaped Evangeline and me. Our attention was focused upon what our mother had promised was to be our new greatest adventure ever, which, translated, meant that she was passing along parental responsibility to our father's parents.

The last time we saw our mother, she wore a cropped red blouse, blue jeans, and gigantic red sunglasses. She drove us in a 1960 blue Corvair and flicked cigarette ashes out the window all the way from Austin to Fireside. Five miles from Walt and Ruby's house, she tossed a final cigarette butt out on the dirt road and spritzed her clothing, hair, and tongue with lemon-scented cologne. Upon arrival, she carried our bag to the front door and waited impatiently for Ruby to answer.

Ruby came to the door wiping her hands on her apron from canning sweet corn, and opened it, little suspecting what was about to happen. If I'd been Ruby, I might have locked the screen door and lay down with a cool rag on my head until our mother had gone away. But Ruby just smiled and seemed overjoyed to see us. Imagine her confusion, however, when our mother proceeded to dump us on her, forever.

"I've got a life to live, and it isn't here. Just isn't. Take care of the girls. I'll be in touch." Then she told us to behave ourselves and walked away as fast as her bare feet could carry her.

As you can plainly see, our delivery to the ranch was more like a drive-by kid dropping, complete with clouds of dirt issuing from squealing tires.

Evangeline and I wondered for years whether it was our penchant for persistent squabbling that had caused our mother to ditch us. If we'd been perfect little angels, would we still be with her?

Like water for fish, hope for our parents' return was what we lived on. It was what caused us to draw in one good deep breath and then to take another. Like salmon, we were always instinctively headed upstream in search of home—a place where we truly belonged.

We had always loved our grandparents, and they us. But changing our home and parents in the space of time it took to drive from Austin to Fireside required some getting used to. I knew, however, that having our doting grandparents to ourselves had a healing effect like Campho-Phenique on blisters when our spirits were raw. Walt and Ruby drew us up close to their chests and held us there for years.

They quickly began to incorporate us into their daily routines and frosted the sameness of the days spent on the ranch with an icing of tenderness and mercy. Like all kids, Evangeline and I had pet names for our grandparents, but in secret referred to them as plain old Walt and Ruby. How could we resist?

Ruby was named for her flaming red mane that did not fade until she reached her late seventies. I've never seen another head of hair like hers since. Truly like her namesake gem, her value was precious. She dearly loved me, even when I couldn't imagine why she would.

Evangeline and I liked to linger over Walt's name like you would a cherished hymn or a cup of coffee with pecan pie. He was our protector. To him, killing a rattler meant picking it up by its tail and popping it against the barn door. The darned snake was dead before it had time to recoil. We watched him do it with huge eyes, realizing that all that prevented the rattler from striking one of us was Walt.

By nightfall, he waltzed Ruby around their tiny living room, all six-feet-four inches of his frame hunched over to hold her close. She would have gazed right into his belt buckle if she weren't looking up into his gray eyes. They were in their midfifties then. This moment is the snapshot I took with my mind. They are dancing to the "Tennessee Waltz," and Ruby reaches up to kiss Walt; they stay like that and time seems to stop.

She is wearing old tennis shoes, striped pedal pushers, and a white blouse. Walt has on his favorites—ancient, faded blue jeans and a frayed denim shirt. In my mind's snapshot, they are a silver Gregory Peck and a ruby Jane Powell. If a real picture like this existed, I'd put in on the front page of my scrapbook where it belongs. Instead, like chocolate rat-holed in a secret drawer, the memory feels selfishly and yet deliciously mine. Through all these years, they are still dancing in my mind, untouched by age or the constraints of time.

Time seemed slower back then. One hour felt like five. A week equaled a year. Christmas was always an eternity away. We marked days by rainfall, by the mysterious births of white-faced calves, and by how many buckets of maize we'd hauled to the chicken yard where we gathered eggs. Mealtimes were spent around Ruby's oval table, picking the tender white meat off fried chicken wings and eating spoonfuls of sweet butternut squash, sliced red tomatoes, and green peas, all vegetables from her blue-ribbon garden.

At noontime, Walt invariably arose briefly from the table to tune in his old white radio to Miss Alma Webster, also known as the Voice of Fireside and the Texas Hill Country, on KOFF-AM. My eyes would droop as I ate lime westerner cake drizzled with powdered sugar icing, lulled into semiconsciousness as Miss Alma droned on about who'd died, who'd had a baby, and who'd had a tractor or combine to sell.

She started every broadcast with, "Welcome to Fireside, Texas—where no strangers are known! Home of the free and the brave, and the everlasting polite person. We never take the last cookie. No one eats beets, but we thank the hostess for them, anyway. Population: eight hundred forty-seven. Climate: cheerful and cozy. Main industry: minding our children and our neighbor's business."

Nap time followed the noon meal after dishes had been washed and white cup towels had been placed over leftovers, still too hot to be refrigerated. Evangeline and I would be led onto a monstrously high feather bed and told to go to sleep. I am quite sure this was done so that the grown folks could stand us in the afternoon. Soon, Walt would tiptoe into the bedroom, put his fingers to his lips, and say, "Shhhh!"

"Hi, Popo!" we'd say, delighted at the diversion.

Walt would smile mischievously as if he were up to something and say, "Don't let your mamaw know I'm in here or she'll skin me alive!"

Then he'd lead us into the kitchen and lower the peppermint jar within our reach so that we could dip our eager hands inside for a piece of candy. He would kiss us on our foreheads and say, "Now, this is a secret between you girls and me. You promise not to tell her?"

"We promise," we'd chime.

Of course, Ruby always knew about the daily peppermint rituals, but would pretend not to know. I believed she thought them an essential ingredient for growing up right, much as a golden meringue is needed to finish a well-turned banana pudding.

Walt soon came to name us after garden pests. Perhaps they were simply terms of endearment, or quite possibly they were revenge for what we called him. He was not pleased when we greeted him in downtown Fireside with, "Hi there, Popo." He would look nervously around himself and pretend he couldn't quite recall who we were. It was as if the name "Popo" was akin to something being expelled by a stray dog, or possibly a word from Swahili meaning baboon lips. And so his exalted reputation as Walt the Fireside rancher and farmer, Walt the election judge, Walt father of a university graduate and husband of a beautiful woman slid down into Popo, the embarrassed.

This was how my name, Juliet Cranbourne, spiraled downward into just plain old Squirrel. In the 1960s, the name was synonymous with the term *goofball.* He called Evangeline Rabbit, a name I thought of as sweet like Sugar Pie or Baby Doll. I felt slighted somehow, as if he'd distanced me from himself by the choice of my nickname. I later realized how mistaken I'd been. Walt loved to play Santa Claus 365 days a year, and he was especially good to me.

Ruby, Evangeline, and I had just come in from delivering a Christmas basket filled with a baked turkey breast with cornbread stuffing, sweet potato casserole, and fruitcake to Adah Mae Applewhite. The prune-like old woman hadn't left the boundary of her crumbling Texas Hill Country cottage for years, due to her advanced agoraphobia.

Afterward, Evangeline and I were seated at the table making a stunning Christmas tree angel out of white wrapping paper, gold glitter, and a toilet-paper cylinder. Sunshine broke through clouds and swept across a bottle of Elmer's glue, Little Child scissors, and two wide-eyed girls. I shivered with delight when I examined my hands and arms. I had glitter-coated my nine-year-old self and much of Ruby's table so that I looked like an electrified human ornament. Neither Ruby nor Walt fussed at me for making such a mess. They just admired my handiwork and let me sparkle, long as I pleased. Imagine that!

That afternoon, Evangeline and I were haggling in the living room over who got to hang the first striped candy cane on the cedar Christmas tree. Twenty-three more were in crunching distance of our tennis shoes. Next to the tree was a life-sized black-velvet painting of Elvis. His hair was *all shook up* over that high black collar of his. It was Ruby's artwork and her man-in-waiting.

Bing Crosby and Rosemary Clooney sang "White Christmas" on the radio as our grandparents made candied popcorn in the kitchen. Although it was a damp and dreary day outside, our own personal thoughts read *warm and cozy* until my sister got on my nerves repeatedly.

Fed up to my eyeballs with her immaturity, I said, "Go on, Evangeline. If you have to act like a big old soggy-diapered baby, you can hang the first one." I was twenty-two months older than my seven-year-old sister, which made me light-years ahead, in my opinion.

"I ain't no baby," she whined.

I fancied myself a champion deal cutter and told her, "I get to hang two in a row if you hang the first one."

Evangeline was bound to work herself up into a Hollywood-class fit; I could feel it coming. She jutted out her chin and fumed, "That ain't fair."

"Can't have your cake and eat it too." I waited for her to fall on the floor and pound the oak planks with her heels, but was surprised when she simply stuck out her tongue. I stuck mine out too and turned my back. We were even.

I hiked up my tan stirrup pants, plopped down on the ottoman, and leaned over to pick up another candy cane from the box on the floor. When I looked up again, I could see Walt and Ruby in the kitchen. They mesmerized me.

Evangeline crushed one candy cane underneath her tennis shoe and muttered, "Whoops!" She scraped the mess underneath the Christmas tree skirt, licked her palms, and slyly issued a challenge, "Juliet, it's your turn. Unless you want me to hang them all, 'cause I ain't waiting!"

"You go on. I'll catch up in a minute." Perched on the ottoman, I held out a candy cane to Evangeline and spied on Ruby's kitchen.

Walt shifted the covered pan of popcorn back and forth across the electric burner. "I heard Nestor say at the hardware store that we ought not to use cedar in the fireplace. That it burns too durned hot and might set the chimney on fire again."

Ruby peered at him and shook her head from side to side as she stirred candied syrup. "Walt, we've been burning cedar logs for fifty-something years. We have had a few chimney fires, but that was on account of soot gummed up inside the flue."

"Well, you might be right."

"I usually am."

Walt studied Ruby and suppressed a smile. "I'd clean the flue myself, but you can see I'm way too big to fit inside. On the other hand, you are not, being slender and five foot with heels on. I'll dangle you upside down and that pretty red hair of yours will act as a Brillo pad. When it's clean, I'll stand you outside underneath the rain tower and drop water over you. What do you think?"

Ruby raised her eyebrows and feigned sternness. "You'll be cooking your own dinner from now on, is what I think."

"You know I'm just funnin' with you." Walt set his popcorn pan off the stove, moved over behind Ruby, and wrapped his arms around her. "You are the most beautiful woman God ever made. All the others were just paste, but you are the true gem."

"You think I'm prettier than, say, Selma Davis?"

"Selma? The one that works at Densesky's?"

"You know the one."

"She's pretty enough, but she isn't you, Ruby. I don't need to graze in another pasture when the greenest, prettiest grass is in my own backyard."

"You don't fool me," Ruby replied coyly. "A man will say anything to spread my watermelon rind preserves on fresh biscuits in the morning. Or to eat my pan-fried chicken at lunch."

"That's true."

"Thunder, Walt. You don't have to agree with me."

"Only thing I know that will help me win this one is a kiss."

I turned back toward Evangeline, who was hanging candy canes willy-nilly, and stage-whispered, "Quick! Come watch. The show's about to begin." Evangeline slid up beside me on the ottoman and watched, hand clapped over her mouth to suppress a giggle.

Walt turned Ruby toward him and kissed her so long and hard we thought she might pass out. But no, she smiled and said, "You're gonna make me burn the syrup."

"Well, I'm burning with love for you, Ruby darlin'."

"Go on. Hush. The girls will hear you."

Then they both looked toward the doorway and caught us spying. "Juliet, Evangeline! You scamps get back to decorating that tree, will you?" said Ruby, flustered.

We snickered and hightailed it back toward the bottom-heavy Christmas tree. Evangeline had decorated it with several packages of candy canes and had hung them all about knee-high to Elvis. Ten days in advance, our Christmas was already made.

Two

By the following May, Ruby must have grown desperate to entertain us, so even as unappealing as the idea may have been on some level, she began to take us fishing on a regular basis.

Some days meant a trip by foot to the Pedernales River or to a fishing tank not far from that. The journey was a good two miles from our grandparents' home and was intended, I am certain, to wear us out. Ruby would help us fish, while we squealed and giggled and scared any self-respecting perch into hiding. The Pedernales was the same river, we were later told, where Ruby had drowned at the age of eighteen on her high school commencement day during a class swimming party and had been resuscitated by an angel in the form of a smelly fisherman.

Other days were spent traipsing around the backyard, wearing Ruby's old red or blue or green stage costumes. She'd played the fiddle and sang and danced along with her sisters, Pearl and Sapphire, when she was young. The Gemburree sisters even performed once at the Grand Ole Opry, but Ruby had long given that all up for a better life with Walt.

She'd altered these outfits, working with yards and yards of netting and satin on an old Singer treadle sewing machine. Along with our fancy dresses, we wore plastic dime-store high heels around the house's uneven sidewalk that often caused us to stub our toes, scrape our knees, and bloody our noses. But in our quest for glamour, we prevailed. Soon it grew too hot to wear our costumes, so we traded them for watermelon and Eskimo Pies. Then we consumed our treats in great quantities on the front porch.

Sweltering summer evenings came often and early in Central Texas, and it was no different in June of 1968. We spent them in the front yard, either playing or sitting in folding aluminum lounge chairs and observing the heavens without the assistance of a telescope. The four of us would lie outside in the darkness for what seemed like hours, swatting mosquitoes and listening to the howls of wild river dogs, the chirping of cicadas, and the occasional gusts of wind rustling the crepe myrtle, pecan, and mimosa leaves.

Walt, who never had the opportunity to go beyond the sixth grade in school, was a self-taught observer of the universe. He pointed up to the constellations and said, "Now, that one yonder is the Big Dipper. Can you girls see it?"

"No sir," Evangeline and I replied.

"You've got to look real close. Pay attention to what's around you in this life. You're liable to miss something important if you don't."

On June first, before time for Walt and Ruby to join us in stargazing, Evangeline and I hanged upside down on the swing set's homemade trapeze bars in the front yard. In truth, we were waiting for our mother who perpetually disappointed us. Dusk was just setting in good, and our bellies were way too full for us to be throwing ourselves around so. Even we knew that no one should pretend to be circus girls after consuming a plate of fried venison sausage and three bowls of ice cream. We were about half sick from it, and yet persisted as stubbornness ran high in our bloodlines.

Upside down, we examined one another's pulled faces as we held our shirts in place. We stuck out our tongues at one another, drool running down our foreheads and into our hair.

"When I cross my eyes, I see a one-eyed ape," said Evangeline, pointing at me.

"A one-eyed ape is what you have when you cut a window from a piece of bread, drop an egg in the hole, and fry it," I said.

"You still look like one, smarty-pants." Evangeline rubbed her head and frowned. "How long does it take for all the blood in our bodies to smack us in the brains?"

"About two and a half hours," I replied, making it up as I went along.

"Will we live?" she asked and burped.

"I don't know. Why don't you try it and I'll watch?"

"That ain't fair!" she whined, her cheeks now red and pooched like a blowfish. Blue veins popped out around her temples.

I chided her, "What are you a fraidycat?"

"Naw!"

"Well, quit fussing then."

I pulled myself back upright and jumped down. The ground spun, and losing my balance made me sit down hard on the carpet of grass. When my vision cleared, I saw the first fireflies I'd seen that summer. They dotted the darkening horizon like tiny flying lanterns.

Evangeline dropped down beside me, and we lay back on the grass, swatting gnats. We grew mesmerized by swarms of darting lights. She said, "Can you make a wish upon a firefly like you can a star?"

"I don't know. I'm not exactly queen of all fireflies."

"Well, I am," she said. "Just call me H-R-H. You can make any wish upon a firefly you want to, so long as you can keep it in your sights. Lose the firefly, lose the wish."

"You can't keep a firefly in sight forever."

"Well, then you have to do it for at least five minutes."

I found my firefly and focused on it until my eyes ached from the strain and my neck grew stiff. Evangeline wiggled on the lawn, crossing one leg over the other and then changing back again. She twisted this way and that, until finally she shouted at the top of her voice, "Time's up. I win!"

"We both win," I said.

"I won first, but you can win second."

"What did you wish?"

"For Mama to come home, and Daddy too. I've been missing them something awful."

"Me too."

I now know that you must be careful what you wish for. Not only might you get it, but it may come to you in a way you hadn't counted on. If I had it to do over again, I'd have been far more specific about how I wanted our parents to return to us. Had I done that, things might have turned out differently. But you can't blame two little girls for not knowing that ahead of time, can you?

Like beads of water flung from a glass, the fireflies vanished. At that exact moment, our attention diverted to the roar of an approaching car and the sound of gravel spun out from tires as it lurched to a stop outside the front yard. They parked underneath the mercury light at the edge of the yard. *US Army* was written on the door of a white government car. Two men sporting burr haircuts got out wearing fancy dress uniforms, including jackets despite the summer heat. They let themselves in the front gate, proceeded down the sidewalk, and crossed through the yard toward us.

We jumped up from the grass where we'd laid watching fireflies, and Evangeline hid behind me. She was ornery until scared by someone larger than herself, and this was one of those times. Furthermore, she was perpetually suspicious of strangers and would not speak to them, ever. Despite my raising, I would usually do just that, lest I hurt a stranger's feelings.

"Sirs, can I help you with anything? Are you lost?" Nobody ever came down our long ranch road at night, so being lost seemed reasonable to me.

"No, young lady. We're not lost. We're looking for Mr. Walt or Mrs. Ruby Cranbourne."

"Just a minute, I'll get them," I replied. I didn't need to bother to get them for Walt and Ruby were already pushing through the screen door and stepping onto the front porch beside the wicker furniture.

"Who is it, Juliet, Evangeline?" Ruby called. Then just as soon as the two husky uniformed men got up into the soft porch light, Ruby turned pasty white and fell unconscious onto the concrete porch like an egg tumbling from a crate.

Walt looked dazed and leaned over his wife where she lay sprawled on the floor. "Ruby! Wake up! Let's hear what these gentlemen have to say first," said Walt, confused. He put his right arm underneath her head and slid another below her knees. He managed to stand and then lifted her into the wicker chair just as soon as she started coming to.

It was all too much for me to take in. My legs started moving fast, the way they do whenever I think a truck is about to roll right over me. I ran through the yard past everyone, burst into the house, letting the screen door slam behind me, and threw myself on the sofa. Still, I could see and hear it all.

"We are sorry to inform you that your son, Lieutenant James Nelson Cranbourne, was killed in the line of duty…"

"Oh, Lord, not him. Not our boy," cried Ruby. Walt stood by her, holding onto her for dear life, like some hold onto a rope as they fall over a cliff. But it was Ruby who Houdini'd out of the blouse that Walt was clinching by its shoulders. Like sweet peas stripped from a pod, Ruby slipped out onto the porch a second time, clad in her Playtex 18-Hour bra and striped pedal pushers. Walt knelt beside her, scooped her up in his arms, arose, and managed to take her inside the house and place her on their bed. I heard the bedsprings squeak as her body sank into them and the wailing that came from both our grandparents.

I didn't understand why or how it had happened, but my heart had absorbed the essence of the matter. Our daddy was dead. My thoughts were this: I am nine and a half, and Evangeline is seven. We are years too young to be without a daddy and cannot make it without him. Walt and Ruby are bound to lose their minds and send us to the orphan home. Surely Mama will feel right sorry for us and come to our rescue.

Three

We did not have a funeral for our daddy; his body did not come home for burial. Since none of us were ready to stomach the idea of a memorial service, we didn't have one. We couldn't believe he was dead.

What was left of him had somehow been lost—misplaced like a set of Edsel car keys or a pair of Woolworth's eyeglasses. It was easy for us girls to imagine that he was still over there in Vietnam, flying Hueys the way some fly kites, checking his G.I. Joe watch, just waiting for the right time to pop into Ruby and Walt's house and surprise us. He always was one to jump out from behind the kitchen door and scare the biscuits outta Ruby—we remembered him doing such, of course. Since Evangeline and I pictured him biding his time airborne, it didn't require a great leap of imagination to believe he could fly all the way to Fireside. If we had not seen him die, maybe he didn't.

Then we got a letter about two weeks after those men in uniforms came to deliver the bad news. It was from a Private Ricardo Sullivan O'Leary Sanchez, whose name was like bookends. He said he had been on board the Huey with our daddy the last time he flew it. Our daddy had just dropped off medical supplies and was waiting to medevac wounded when he became a sitting target himself.

When the Vietcong shot him through the shoulder as he sat strapped into his pilot's seat, the bullet stayed in his chest. He did not lose consciousness then, and he did not moan or complain of pain. The only sounds, Private Sanchez said, came from gunfire, other wounded soldiers, and chopper blades that whirred like a thousand birds' wings.

Even with a bullet inside him, he was able to take off and fly those wounded men to safety before he died. This made me believe that, like a kite on a string, more time had been unrolled for him that he might save those men. Why then couldn't our daddy have been delivered home alive as well?

Through his letter, Private Sanchez became our eyes. Now we could see that our daddy wasn't sitting in the Huey. He was never flying home.

"Well," said Ruby, sniffling after she finished reading us the letter in the living room. "It paid off for James to be so darned hardheaded by nature. I remember when he sat at the table for four hours after we'd gotten up because he refused to eat the cooked spinach and boiled egg dish I'd copied from Adah Mae's cookbook. He never took a second bite, and there just wasn't anything I could do to make him. It was that same stubborn, hard head of his that he used to save the lives of all those men."

"He's a hero, Ruby," said Walt, brushing away his tears with the back of one hand and pulling his tattered ranch hat off the stand with the other. "Goin' to check on the cows, girls."

"Can I come too?" Evangeline pleaded with big, sad eyes, but Walt didn't turn to look.

"Not this time, Rabbit. Tomorrow."

Ruby, seated on the ottoman, was in another world. She blew her nose, wiped it, and sniffed, "Yessir. When James made up his mind he wanted brown sugar on his Cream of Wheat, he'd sooner walk to town to buy it than give it up. And when he was a little feller, he wrapped abandoned chicken eggs in a cup towel and warmed them next to his belly, determined they'd hatch with his help."

"Did they?" I asked.

"No, they weren't fertilized. I tried to tell him that there were no chicks inside to begin with, but he was stubborn. Warmed those eggs for a solid weekend till he broke one and saw that it was just a regular old egg."

"How do they get fertilized?" Evangeline had a great curiosity for science, even as a girl.

Ruby squirmed uncomfortably. "Well, you've got to have both a rooster and a hen, and that's all there is to it."

"Why?"

"'Cause I said so."

"Oh."

Years later, I came to realize that this diversion about roosters and hens had a double purpose. It helped Ruby to get her mind off the loss of her boy for a moment, on one hand. On the other, the brief exchange served as the only birds-and-bees talk we'd ever get.

The months that followed the death of our daddy were a long test of endurance. July and August were without rainfall. Every blade of grass had been bleached by 109-degree days, making our fields seem like boneyards for hay skeletons. We let the windmill run for hours during the day so that water could be pumped into the tank and troughs for cattle. It screeched and clanked endlessly, working our thin nerves into cords of irritability and frustration.

A grassfire exploded onto the ranch next to Walt and Ruby's requiring every able volunteer firefighter's assistance. We were alerted to the fact thanks to the party-line system on the telephone. Walt barreled off in the old ranch truck on that Friday afternoon, only to return nine hours later, nearly too tired to undress for bed. As Ruby helped him late that night, I listened to the gentle murmurs coming from their bedroom.

"So worried 'bout you, Walt. I'd just as soon you let the other fellers fight fire."

"Got to be worth something at this age, Ruby."

"You're worth plenty to me and the girls."

"Have to do my part to help my neighbors. We sure didn't need that fire crossing over here to our place."

"If we lost this house, we could build again. We can't get another you. The good Lord only made one, and he did a fine job."

"Ruby, what'd I ever do to deserve you? Give an old firefighter a kiss, will you?"

After that my mind snapped shut, and I went to sleep.

The next morning, a hot wind carried ashes inside the house, and the acrid smell of burned tire rubber and brush smoke lingered throughout the ranch, irritating our eyes and causing our noses to run. Dust devils whirled in and out of Fireside, thrusting dirt into our eyes whenever we helped Ruby deliver eggs on Saturday afternoon as usual.

Ashes to ashes. Dust to dust.

When we returned from our egg-delivering mission to Fireside, Evangeline went straightaway and etched a portrait of Daddy on our bedroom wall with a pair of dull scissors. It was not a handsome likeness of him; she'd cut his teeth long and narrow and had made one eye monstrously bigger than the other.

"That just don't do him justice," I complained. "Our daddy was good-looking. Nobody in Fireside would recognize him by this picture."

Evangeline stuck her tongue out at me and grimaced. Her cocoa eyes burned a hole right through my head, and then her tears started to fall. "It was the best I could do, dammit," she said. Then she carved D-A-D-D-Y underneath the picture to clarify the matter.

Under normal circumstances, Ruby would have had a piece of both of us for such destructiveness. She'd have paddled us for messing up the wall in the first place, and for not using our *noodles* in the second. But when she came into our room unannounced with an armload of clean underwear and socks, she just put away the clothes, stared at her son's crude portrait, and left the room without a word.

That evening, Ruby forgot to add baking powder to the biscuits. They emerged from the oven like smoking lethal weapons and could have killed a wild river dog, a skunk, or maybe even Walt from thirty paces. Ruby just dumped the entire baking sheet of evidence into the trash can and put sliced bread in the toaster. After dinner, she left the dishes in the sink and went for a long walk in the pasture.

While she was gone, Walt and we girls cleaned up the kitchen and went into the living room to watch *Gunsmoke.* We decided that Marshal Matt Dillon ought to have married Miss Kitty and given her a proper home. He must not have been of a mind to do that as they just stayed sweet on one another, and never really got anywhere.

When Ruby returned from her walk, she went directly to the bathroom, filled the tub with water, and did not emerge for hours.

"Popo, Mamaw didn't go down the drain, did she?" asked Evangeline fearfully as we hugged our grandfather good-night.

"Ruby is fine. She just needs some time to herself."

"Well, gosh, she missed out on Miss Kitty."

"That might have been the point," he replied. "Sometimes folks need some space to get their thoughts squared away. To put things in their proper places."

"I know what you mean, Popo," I said. "Sometimes when I'm straightening my desk at school, I need lots of room. Trash does tend to fly when I'm doing that."

"Trash does tend to fly. You're right about that, Squirrel."

The next morning, we packed a box of food for Adah Mae Applewhite and drove it over to her mildewed, imploding house on the west side of Fireside. The dilapidated, white frame house was nearly covered over by ivy, dirt-dauber nests, and grasshopper droppings, and squared off with Selma Davis's house across the street. Ruby maintained that, at the very least, Adah should have had the house painted blue to ward off dirt-daubers who were opposed to the color. Adah, however, didn't want strange painter types hanging around her place. No, a few dauber nests never hurt anyone.

Her daughter, Mable, had once been Ruby's best friend. She died on their high school commencement day. They'd both been showing off in front of their classmates down on the Pedernales River, doing handstands and what have you. The watershed way upriver had received an abundance of rainfall really fast, which roared downstream in one mighty wall of water. They simply could not get out in time. Mable died, and Ruby was fetched back from the beyond somehow. Poor Adah Mae had seen it all from the riverbank where she'd just set out a picnic for the graduates.

After she attended Mable's funeral, Adah never again set foot into the outside world. She held herself prisoner in her own home, fearing the unknown tragedies that lurked beyond her door. Ruby was her one source of information of all things that had since passed. She clung to Ruby's every word, alternately treating her with adoration and contempt. Ruby never knew what she would have to face during a particular visit, but forged ahead anyway. I knew firsthand that Ruby was in the habit of loving people despite their faults.

The only time I ever observed Adah's weathered wooden door to be open was when she was expecting Ruby. The rest of the time, she had it bolted shut, no matter the temperature. This, combined with the general run-down look of the place, made lots of folks think it was abandoned. Now the screen door was all that stood between the hermit of Maitlin County and the real world.

As usual, Ruby had told us to sit there on the front-porch swing while she carried in her groceries and not to even try to come inside. She would be back directly.

That was no problem to us, since we had no desire to enter that dreadful house. We were dead certain it was haunted by at least nine different kinds of haints and goblins. We'd heard that dead people were rotting in the cellar, while rats as big as children perched on her bedposts where they lived off the wads of chewed gum she'd stuck to it. Why, everybody in Fireside knew she kept a Colt .45 in her apron pocket and used a Spanish saber to part her hair after a shower—that is, supposing she ever took one. She snacked on beetles and scorpions between her regular meals, which normally consisted of cannibal's delight, except on the days when Ruby came to visit.

Every child in Fireside knew that cannibal stew consisted of the fingers and toes of babies, mixed with mashed beets. Wasn't anybody in his or her right mind going to eat a beet in these parts. Everybody in town was practically kin, and all of the kin were allergic to those nasty red vegetables.

I heard old men playing dominoes by the courthouse say that Adah liked to draw a bead on children through her Winchester rifle cross hairs as they walked home from school. She had her own artillery of weapons, some of which she'd stolen when she was a spy for the communists during the Great War. She had a huge black kettle, which she stirred all the livelong day and through the night without ever stopping to sleep.

Going without sleep never bothered her one whit because she wasn't human to begin with. It just gave her more time to peel beets and come up with mumbo jumbo to torture people with. For instance, she had a spell that could force a child to walk backward and whistle, "The ants go marching one by one, hurrah, hurrah." That wouldn't have been so bad except that the afflicted child would not only walk and whistle backward, but he would age backward as well. Before he knew it, he'd be back in his mother's womb and then, one day, would shrink up into a speck so tiny that even ants were giants in comparison.

If the moon was full, Adah Mae liked to howl. When she opened her huge mouth, which was filled with rotting teeth, and commenced calling coyotes, like nails on a chalkboard, it set all of Fireside's canines on edge. They couldn't help but howl too, and then neither child nor adult got any sleep. This was another reason, I believed, she never left her house. All those dogs would be waiting for her on her front porch with their bare teeth flashing and growling. Nobody liked a howler.

Furthermore, she'd gotten the name Applewhite because of her relationship by blood to the wretchedly wicked queen who had given the poison apple to Snow White. You cannot trust a wicked witch bearing a red apple. Trust me on that one. All these stories about Adah Mae I'd either heard in town from other children or adults, or had derived by my own brilliant reasoning.

So, although I'd heard Ruby's version of what made Adah Mae act like she did, I chose to believe what I'd heard in town. Those stories made more sense to me on account of her oddball ways. I made it a practice to stay away from people like that.

Even Elvis didn't have enough money or charisma to talk us into entering Adah Mae's house. Furthermore, we feared mightily for our grandmother, wondering whether she'd be swallowed up whole by the strangeness of the place, never to be seen again.

Ruby took in a good deep breath. "Lord, let it be a good day!" she said. Then she squared her shoulders and called out, "Mrs. Applewhite, I've got a box here filled plumb up with the groceries you asked me to bring."

She pushed through Adah's screen door and stood in the parlor, resting the cardboard container on one hip. Evangeline and I peered through the screen, making sure the old woman didn't devour our grandmother. We were ready to bolt for the highway ourselves, if need be. Adah Mae shuffled into the parlor, her white hair thinly covering her pink scalp. She wore a gray empire dress and blue corduroy house slippers. She had a great swollen stomach, and her breasts sagged over her high belt. Her fluid-filled legs were purple with phlebitis.

She leaned over Ruby's box and said abruptly, "I don't see my pickles. Where are they?" I pictured Adah Mae eating my grandmother alive just as another famous wicked witch tried to eat Hansel and Gretel.

"Oh dear," Ruby sighed. "I left them at home. I'm so sorry."

"You ate them on the way over here, didn't you?" Adah Mae accused as she crossed her arms over her great belly.

"No, of course not." Ruby pressed her lips together in a firm line, but kept them sealed. I thought she ought to deck her one right on the spot for having accused her of such.

"Why, I ought to paddle your britches but good. I bet you didn't do your homework, did you?"

"Mrs. Applewhite, you know I don't have homework at my age." Ruby's voice just sounded tired, as if she'd been through all of this too many times to count. "I'm fifty-two years old."

"I hate it when you girls lie to me. Lie! Lie! Lie! I'll bet that even President Hoover doesn't lie as much as you. He keeps saying for us to hang on and that the Depression will soon be over. Ha! Can't trust tricky politicians or children. That's what I always say. He just wants to get his hands on the great big ball of string I've been saving for all these years!"

The only reality that Adah Mae had touched upon involved one humongous ball of string sitting square in the middle of her parlor floor. It was roughly the size of a recliner and emitted a great moldy odor due to the leak in the ceiling above it. I could smell it all the way outside—along with the five jillion mothballs the old woman kept scattered around.

"I'll bring you a jar of bread-and-butter pickles tomorrow, Mrs. Applewhite. Don't get so upset, please."

After that, Ruby had eased out of the house with Adah Mae close behind her. The red-faced woman stopped short on the inside of the screen door and glared at us.

"Did you bring those little spies with you again?" she fumed, eying Evangeline and me with great suspicion.

"Mrs. Applewhite, these are my precious granddaughters. They are not spies."

"Well, whoever they are, tell them they can't have my string either!"

I politely told Adah Mae that Evangeline and I didn't want her durned old string. Not, of course, that it wasn't really nice durned old string.

"Are you trying to trick me?"

"No, ma'am," I swore and, at the same time, visualized her handing a poison apple to an innocent Snow White.

"Well, I know a spy when I see one. I wasn't born yesterday."

On the way home, I asked Ruby why she bothered to help a woman as mean as Mrs. Applewhite.

"Because she can't help herself. My conscience tells me I ought to help those who can't help themselves." Ruby looked at us in her rearview mirror to see how we reacted and whether we'd digested her moral lesson. I gave her my best smile and sat up straighter in the seat, confident that I was winning points. My sister, however, did otherwise. She scooted down low in the seat and twisted her hair back and forth. Then she flopped over on her side and stuck her feet in the air, hoping to touch the car's headliner with her tiptoes.

Evangeline giggled and said haughtily, "Well, my conscience tells me I ought to have a cherry Popsicle!" Upside down, she clapped her feet together over the backseat of Ruby's Thunderbird, laughing at her own joke.

Ruby looked dismayed and shook her head. "Oh dear. I'm gonna have to sand some rough edges off you, Rabbit."

Evangeline's eyes grew wide. "With Popo's wood sander?" she asked, obviously thinking of the electric sander that hung from a nail in the tool shed.

"Just a figure of speech," said Ruby.

Four

The Cranbourne females were not the only ones to have rough edges or offbeat days or suffer from forgetfulness since the death of our loved one. Walt had been affected as well. He had failed to close the pasture gate when he drove through it on the way into Fireside. Before he'd returned home, thirteen heifers moseyed on down the road and got into Helmut Kugel's pasture.

All those cows and Helmut's one-eyed Charolaise bull spelled nothing but trouble and meant calves in the coming season, which were not of the intended breed. That meant poor prices at the auction. The old bull, named Babylon, was good for nothing, except as Helmut's pet. He was too sorry a specimen to rent for breeding, but I supposed he stood in for a watchdog now and then. He liked to be scratched behind his ears so long as no one got on the side of his bad eye. Whenever that happened, it made him nervous, and he backed up fast as a freight train and trampled those behind, or charged ahead, butting whoever was in his way.

Helmut had tracked Walt down in Nestor Klein's hardware store, where he usually stopped in to drink a Dr. Pepper with the local men and visit. Walt stopped what he was doing and came home right away. Evangeline pestered him to let her go too, and he finally relented. They put a sack of feed in the back of his old ranch truck and took off.

All Walt had to do to call the cows home was to go up within earshot and sit on his truck horn. When the first few cows started to arrive behind the truck, Walt told Evangeline she could toot the horn while he climbed in the back and threw out a few handfuls of molasses and alfalfa pellets, which were as attractive to them as cotton candy to children.

Evangeline sat in the driver's seat of the truck, fantasizing about the banana pudding with mile-high meringue Ruby had promised to make us for dinner that night, supposing we had good behavior. Oh, both of us knew the dessert well. We had sleepwalked through the day, dreaming only of its unforgettable sweetness. It was to become part of her confession, later.

Old Babylon was soon lumbering toward them in the distance, and Evangeline saw him coming through the side mirror. She put the old truck into gear to speed things up. The fact that she was eight years old and ought to have asked permission first did not dawn on her. As the truck lurched forward, Walt was thrown from its bed. When he arose from the ground and dusted himself off, he was dismayed to find himself on old Babylon's blind side.

It was an out-and-out miracle that Walt survived with no more injury than to be knocked down again by Babylon's swinging head. That he wasn't trampled by the other heifers was yet another thing as they'd all crowded close to him, expecting a further reward of more pellets.

Evangeline hadn't known the first thing about steering an aged ranch truck, breaking one, or making it stop. But that was no matter, as a tree stump bigger than most barrels stopped the whole thing dead in its tracks. Evangeline bloodied her nose on the steering wheel at impact, and the truck's grill was caved in something awful.

An hour later, Evangeline confessed everything in jagged bits and pieces during sobs of remorse. I was able to reconstruct a pretty good idea of what had happened. But after her punishment was levied, she changed her tune and became sullen and defiant. Ruby had a hard time making her sit still as she tended her bleeding nose. When Ruby doctored Walt's skinned knees and elbows, she pitched a good fit.

"I was just trying to help Popo, dammit!" she said.

Ruby looked up at her from her bottle of reddish-brown mercurochrome that she'd just painted Walt's right knee with and said, "Evangeline Lynette Cranbourne! You ever use that word again, and I'll get a bar of Lava to soap your mouth out with."

Walt pleaded with his wife, "Ruby, it was my fault more than hers. Don't—"

"And you, Walter Scott…Don't contradict me in front of these girls. The battle will be lost before we get going good."

Walt hung his head, and Evangeline just did what came naturally to her whenever she was upset, which was to throw up on the kitchen floor. Ruby calmly got up from her kneeling position, set the bottle of mercurochrome on the kitchen counter, and went for a good long walk outside.

Ruby did not cook for any of us that evening. She got out a box of Kellogg's Corn Flakes and a bunch of bananas and set them on the kitchen table. Next, she pulled out a bowl of leftover strawberry Jell-O with its suspended fruit cocktail and a can of Reddi-wip from the Frigidaire. She ceremoniously plopped them with a dull thud next to the other food and said, "Like they say on the commercial, 'There's always room for Jell-O!'"

Clearly, there was an absence of the promised banana pudding with mile-high meringue. Our hearts sank. We hadn't passed the good behavior test, not that it was unusual. Still, forgiveness normally ran high in Ruby. Evangeline waited until Ruby's back was turned, winked at me, and mouthed, "Gosh durnit."

It was to my credit that I did not rat on her for her second offense. I did not think that Ruby or Walt could take one more thing that day. Part of me worried that they'd eventually grow tired of our shenanigans and throw us out for good like crusty leftover custard. Things had changed so quickly in our lives that we'd not had the chance to draw in a good, deep breath. I, for one, wasn't taking anything for granted.

If there was one thing we could depend on, however, it was that every Saturday was egg day. I helped Ruby wash, dry, and grade every egg, one by one. Then we placed them in cartons and loaded them up in the back of her green Thunderbird. Ruby's Thunderbird was so famous around Fireside and beyond, it was practically regarded as a national treasure. In 1959, Ruby had baked Elvis a rum fruitcake on account of him being sad about his "Blue Christmas," and shipped it to him. Two weeks later, the Thunderbird arrived with a card that said

Dear Ruby,
Thanks. Thank you very much.
Sincerely,
Your ever-loving Elvis

Folks around Fireside had been known to voluntarily polish the Thunderbird whenever Ruby left it parked along Main Street. You see, since Ruby was one of Fireside's own, so was the car. They took pictures of their children and grandchildren standing in front of it because it was the next best thing to having their picture taken with Elvis. In parking lots, folks were downright respectful and left double the ordinary amount of room between their car and hers, just to protect its doors from dings and scrapes. On account of its fame and V-8 engine, plenty of men and teenagers tried to buy it from her, but Ruby always said, "No, I'm sorry. Just can't part with it."

That afternoon, before we drove the eggs into town, we each took turns taking baths, cleaning our faces with Noxzema, and then sprinkling talcum powder over our semidamp bodies. While I simply put on my Saturday blue gingham dress with its white lace and then my Oxford shoes, Ruby went all out. She put on beige foundation, powder, mascara, blush, and cardinal-colored lipstick. Her fiery hair was swept up into a chignon and pinned with the mother-of-pearl combs Walt had given her long ago for their fifth anniversary.

Here's where the Jane Powell look comes in—those aquamarine eyes and her perfect, diminutive form. Even with her in mourning for our father like she was, and in her fifties to boot, I often thought that Walt ought not leave her unattended for long. Whenever she put on that green calico dress that was belted at the waist, I felt like I was in the presence of Hollywood royalty.

When we finally arrived in Fireside, Ruby pulled the Thunderbird to a stop in front of Densesky's Groceries, Dry Goods, and G.E. Appliances. Just as we emerged from the car, a trim, graying Mr. Densesky held the store's heavy glass door open for Selma Davis. He towered above her and seemed pleased with himself for his good manners as he watched her pass. She wore humongous white sunglasses, piled-to-the-sun blonde hair, and tight beige slacks. Her low-cut cotton sweater revealed most of her considerable inventory. Headed down the street away from us, she sashayed from side to side like Marilyn Monroe in *Bus Stop*.

Ruby said, "Well would you look at the swing set in her backyard!"

Thinking that Ruby meant Densesky's had added swing sets to their line of merchandise, I asked, "Does it have a slide?"

"No, child. Just a bed that takes quarters."

"Really? Where?"

"Never mind. Help me carry in the eggs, please. They want twenty dozen this week."

It took us two trips to the Thunderbird to carry in all the eggs. We placed the cartons in front of the cash register where Mr. Densesky stood smiling. He had a No. 2 pencil behind one ear and a receipt pad where he hen-scratched a figure. He gave one copy to Ruby and slid the other underneath the cash drawer. He counted out seven dollars and then double counted to make sure that none of the bills had stuck together. After thanking her, he peered down at us. "You girls want some Necco Wafers?"

We looked dreamily at the rows of candy and gum behind him.

"Yessir!" we said.

"Just promise me one thing," he said.

"What's that?" I asked.

"You girls wind up in the egg business one day, you got to make me your first customer."

"We promise," we said.

"And another thing, you've got a beautiful grandmother. Back when we were classmates, none of the boys could keep their eyes off her. Still that way today. You girls take care of her. She's a sweetheart."

Ruby just rolled her eyes and ducked her head. She was smiling though, and I knew her spirits had been lifted.

After we left Densesky's, Ruby drove us over to the drugstore to deliver eggs to the pharmacist. It was an old store with a Western front and big plate-glass windows filled with advertisements for beauty products, vitamins, and one old poster of last year's Fireside homecoming football game.

We parked next door at a pecan tree–covered lot that was occupied, as usual, by old men playing dominoes at card tables. When Ruby stepped out into the sun, I realized she'd forgotten to wear her slip underneath her thin calico dress. Light illuminated her legs so that the metal hooks of her garter belt glistened through her calico. I had not noticed her relative nakedness when we'd gone into Densesky's because I hadn't been walking behind her.

In a rusted folding chair sat old man Ernest Boone with a huge Sylvester-who-just-swallowed-Tweety-bird smile. He'd been widowed at the age of eighteen, never remarried, and was now coasting through his seventies in search of chicks. He looked up at Ruby, mopped the sweat off his brow, and wolf whistled, "Aw, Ruby, ba-ba-ba-baby! How'd you know it was my birthday?"

"Go on back to your game, you old codger," she retorted.

"I can see clear to Kalamazoo, and I don't mean Michigan. How can I concentrate with a naked woman in front of me?"

Just then Ruby looked down at her dress and dropped three cartons of eggs on the August sidewalk where they all set to frying.

"Darlin', you can cook too? All them frying eggs just make me want you more!" yelled Ernest.

"Go to the devil, you old jackass!" fumed Ruby. She grabbed me by the hand and cha-cha-cha, our egg delivering was over for the day.

Five

So you can see that all of us living Cranbournes were a mell of a hess after Daddy's death. There had been Walt and his cows, Ruby and her slip—not to mention all those smashed eggs on the sidewalk—and the generally tangled and continuous disaster afforded everyone by Evangeline and me.

But then a bad epidemic of head lice brought us crashing back to our senses. It was the first week of school in Fireside, and thirteen children in Evangeline's second-grade class were infected. None of us could get over the fact that it had happened so early in the school year too. What an ever-loving shame!

We sat around the kitchen table at the Saturday noon meal listening to Miss Alma on the radio. Walt poured a saucerful of coffee to cool and leaned back in his chair, one ear tuned into the radio, and the other into us.

Evangeline reached into the center of the table to get a date cookie off Ruby's milk-glass platter.

"You're a big enough girl to have manners!" said Ruby. "Ask somebody to pass it to you, next time."

"Mamaw, would you please pass me the cookies?" I asked smugly.

"Show-off," growled Evangeline, crossing her eyes.

When Ruby passed me the platter, I leaned over it to select the biggest one, naturally, and then passed it to Ruby. She glanced at the dish and then took a second, startled look.

"Glory! Look at what's crawling on this platter. Walt, looka here!"

Walt settled his chair back on all four legs and then took the platter when Ruby passed it to him. "I don't see nothing but cookies."

"Put on your glasses."

Walt took his dark-rimmed glasses out of his breast pocket and settled them on his nose. "Well, I see them now." He looked up at us girls. "Which one of you monkeys has got head lice?"

"Not me," I said.

"Didn't you just lean over the cookie plate?" he asked.

"Yes, sir." I looked down at my lap, ashamed.

"Juliet's got cooties. Juliet's got cooties," sang Evangeline.

"Don't get too high and mighty," said Ruby. "Come on over here, both you girls, and let me have a look."

Ruby rose up over us and picked through our hair, first checking the spots above our ears and then at the nape of our necks. "Both you girls have got head lice."

"Want me to shear 'em?" asked Walt.

We were horror-struck at the mention of Walt using his sheep-shearing equipment on our tender heads. Furthermore, we would be laughed right out the doors of Fireside Elementary.

"No, not just yet. Why don't we try mayonnaise first? We'll suffocate the little devils, and I'll pick them out, one by one."

The next thing I knew, both Evangeline and I were perched on the kitchen counter while Ruby scooped out tablespoon after tablespoon of mayonnaise and put it on our heads until we looked like miniatures of Medusa or like mounds of coleslaw. When Ruby was satisfied that we were well coated, she put shower caps over the whole mess and said, "Girls, you'll have to wear this all day and sleep in it too."

"But Mamaw!" we protested.

"No, I mean it. The school nurse won't let you go back to the elementary until you're lice free. It's in the handbook."

"My mama wouldn't make me sleep in this darned old stuff," whined Evangeline.

"Mama ain't here, Evangeline," I said.

"When she comes home, I'm gonna tell on all of you," said Evangeline, tugging at the blue-flowered plastic shower cap that covered her head.

"You do that," said Ruby. "Until then, I'm in charge."

Tears streamed down all our faces, Ruby's included. Only Walt escaped the tears when he plucked his straw hat off the bread box. "Gonna go to town and get the mail," he mumbled.

"And leave me alone with all this?" asked Ruby.

"Thought I would."

"Don't let the screen door hit you on your way out," said Ruby between gritted teeth. It didn't take much for me to figure out that Walt wouldn't be getting any sugary kisses from Ruby that night.

After Walt left, Ruby said, "Girls, I'm gonna let you in on a little secret. Mayonnaise is a first-class beauty conditioner. It's what all the movie stars use to have that shiny, silky hair you see in the commercials. Who's to say but that the next time we go into Fireside that some Hollywood talent agent passing through might just snap up the two of you for one of his television shows."

"Really?" we said, and stood a little taller.

"Why sure. If I was some big-shot talent scout or producer, I'd be interested in signing you two Cranbourne beauties. But let's work on getting rid of those frowns first. A frown will cause anyone, even a child, to wrinkle ahead of her time. I personally never knew blues that couldn't be chased away by a little music, some grape Nehi and a bag of Cheetos."

"Yeah!"

Ruby disappeared into her bedroom and emerged with a turntable and a stack of forty-fives that had belonged to our father. "Rock Around the Clock," "Blue Suede Shoes," "My Girl," and more were played so loudly the house vibrated. We all danced, threw ourselves around the living room, and became human mixers for the masses of soda pop and Cheetos we consumed.

We could not hear the old black Ford sedan lurch to a stop in front of the house amid a cloud of caliche dust. There was no warning, no clue that Itasca Cranbourne and Walt's brother, Melville, had arrived with no good intentions.

We were in the midst of doing the twist and singing at the top of our lungs with grape-rimmed mouths and orange-tinged fingers when a vision of eternal blackness suffocated the living room, depriving us all of our next breaths.

Ruby froze as if she were about to step on a rattler. After she composed herself, she switched off the record player, wiped her hands on a Kleenex, and said, "Hello, Mother Cranbourne."

Itasca merely glared. Then Ruby looked at her brother-in-law and said, "Hey, Mel, how ya doing?"

Mel just looked down at his feet like a guilty dog with the family's Thanksgiving turkey in his mouth.

Then Itasca started in, "Have you completely lost your minds?"

She wore what I later determined was her battle wear: a moth-eaten, black pillbox hat with torn veil, peeling black leather gloves, a long-sleeved shirtwaist with pleats, and patent-leather shoes. She smelled of mothballs, though they hadn't apparently been used in time to save her wardrobe, and of a depilatory.

"Maybe," replied Ruby nervously, as she picked at imaginary hangnails.

"What have these girls got on their heads?"

"Hellmann's and shower caps."

"Whatever for?"

"Head lice."

"Oh for Pete's sake. Why didn't you just bob them really close to the scalp?"

"I'm not that mean. There's better ways these days."

Itasca plopped down into Walt's favorite chair, the one with wheels. I started to warn her, but she shot back against the living room wall and then snapped back like a rubber band. She was not harmed, but her veil fluttered upward over her hat and locked into an upright position.

Ruby managed to keep her face straight and turned her attention toward Melville. "How's Nadine?"

"Just tolerable."

"Oh? Sorry to hear that." Then Ruby apparently didn't know where to take his response so she looked back at Itasca and asked, "Mother, how are you?"

"'Bout dead of a broken heart," she said, sniffling.

"Oh, Mother Cranbourne, surely not."

"Do you doubt my word?"

"No."

"Melville, go out to the Ford and get my luggage. I can see that this household needs my supervision and unfailing good judgment. I'll be staying here for the rest of my dying days."

Ruby looked as if she'd just been punched in the stomach. I thought we might lose her to the floor, that she'd just been KO'd in the first round by Itasca, but she managed to stay upright.

Mel said, "Ruby, could you please come outside and help me with Mother's luggage? There's quite a bit."

Like a sleepwalker, Ruby followed him out the door, down the porch steps, and toward the 1961 Ford Falcon with bald tires. I pressed my nose against the screen door and watched and listened while Itasca dragged Evangeline into the kitchen to wash her hands.

"Mel, you can't leave that woman here. She hates me!"

"Ruby, you got to take her in. Nadine said she'd leave me if Mother spent one more day in our house. It's true that Mother is dying from congestive heart failure. Her lungs fill up so in the night that she has to sleep practically sitting up. She won't last more than a few months."

"A woman that mean could last forever out of spite. If Komodo dragons live for as long as fifty years, Itasca could make at least another thirty. Having her here with us will be like having a cobra for a pet. And I have these two sweet girls to look after now. Mel, we haven't got but a two-bedroom house. You know that."

"Same as us. Remember, we've got Ralph at home."

"He *still* in college?"

"No. Looking for a job."

"That son of yours is nearly old enough to apply for Social Security by now."

"He's just twenty-eight. You're his godmother; you ought to be more understanding of his plight. Don't take this out on me, Ruby. Please."

"You didn't even call me first." Ruby was starting to cry.

"Would you have let her come?"

"Hell, no."

"That's why I didn't call. Period!"

"Take her back, Mel. I'm not kidding!"

"Sorry, I just can't do it, Ruby. It's yours and Walt's turn."

"Texas ain't a bit like Arkansas. She'll never be happy here."

"Mother will never be happy anywhere, Ruby. She might as well be miserable here with you."

Mel set Itasca's luggage down on the sidewalk and one cardboard box square in the middle of Ruby's snapdragons. Without so much as a nod in Itasca's direction, Mel climbed inside his junkyard Ford, started the engine, and roared off in a cloud of caliche.

"Damnation!" yelled Ruby as she kicked one of Itasca's hard-sided suitcases. "I get one fire put out and another one springs up in its place."

What I saw written on Ruby's face that day was that she didn't think she could take another blessed iota. That feeling of just not being able to handle anything more guaranteed one thing—that like metal filings on a magnet, more weight would land on her shoulders.

Six

After Itasca had been with us for six weeks, I came to expect her to do certain things each morning without any detectable variation. At 5:30 a.m. sharp, she began blowing her nose and hacking up phlegm, as if none of us could hear her. Next, she went into the tiny closet of what used to be Evangeline's and my bedroom and began rummaging for what stunning outfit she would wear. Would she pretend to be Gloria Swanson in flapper attire, Eleanor Roosevelt in her inaugural ball gown, or plain old Emily Dickinson in a Gibson-girl outfit with a fake cameo pinned at the neck?

Evangeline and I were now sleeping on the living room hideaway bed, a great vantage point to keep an eye on Itasca when she shuffled into the kitchen. She liked to start her day off with orange pekoe tea mixed with four tablespoons of clover honey. Next, she'd drink several teaspoons of Ruby's pickle juice so that, in no time flat, all the cucumbers stood naked and withering in the jar. This infuriated Ruby to no end, but our great-grandmother was convinced that pickle juice helped to thin her thick blood. I often wished that it had done something to help her disposition—a greater problem, as far as I was concerned.

Next, Itasca began making a gigantic pot of oatmeal. My stomach lurched into my throat each time I saw her commence to pour oats in that cast-iron pot. Then she sermonized the bubbling concoction saying, "Hail Mary, full of grace…" Itasca was not a Catholic, at least not a Catholic in good standing, but it was a dramatic way to cook breakfast—a little theater with the meal preparation.

Since I did not understand anything of the Virgin Mary at the time, I had it in my mind that, like the witch she seemed, Itasca must be casting some sort of spell. The oats began to bubble wildly until the whole bottom of the pan was scorched. The smell permeated the living room and our nostrils. In my opinion, the only worse odor was that of singed chicken feathers.

At the top of her lungs, Itasca called, "All you lazy Cranbournes rise and shine. Your breakfast is ready. Come in the kitchen and eat before I throw it to the dogs."

Evangeline and I played sleeping opossums and ignored her. We wanted to buy ourselves a little more time before facing scorched oatmeal, to which she added malt.

Next came Ruby, wild-haired and in her Eva Gabor frilly robe. She snapped on the living room lamp and then drew our covers back. "C'mon girls, time to get up and come to the table for breakfast."

"Tell her I done died," said Evangeline, as she reached forward to try to pull the quilt back on top of her. Our grandmother wasn't having any of our nonsense and held firmly onto the bedcovers.

"I will do no such thing," replied Ruby.

"I got a bellyache," I said.

"Then a bowl of oatmeal will clean out your pipes," replied Ruby. She put her hands on her hips and grimaced, "Now, mind me and get out of bed."

Like prisoners of war, we marched slowly into the kitchen and sat halfway on our chairs. We each kept one leg draped over the side with a bare foot pressed firmly on the floor, ready to bolt. A smelly bowl of oatmeal had been placed in front of each of us as well as brown sugar and raisins. Ruby went over to the toaster and began to put slices of bread inside and then poured herself a cup of coffee.

While she had her back to us, Evangeline reached for several napkins and put them in her lap. She dumped the entire contents of her bowl of oatmeal into them and then excused herself to go to the bathroom. Shortly thereafter, we heard her flush the toilet and then emerge, smiling.

She slid back to the table just as Ruby slid saucers of buttered toast with peach jelly in front of us. Evangeline smiled like a cherub and said, "Grandmother Cranbourne, that was the bestest oatmeal I ever ate."

"Of course it was!" beamed Itasca.

Ruby looked baffled, but said nothing. She poured a cup of coffee for Walt and took it to him in their bedroom, where he dressed for the day.

I leaned across toward Evangeline and hissed, "Liar, liar, pants on fire. You're a cheater eater if I ever saw one." I thought about ratting on her and telling Ruby about Evangeline flushing her breakfast, but I thought better of it. I might want to do the same thing myself.

After breakfast had been endured by all, Evangeline and I dressed for school, brushed our teeth, took our vitamins, and then set out for the mile walk to the bus stop. This was one of the best parts of our day, especially since Itasca had arrived. We could avail ourselves of all the walk had to offer, without our great-grandmother's valuable insights.

There were jackrabbits we tried our best to creep up behind. Mexican blue jays swooped here and there while mourning doves cooed nearby. Occasionally, a coral snake, rattler, bull snake, or coachwhip would lie on the road ahead. We'd make the broadest possible detour around any snake, sometimes walking an acre or two away. We were terrified of snakes of any sort and ranked them right up there with beets on our list of horrors to avoid. Smells of juniper, smoke from distant fireplaces, and maybe a hint, now and then, of rain made the air an elixir that semicompensated for the burned oatmeal we'd just not eaten. For forty-five minutes to an hour each morning and afternoon, Evangeline and I were free to do as we pleased.

Sometimes, when we returned home in the afternoon, Itasca and Ruby waited for us on the front porch in the wicker furniture, drinking tea or lemonade.

Once, when Itasca was dressed as Emily Dickinson and, therefore, in her literary mode, she said, "Here come my little Shakespeare and Longfellow."

"Your what?" Evangeline asked. Then my sister turned toward me and whispered, "Is she calling us ugly names?"

"No, ignoramus," I replied. Evangeline stomped her grubby tennis shoes, full of freshly acquired pothole sludge, on top of my new plastic go-go boots. "Dummy," I added.

Itasca frowned in disbelief, not because of the interchange between my sister and me, but because of our appalling lack of literary knowledge. "They are the authors from whose works your names came, of course."

"Well, my nickname," started Evangeline, "is Rabbit. Hers is Squirrel."

"Dear me. Who gave you those?"

"Your boy. Our Popo," said Evangeline as she kicked embarrassedly at the ground.

Ruby rolled her eyes as if to say, don't get this woman started, please. She then arose from her chair, passed through the screen door, and disappeared into the living room.

"It's that sixth-grade education showing. He had to drop out to work to help support us. That's his father's fault. I'm talking about your great-grandfather and my husband, George, who left us when Walter and Melville were little boys."

This was news to us. We'd never thought about Walt having had a father, but of course, that was silly. I tried to imagine what kind of a father would have had Itasca for a daughter, but couldn't. Maybe she had been the one exception to the rule. Maybe she was an alien who'd kidnapped our *real* great-grandmother and sent her on a rocket to Pluto, or some such. I doubted whether she'd had a human mother either. No, there were some people who simply appeared on the planet without having taken the usual route.

"Girls, never marry any man named George. He will leave you, and you will grow to hate and miss him at the same time." She adjusted her Emily Dickinson bonnet and folded her wrinkled, sagging arms over her bosom. "I think there's something to names—a predestination."

"No, I already know that I won't," said Evangeline. "I aim to marry a man named James, like my daddy."

"Good choice. James is the name of a king," said Itasca. "How about you, Juliet?"

"I won't marry at all."

"Then you have the potential to fulfill your destiny!"

At the time, the word *destiny* meant a makeup vanity table, complete with powder, false eyelashes, and worlds of rouge. This is because I'd so often heard my mother talk about her *date with destiny* while she applied cosmetics seated in front of her glamour mirror and table. I envisioned myself in tap shoes and calf-length black tails, fishnet stockings, and a top hat.

"Oh, I don't think I have any talent," I said as Itasca snickered.

I often tried to picture my parents—my mother tap-dancing on Ed Sullivan's *really big show*, and my father perched on white clouds like in the

Charmin commercials. While the image of my father playing the harp didn't really fit with how I remembered him in the flesh, the picture of my mother did. I didn't blame her that she had left us.

I, myself, couldn't sing "Jingle Bells" without blowing it. Evangeline liked to do the twist and the swim along with me, but I can't say she could sing well either. We were two untalented kids—obvious embarrassments to a Broadway mother. Still, I missed certain things about her so much that I could hardly take in a good, deep breath at times.

She had often smelled of gardenia perfume and Chiclets—sort of a fruity, flowery smell that was an acquired taste. Whenever she was in *hormonal disarray* in the midst of Texas summers, she was known to open the icebox, snap on the rotating fan that sat in the middle of our kitchen table, and perch on a yellow vinyl chair. Wearing a Playtex Cross Your Heart Bra and a Wonder Girl Girdle, she looked like no other mother I'd ever seen in Austin. I wondered why she didn't think to do commercials like that and make us a mint. Then maybe she wouldn't have felt like she had to run off to Broadway.

"Mama, don't you think you ought to put some clothes on before the milkman comes?" I asked her when I was five.

"Honey, I don't care whether the milkman comes and brings the rest of the neighborhood with him! It's too danged hot to breathe in this town."

"You can have one of my Popsicles. That will cool you down."

"Maybe if I bathe in a tub full of them."

"Oh, don't do that. They've got to last me and Evangeline till grocery day."

Obviously, Evangeline and I didn't hail from regular stock. Not from either side. I don't know a thing about my mother's people—she never spoke of them. I figure that the news couldn't have been good. But anything you want to know about my dad's side, just ask.

When fall came and the days of lice and grape Nehi lagged in the distance, Itasca became queen of all she could see. Her queendom existed within her own exalted opinion of herself, and its square surface occupied everything she thought of, touched, or smelled. We allowed her to maintain that delusion up to a point.

The way I saw it, however, was that Ruby was the star attraction, and Itasca was a daffy sidekick intruding upon her limelight. Ruby was who I looked to when I needed someone to love me. Evangeline was valuable in that, if I picked a good fight with her, I could still keep my head up when it was through. I couldn't fight with Itasca. That was Ruby's job. Walt's job was to spoil us Cranbourne girls and to drive us through the pasture in search of new calves so that whosoever saw a new one first, got to name it.

He kept Evangeline out of my hair when my nerves couldn't take it. That was mainly when I'd get to missing our parents. Whenever that happened, he'd lead her out to his old blue ranch truck, and they'd knock around the pastures until dinnertime. She liked to help him gather firewood, and I would help Ruby around the house and garden.

We soon learned that the best way for me to work through my anger was to have at the hen house with cartons of eggs. Ruby would ask, "Juliet, is this a one- or two-carton day?"

"Three, just in case, Mamaw," I'd say because running out of eggs before the anger had splatted into nothing against the wooden hut was like leaving a grass bur halfway stuck to my derriere. I would carry the cartons out to the hen house and throw the first batch as fast as I could hurl them. By the time I got to the second carton, I'd forgotten what I was mad about and was just enjoying watching them slide down the tin walls. Finally, I got into the art of it and enjoyed creating various images in egg against weathered wooden boards.

The pullet hens would run to the mess I'd made and start pecking at the shells. Later, after having consumed so many, the pullets would produce sturdier eggshells themselves. I would like to point out that this is not cannibalism among chickens because those eggs were not fertilized. So you see, there was method in Ruby's and my madness. It always cracked down to this: Ruby had helped me throw myself out of the depths of despair once again, and I helped those pullet hens to lay better.

Ruby was the real monarch of the ranch. To look at her delicate frame, her red updo often pinned back with combs, and her penchant for wearing lipstick even while hoeing weeds in the shade of her bouncing, broad-brimmed straw hat, no one would have guessed how much her garden meant to her. While she might appear elegantly misplaced by an unseen hand between the rows of tomatoes and squash, we knew better. She lived to grow the world's best Beefmaster tomatoes, which won the blue ribbon each July at the Maitlin County Fair. Even in the fall and winter, she combed through seed catalogues, wistfully eyeing photographs of old, scraggly coots in overalls standing next to gigantic Beefmasters still attached to the vine.

One afternoon while Evangeline and Walt were out checking cattle for worms, Ruby and I sat on the eggplant-colored sofa. We could hear Itasca's great snores coming from our bedroom as she took her regularly scheduled two o'clock nap. I traced my finger over the maple leaf design on the sofa's velour and listened to Ruby breathe and sigh contentedly. She would let me lean my head on her shoulder until I put her arm to sleep. With just the two of us sitting there like that, I could think her into that Mama spot.

She pointed to this year's winner of the tomato contest in the *Seed Outfitter's Catalogue*. "Bet you five dollars and an Eskimo Pie that the bottom of this giant Bragger tomato is rotten as a year-old egg. That's why they didn't move it to take this picture."

"Mamaw, you've grown tomatoes a powerful lot bigger than that one," I pointed out.

"That's true. And mine taste fit for Ingrid Bergman or Jack Lemmon any day of the week. Some of these in the pictures taste about like candle wax."

"Why don't we take a picture of you next summer at the county fair with your new blue ribbon and send it in?"

"I could win a trip to Gary, Indiana, to meet the head of *Seed Outfitter's Catalogue* and maybe Horton Hall, star of all the Supersonic Garden Fertilizer commercials."

"They might even want you to star in one of their advertisements. You could wear your sunflower party dress, garden hat, and white gloves and point out your Beefmasters one by one, like they do patio furniture on *Let's Make a Deal*."

Then we were startled by a great deal of racket issuing from Itasca's room. Her snores halted with an abrupt snort as she thrashed around in her bed and started coughing up Tibet.

Ruby stiffened and called, "Mother Cranbourne, you all right?"

No answer. Ruby moved the magazine off her lap and gently slid her arm from under my head. "Stay here," she said.

I was half afraid of Itasca anyhow, but when she commenced to hacking and coughing up whole nations like she did, I flat out avoided her like some might cholera.

Her plague was hard to put my finger on. Some days, Itasca got around like aging royalty, ordering us to fetch this afghan or that piece of peach pie. At other times, she would hole up in her room and act like she hadn't the energy to lick a stamp. Eventually, I thought I saw a pattern. On the days when her condition seemed most severe, I recalled that she had eaten her oatmeal in the morning. This realization doubled my conviction that oatmeal will kill you if you eat it for seventy-plus years.

Partially muffled bits of discussion seeped from Itasca's bedroom.

"Ruby, don't you call that moth-eaten old quack. Nothing he can do."

"He's a good man. Check you over good. What he's there for."

Ruby emerged from Itasca's bedroom and called me up from the couch. "Go get Grandmother Cranbourne a Dr. Pepper with ice, Juliet. Take it to her while I call the doctor."

I froze, trying quickly to think of a good excuse not to go to Itasca's bedroom. "How 'bout I set it on the floor outside her room?"

"You afraid of something?" Ruby raised her eyebrows.

"Of catching that oatmeal disease," I replied, looking at my folded hands.

"There's nothing that poor old woman has got that you could catch," Ruby said. "Go on now, do what I told you."

I went into the kitchen, got an ice tray from the freezer, and walked at a snail's pace to the sink. Oh, I ran water over the tray, this way and that, taking my own sweet time. Then it occurred to me that I could practice reciting my favorite poem: "To A Louse, On Seeing One On A Lady's Bonnet At Church," by Robert Burns, which I had memorized after the day of the mayonnaise:

Ha! whaur ye gaun, ye crowlin
ferlie!
Your impudence protects you
sairly;
I canna say but ye strunt
rarely,
Owre gauze and lace;
Tho' faith! I fear ye dine but
sparely

On sic a place.
Ye ugly, creepin, blastit
wonner,…

I was truly just getting wound up good when I felt two clammy old hands upon my shoulders. The tray of partially defrosted ice cubes clattered into Ruby's sink.

"Child, I didn't know anybody from Texas could read well enough to know Burns, much less memorize him." Itasca, piqued-faced and weak like mop string, had risen from the dead while I'd fiddled around the kitchen trying to avoid seeing her. I was suddenly filled with shame.

"I'm sorry. I should have come right away. I know better."

"Bring me that Dr. Pepper, and you can finish reciting your poem."

So the days passed, with Itasca clothed in costumes on some, and in fairly normal nightgowns on others. On the bad days, I was summoned to her tiny quarters to read to her whatever I'd checked out from the school library.

She'd turned our bedroom into a museum of memories. There was the oriental fan she'd used while attending the dinner theater in Boston; the remains of two tickets for the train from Washington, DC, to New York framed with a menu from a restaurant called La Petite Fille; and a black silhouette of Itasca as a young girl pressed against red velvet and framed. To think that Itasca had ever been a girl was shocking news to me. Wrinkled, bizarre, eccentric Itasca made me believe she'd been born old. The idea that she just might have been a fun person who'd done interesting things was otherworldly—like a meteorite hurled from the end of the universe, alien and miraculous.

Furthermore, Itasca's memorabilia reminded me of something my mama might have placed on her walls had she been young at the same time as Itasca. Just thinking of her made me feel like I needed to go lie down on the sofa with an ice bag to soothe my aching head.

Evangeline and I missed our parents so much that we came to make them into faultless champions of goodness and morality, which they were not. I told every child who would listen that my mama had been invited to the White House to sing for President Johnson and Lady Bird. After she finished with that, I said, she flew to India to raise money for the poor with her one-woman show. You can't beat that with a stick, I informed a row of fourth graders as we stood in line for the playground slide.

Fireside Elementary was flanked on either side by the junior high and high schools, creating the shape of a horseshoe. Its front faced Densesky's, the store that unfairly enticed us with the strawberry ice cream, bubble gum, and jawbreakers we were forbidden to leave campus to purchase. Behind the elementary school was the playground that consisted of four pieces of equipment embedded in a sea of sand and gravel. The fourth and second grades shared the same playground period, which was 2:10 p.m. every day. I liked to watch my sister fly from the teeter-totter to the swings and metal slide and then on to the monkey bars like a banshee.

One afternoon in October, Evangeline carried on about how *her daddy* (never mind that he was mine too) flew all kinds of lifesaving missions in that Huey before he got shot down. Well, there was some truth to that one. Then who started his bullying act but scab-headed Nathan Wilcot. He'd said that, no, our daddy durned sure hadn't and that everybody knew he was a lying pissant to boot. Nathan drew back his right boot and kicked a storm of dust and sand into Evangeline's eyes.

"Leave her alone!" I shouted and ran toward him. "Haven't you got a lick of sense?"

Nathan put up his fists as if he meant to fight me. His filthy olive-green knit sweater was coming unraveled at the bottom. Frayed yarn coiled against his worn leather belt that was four sizes too big for him. He spat on the playground, looked back up at my sister, and sneered, "You calling me stupid?"

My classmate, William Bartlett, left his circle of friends over by the sycamore tree and ran up by my side and stared down at Nathan. "Nobody wants to fight with you, Nathan. Why don't you leave them be? Tell you what, I've got some jawbreakers in my pocket. I'll give them to you if you'll go on." The bully paused and seemed to consider what William had offered.

Nathan had a reputation for fighting anything or anybody that moved. His shadow. Boys who bumped into him while in line for the water fountain. Six graders who had a pair of shoes he wanted. He'd once fought a rooster and had come out scratched to pieces, but undaunted. That rooster, tough as an old saddle, wound up on the noon table fried in egg, flour, and milk batter. Everyone knew he'd locked his brother in the outhouse for three days before a neighbor found him.

Nathan and his odd family lived on the edge of the wrecking yard, selling salvage off old refrigerators and cars. They had electricity, but no running water—an inconvenience that hardly seemed to bother Nathan, his lazy mother, or his delinquent older brother. Like barnyard cats, they did not take to washing themselves except for weddings and funerals. Dirt was no problem to them. Neither was rust, as they lived in a sea of corroded wreckage.

"I'm saying that we miss our daddy." I stared a hole in him, knowing better than to let on that I'd rather not fight. "If Evangeline wants to brag all the livelong day about him, you let her. Wouldn't you miss your dad if he up and died?"

"I ain't never had no daddy." He paused and looked into the distance. "Least ways, I don't remember if I did."

True to his word, William dug into his jeans pocket, pulled out a handful of miniature jawbreakers, and offered them to Nathan. He grabbed them greedily, stuck three in his mouth, but punched at the air with his fists, anyway. "Thanks for nothing, sucker!" he mumbled through his mouthful.

"A man's word ought to mean something," said William.

"Guess I ought to knock some smarts into you, you sorry momma's boy," said Nathan, as candy dye dribbled down his chin. "First, I got to learn these girls a lesson."

William stepped between him and us, and said, "You'll have to whip me to get to them."

The grit in Evangeline's eyes made them itch. She began crying and rubbing her eyes, and the more she did, the more they smarted. "C'mon," I said. "Let's go over to the water faucet by the front steps, and I'll help you get the sand out."

Nathan just stood there with his fists raised, but let us all walk away, including William. Then, because he was all dressed up and had nowhere to go, he reached out and punched a fourth-grade boy on crutches in the stomach.

Within moments, Nathan was hauled off in the direction of the principal's office by fourth-grade teacher Judy Fishhook Whisenant. At six feet five inches, Judy was the only person on campus whom Nathan both feared and respected. William waited until Nathan was gone before he returned to his group of friends.

Just as Evangeline and I rounded the school building toward the front, my attention was drawn to a silver-haired man in Densesky's parking lot.

"Good heavens, there's Popo," I said.

"Shout for him to come fetch us," said Evangeline, with both eyes squeezed shut.

"He's busy."

"Doing what?" Evangeline whined. She was working herself up into a champion-class pout.

"Just a minute, let me look."

Walt was dressed in his finest going-to-town khaki clothes, ostrich-leather Tony Lama boots, and a Stetson hat. He and Selma Davis stood next to his truck, just one measly arm's length apart. Selma was wearing a tight-knit sweater and matching purple miniskirt. Her way-too-blonde hair was teased like nobody's business, pinned into a Pisa-like architectural miracle, and sprayed into a concrete permanency that only a can of Aquanet could provide. Autumn's afternoon sunshine glinted on her gigantic hoop earrings. Luminous pink lipstick and white sunglasses were frosting on a Southern wedding cake of a woman.

Walt reached into his open truck window, pulled out a small package, and handed it to Selma. Pressing it to her ample bosom, she reached out, touched his arm, and let her fingers linger there before she patted him and stepped backward. A moment later, she hurried into Densesky's with the package still pressed against her.

"Well, slowpoke, what's he doing?" Evangeline asked impatiently. Tears from tightly closed eyes still streamed down her dirt-streaked face.

"I was wrong," I said. "It was somebody else who looked like Walt. But it was definitely, *definitely*, not him."

"How could you tell for sure?"

"Wasn't near as handsome. And he sure as shootin' didn't act like him."

All I could think about as I helped Evangeline wash the grit out of her eyes was Ruby. How she was back home up to her ears in house- and farm work. No doubt she was listening to Itasca going on about this and that and waiting on her hand and foot, all for a man who cheated on her. No, he was not at all the Walt I thought he was.

Seven

From Evangeline's view of things, her mistrust of me was rooted from my having withheld certain key bits of information. I have always believed that what I'd done was the right thing to do, given the knowledge I'd had available at the time. I had thought long and hard about the situation and found myself blameless for the most part. That's it, *blameless* little me. You'd have done the same if you loved your little sister, wouldn't you?

Thinking back, it was to my credit that I didn't breathe a word about what I'd seen go on between Walt and Selma Davis that day at Densesky's. It isn't easy, you know, for a child that age to keep a secret of any kind. But me, I am verifiable, certifiable CIA material. I could be a spy in any country and keep national secrets tucked inside my sealed lips like peanut butter between two slices of bread. You have a secret that needs keeping, just tell me.

In my opinion, Evangeline was too big a baby to sort through such a thing. She liked to think she was a tough tomboy; she could even look that way on the playground. I knew better. She was like a Twinkie on the inside, soft and gooey. Furthermore, she could not keep a secret for all the Milk Duds in the world. Had I told her, the next thing you know, she would have been wrapped around Ruby's neck like a howler monkey, crying noisily into her cotton blouse, and telling her the whole durned mess. Ruby just plain hadn't needed to hear it. I had been ashamed, though, to have kept something from the grandmother I'd adored. I felt as if I, too, had betrayed her, and that, on some level, I was just as guilty as Walt.

I had featured the consequences of our grandparents' splitting apart. Like a rock thrown through a plate-glass window, the image I conjured up was jagged and unsightly. Ruby would have no husband to sit next to her in the pew at the Methodist church, or to fan her when she got overheated at the annual Fireside parade. Whenever she bought chocolate-covered Pinwheels at Densesky's, who would fight with Evangeline and me over the last one if Walt no longer lived with us? Who would air up the tires on the Thunderbird and see to it that the oil got changed on a regular basis?

I liked to think that Ruby would get by in the night without a man cuddled up, snoring in her ear, but who was to say she could? There would be no more plotting about burning Walt's hole-infested blue jeans while he was in town at the hardware store. You know the pair of jeans I mean. The ones Walt wore the seat out on by scooting across the front porch's concrete floor as he cracked pecans with a hammer and sent pecan shells flying like shrapnel.

What other adoring man would remember Ruby's birthday and deliver an armload of red-velvet roses and a bag of candied orange slices, just the way she liked? Who would dry dishes while she was up to her elbows in Joy dishwashing liquid and then smile and snap her on the behind with a wet towel when they'd finished? I thought just maybe I could recruit some high school boys to check the Thunderbird's tires and even to donate their sorry, worn-out jeans for her to burn in the wood stove for old time's sake. For the life of me, though, I just couldn't dream up anybody else in the world who could fill in the other holes.

How could one grandfather cause so much trouble?

I had a devil of a time reconciling the Walt I'd always known with the Walt who could be untrue to the best woman in the world. Walt, who'd carried me to the doctor to get stitches in my chin, an injury that had come from an aerial lift at the roller rink. Walt had lifted and twirled me around to the tune of "Spanish Flea" by Herb Alpert and the Tijuana Brass, and then we'd both cratered. I'd bled on the floor, down my white shirt and gold-plaid pants, and was certain that my own brief moment of roller blade stardom was about to be snuffed out, permanently.

Then two weeks later, he'd taken me again, this time to get stitches in my knee. Evangeline and I had fought on the back steps over who got to carry in the giant bottle of Dr. Pepper. I had won the battle, except the bottle had broken, and I had fallen on the glass. So what I had really won was seven stitches.

After that, I let Evangeline carry in the soda bottles all by herself. Ruby had always said that discretion was the better part of valor. That worked for me.

There was the Walt who'd driven us to school one morning when it was too messy outside to walk to the bus. Evangeline and I had run from his Chevy truck toward the front of Fireside Elementary School. I had skidded on the slippery sidewalk and fallen into a huge muddy puddle. My robin's-nest-print dress had turned from pale blue to wet and dingy brown in the front. Walt had been headed to the Tuesday cattle auction to socialize with his pals, but he drove me home like lightning, just so I could change. Then he let me cry as long as I wanted and didn't fuss a bit about the ruination of his own plans.

When his son died, and Evangeline and I lost our precious daddy, he put his own grief on hold to just plain love us. How then could a man that good have gone bad?

I needed to come up with a plan, but wasn't sure what would work. Oh, I had my ideas all right. I pictured propaganda designed to convince Ruby that we needed to change religions. I knew that Baptists were into repenting, big-time, and that Catholics were into confession. I thought that Walt could do with a little of both those things, so what I was looking for was a combo religion. A Cathoist or a Baptlic, perhaps? As Methodists, we did not, as far as I knew, go in for remorse on a grand scale. Not only did I desire a religion of remorse, but one that would boomerang Walt back into the faithful person he'd always been.

Then there was Selma, whom I thought was the cheapest thing outside of a carnival. Oh, I'd heard all about temptation and knew that Walt was the best-looking man in Fireside, no contest. But, well, she would just have to get over him, wouldn't she? I wasn't sure what my responsibilities were in this situation, or exactly how to proceed when it came to Selma, but I knew I had to do something.

Since I couldn't think up anything better, I wrote Selma a letter telling her she ought to go on over to Austin where there were plenty of handsome single men. I thought of signing Itasca's name, but thought better of it. Instead, I signed it, *Mellorine Wannamaker, new girl in town.*

In November, Itasca's health rallied. On the Monday preceding Thanksgiving, she dressed in her Eleanor Roosevelt outfit and issued orders as if she were the First Lady with the White House staff waiting on her. Spreading out her long skirts, she sat down on the firewood box that stood catty-cornered to the cast-iron kindling stove and the 1955 Frigidaire oven. Ruby was the only person I'd ever known who needed two stoves, but I could vouch that she used both all the time.

Itasca's getup was a nifty two-piece sailor outfit with a full skirt and blue ribbon trim. She wore a smart straw hat, which everybody knew was out of season for November, and cocked it low over one eye. As a mature ten-year-old, even I knew better. There was an unwritten law in Fireside that you could not wear white or straw after Labor Day, under penalty of violation of some law. While I did not know of any hardened offenders serving time in the Maitlin County Jail for such an offense, I was sure that Itasca was going to be the first jailbird in the Cranbourne family. Furthermore, if you wanted to wear your new white patent-leather Mary Janes before Easter Sunday, forget that too. White before Easter could probably earn a violator fifteen hours of community service at the very least.

Itasca seemed immune to most of Fireside's conventions. She did what she wanted, when she wanted. Nobody argued with her much—you couldn't argue with a crazy woman and win. Now, as if she'd just remembered something important, Itasca touched two fingers to her temple and launched right into Ruby's business.

"Ruby, have you purchased the Thanksgiving turkey? I don't see it in the freezer."

"No," Ruby said. "We prefer to eat one of my hens over turkey." Ruby pulled a baking sheet of soft molasses cookies from the electric oven and set it on top to cool. She switched off the burner underneath a pot of percolating coffee and poured a cup for each of them to drink. I stood pressed against the cupboard, waiting for an invitation to get a cup for myself.

"That simply will not do." Itasca sniffed disdainfully and blew the straw hat's blue ribbon out of her face.

"Why?"

"That isn't what the Pilgrims ate. I like to do things authentically." All this, I thought, coming from a woman dressed like Eleanor Roosevelt.

"We are not Pilgrims." Ruby set the coffeepot down with a clank on the stove. A bit sloshed out through the spout and sizzled onto the burner's coil.

"Nevertheless, that is what we will serve."

Ruby closed her eyes in exasperation, but didn't say a word. She simply picked up her cup of coffee, put on her green corduroy jacket, and disappeared. That left me alone with Itasca, something I never let happen on purpose if I could help it. Like a gecko, I flattened out against the cupboards and vanished through the door. I went outside and looked high and low for Ruby. She wasn't in the garden or in the potato and canned goods cellar or even in the potted plants pit. I walked out to the pullet house and checked in the feed shed, yelling, "Mamaw!" at the top of my lungs like a child lost in the wilderness.

I later found her in the washhouse reading old *National Geographic* magazines. The washhouse was a rock building situated next to Ruby's famous garden. It sagged to the right next to the smokehouse where Walt smoked venison sausage rings each December and January during hunting season.

Since Ruby couldn't stand to throw anything away, part of the room was piled chest high with old *Reader's Digests, Farm and Ranch Journals, Guideposts,* and the *National Geographics.* Odors of moldy paper, laundry detergent, and mice filled the air. If a person who wanted to hide was still enough, he or she could easily be overlooked. But Ruby gave herself away.

Grayish November light filtered through the window, illuminating a thin trail of cigar smoke. Ruby sat with her feet curled up underneath her, drinking coffee and smoking one of Walt's occasional Muriel cigars. Music from the cigar commercial came to mind with Ruby replacing Edie Adams in the slinky, sequined evening gown and feather boa, all to the beat of Bob Fosse's play, *Sweet Charity*:

The minute you walked in the joint
I could see you were a man of distinction
A real big spender, good-looking, so refined…

This flashback to the commercial deepened my shock at seeing my grandmother smoke. They preached against this kind of thing on Sundays at the Fireside Baptist Church, didn't they?

"Mamaw! I didn't know you smoked."

"I don't," Ruby said, dropping the cigar into the ashtray like a hot dish. "At least, I didn't till now."

"Well, is it nasty?"

"That depends on what you want to compare it with," she replied, picking up the cigar and taking another puff.

"Nasty, as in, say, smoking a cow paddy?"

"No, it's way beyond that." Ruby took a swig of cold coffee from a rooster cup with one hand and lifted the machine-wrapped cigar up to her lips with another. As the smoke drifted upward, she blinked her eyes a number of times and then sneezed. "Sort of like smoking the bottom of a septic tank. Apparently, it's an acquired taste. Can't figure out for the life of me what Walt sees in this stuff."

"Then why do it?" I asked.

"So you won't have to, Juliet." She stared me down like a science teacher examining a witch-tree bug under a magnifying glass. "I'm setting the example of why smoking is no good. Later, if you are truly tempted, you can just refer to this occasion, rather than trying it yourself. I've saved you from the agony of learning the hard way. I've done you a favor."

"Oh," I said, not terribly satisfied.

It was then we heard the sound of Ruby's Thunderbird starting up and backing out of the garage at the speed of light. Then there was the screech of tires and the revving of a motor as the car was mistakenly shifted into neutral. The drive gear was found, and a hot-rodding thief was off to the races.

A horrified look crossed Ruby's face. It was the same expression that might be worn by a mother who'd left her baby in a grocery cart and realized that fact as she unloaded the last bag of groceries from her car at home. We dashed out of the washhouse, slamming the screen door behind us like a swat against a bully's behind. Racing past the water tower on the north side of the house and through the side-yard gate, we arrived just in time to witness Itasca roaring off in Elvis's gift.

"Ahhhhhhh," Ruby screamed. She threw herself down on the muddy ground like a two-year-old pitching a walleyed fit in the candy section of Densesky's. I felt cheated somehow. If a fit were going to be pitched, it was my place to do it. I was the kid. Maybe I could have outdone her, kicked harder, or screamed louder, but Ruby was doing a pretty good job on her own for a grandmother.

"C'mon, Mamaw, let's go on into the house and wash your face and hands," I said. "She'll be back directly."

Ruby looked at me with clumps of mud and grass stuck to her red hair and clothes. If it had been me, I'd have picked a cleaner spot to pitch a fit. I guessed my experience in that department was fresher than hers. Ruby was old—at least in her fifties. Old people forgot how to do things. Couldn't remember how to jump a double rope. Maybe sometimes failed to lift their feet when we drove over railroad tracks. Old people didn't understand the need to shut closet doors at night to keep vampires and bats from coming into the bedroom. They never walked backward to undo a mistake and didn't believe they could flap their wings and make it to the moon by jumping off the cement table in the yard.

The older folks got, the slower their blood, the more ignorant they became of our gospel—the truths we knew that saved us from all sorts of disasters, taking into account the current one.

Ruby let me lead her through the gate, up the steps, and into the side door of the house. "Where's Walt?" she asked.

"He and Evangeline are out feeding the sheep and goats. They fed the cows last night, so this morning they went to the south pasture where the Corriedale and Angora are."

"Why'd they do that?" Ruby asked, pouting.

"I think it's color-coded. They feed the brown ones in the afternoons and the white ones in the morning."

"No, I mean why couldn't he be here when I need him?"

"Well, I'm here," I replied hesitantly.

"Yes, Sugar Foot, you sure are." Ruby's voice was tender for a moment, but then she caught back up with her furor. "I want him to go and lasso that old heifer. No one drives my Thunderbird except me."

Walt and Evangeline must have had a sixth sense about Ruby's condition because they stayed away. Two hours later, Itasca came creeping up the road in Ruby's dented Thunderbird. The front fender was catawampus, and the imprint of an animal lay across the hood. Bits of blood and white hair were plastered against the grill. Ruby's face went funeral-parlor white just as Itasca emerged from the car, triumphant.

"I bought the Thanksgiving turkey and got the mail! You left your keys on your dresser, so I thought I'd help out a little in preparation for Thursday's dinner." Pleased with herself, Itasca smoothed down her First-Lady sailor dress and adjusted her ridiculous hat. She beamed at me and said, "Juliet, please bring in the turkey and the mail. I think I deserve a cup of tea."

I looked back anxiously at Ruby, waiting for the volcanic eruption I knew was her due, but she stared into space. "C'mon, Mamaw. Popo can fix your Thunderbird. He can fix anything."

Eight

Itasca never once apologized to Ruby for damaging her precious car. She never even made reference to it. I wasn't really sure she even knew she'd hit anything—considering the shape her mind was in those days. Anyway, it was too late to change anything. Even walking backward and speaking pig latin couldn't undo it. And if that wouldn't work, then I didn't know what would.

I opened up the passenger side of the Thunderbird, pushed forward the seat, and managed to pull out the fattest old Butterball I'd ever seen. On the seat beside it was the mail: an advertisement for a life insurance and burial policy, a bill from the electric company, and a package with Evangeline's and my name on it! It had a New York City postmark. At last, our mama had remembered she had two girls.

I knew it wasn't right, but you see I just couldn't help myself. I set the turkey on the floorboard and opened the package right then and there. I should have waited for my sister.

Instead, I tore the outer layer of brown wrapping paper off to find a red-and-black check carton, like the kind the bank sends when you reorder a new batch. Inside, nestled against cotton, were two buffalo nickels in silver bezels with slender matching chains.

"Oh, what beautiful necklaces!" I said, fingering them as if they were made of platinum and diamonds. Of course, to me they were worth far more than that. You cannot place a value on word from a mother who seemed to have forgotten you. Underneath the necklaces and cotton was a short note, written by an elegant hand. The penmanship was sweeping and grand and graceful as a doe leaping across a fence.

Dear Juliet and Evangeline,

I have missed you both. Here are the necklaces I had made to let you know I am thinking of you. You two girls are the apples of my eye. Remember that I love you with all my heart. Mind Ruby and Walt. Do your best in school and don't let the skeeters bite you in the night.

Love,

Mama

I turned the paper over and over, hoping to find the words I wanted to read most of all, like, *I'll be home for Thanksgiving. Have your bags packed girls, because I'm bringing you both back up to New York with me.* I could see nothing else, so I crossed my eyes to see if it helped to look that way. Then I cocked my head to one side and looked out of the far corner of my right eye. Nothing. I tried the same from my left eye, and finally gave up. What I'd hoped for just wasn't there.

After I'd managed to get the turkey into the house and hide our package behind the sofa, Walt and Evangeline drove up in his pasture-beaten truck with the shocks nearly shot. They stopped outside by the smokehouse where Walt opened the tailgate and pulled out a bloody, dead-as-lead angora goat. I'd run back outside as soon as I'd heard them, eager to tattle on Itasca, but watching Walt took the wind out of my sails.

He tied the hind legs of the goat together with rope and then strung the whole mess up on a pulley, upside down. He hoisted the carcass up to eye level and proceeded to gut it, dropping the steaming entrails into a metal bucket.

"Aw that stinks," Evangeline said, cupping her hand over her nose.

"You'll get over it before you're married, Rabbit," Walt said and winked.

"Married! I'm in the second grade," she said, indignantly.

"In that case, you're getting a little long in the tooth to still be single."

"I'll just marry you then, Popo."

"Sorry, Ruby beat you to it."

Walt proceeded to skin out the goat, starting at the hind legs and moving downward the neck. When he'd finished, he washed the whole mess with the garden hose.

"Now, Squirrel, go inside and fetch me a clean old sheet to wrap this up in."

I disappeared into the house, got into the linen closet in the bathroom, and returned with something stained and yellowed that looked as if it was about a thousand years old. After Walt took the carcass down from the pulley, he wrapped it in the sheet, carried it into the house, and placed it on Ruby's kitchen counter.

I pulled Evangeline into the living room and dug out Mama's gift from behind the sofa. "Here you go," I said. "You can have the pick of which one you want for yourself." That was big of me, I thought.

"They're exactly the same," she said, regarding the necklaces with suspicion.

"Well then, I'll pick, smarty-pants."

"No, I want to." She reached into the red-and-black box and lifted one necklace out of the cotton. "This one's calling to me."

We helped one another fasten the new jewelry around our necks and admired ourselves in Walt's magnifying mirror.

"We could wear these to one of Mama's plays," I said.

"Is she coming to get us?" Evangeline's eyes were brown and wide as a doe's.

"She didn't say she was. I'm just hoping she will."

"I'd rather have her than this darned old necklace."

"Me too," I said. "But at least we know she's thinking of us."

"That ain't good enough."

"No, it isn't. Sure isn't."

That night, Ruby worked her fingers to the bone. She cooked a mess of frozen black-eyed peas, butternut squash with cream, red sugar beets (which you could not make me eat, even if I was starving to death), and baked cabrito in barbecue sauce.

After dinner was on the table, Evangeline and I sat down next to one another, wearing our new necklaces. Directly across from me was Itasca between Walt and Ruby.

"Let's say the blessing," Walt said and bowed his head. "Father, we thank you for this bounty we are about to receive. Amen."

Walt opened his eyes and reached out to serve himself some cabrito. He then stuck the serving fork into strips of tender young goat meat and placed some onto Evangeline's plate and then some on mine.

"Plate's too heavy and hot to pass," he said.

Evangeline put her head into her hands and set to bawling.

"What's the matter, Rabbit?" Walt set the fork back down and looked at her in surprise.

"I can't eat none of this!"

"Why on earth not?" Ruby said.

"It has tire tracks on it."

"For heaven's sake," Itasca said and pursed her wrinkled lips.

"Well, Grandmother Cranbourne ran over it in Mamaw's Thunderbird, didn't she?" Evangeline folded her arms across her chest and gave Itasca the evil eye.

"Popo," I said. "*She* drove Mamaw's car without permission and ruined it!" There, I'd said it, and hoped I'd gotten Itasca in double big trouble.

"Squirrel! Rabbit! Don't be tattling," Walt said.

I looked up at Ruby who was smiling at me, big as you please. I knew at that moment she loved me more than she ever had.

On the opposite side of the table, Itasca glared at me as if I were a scorpion she was about to splat with her shoe. She was about to get even in the worst way I could imagine. "Juliet, you're not eating the sugar beets."

"I can't abide beets, no offense to Mamaw's cooking."

"Eat them, all the same," Itasca said.

"No, ma'am. Thank you, though."

"You do not tell your elders no, child."

Itasca stood up from her chair and came to my side. She stabbed a forkful of beets and tried to force them into my mouth. I made myself go limp as a noodle and slithered to the floor. You cannot make a noodle eat.

"Mother, stop it! You leave the girls' rearing to Ruby and me," Walt said, his face reddening.

"What a poor example you have set for your grandchildren, Walter Scott Cranbourne."

"The girls have been through a lot. They don't need to go to war over beets and goat meat."

"In my day…" Itasca said. Blah. Blah. Blah. Her words ran together until they became like the droning noise of an oscillating fan. I picked myself up off the floor and proceeded to eat my cabrito and Evangeline's too. Oh how sweet the taste of young goat after battling an old one. Even so, I was careful to use my best manners and avoided looking at Evangeline for fear we'd giggle.

That night, Evangeline and I were pressed into place under a mountain of quilts, like petals between the pages of a family Bible. The old sleeper sofa had coils that stuck me in the back when I rolled into the sloping middle toward my sister. I could hear Ruby and Walt in bed in the next room. Ruby cried, blew her nose, and then cried some more.

"Ruby, don't worry, darlin'. I'll take it down to the Fireside Body Shop and have it fixed and repainted," Walt said.

"It won't ever be the same," she said.

"No, it will be better. Remember the hail dents?"

"Yes, darlin'."

"Well, they'll be gone too."

"They will?"

"You betcha." Then I heard them shift in the bed. "Ruby, you are the light of my life. I'm a lucky man to have you. You do so much for all of us. I can't think where we'd be without you."

"Oh, Walt. I love you more than Elvis." Ruby giggled like a schoolgirl.

Before I finally drifted off to sleep, I thought, just so Selma Davis hasn't been lighting up your life lately. That's all I care.

Nine

Stubbornness runs high in my family, except that I am practically perfect. I work hard at that. I have wondered, though, where the *others* inherited theirs. It could have come from our daddy, mother, Ruby, or Itasca. There are as many hard heads in our family tree as there are acorns on a live oak.

Ruby refused to cook Itasca's Butterball on Thanksgiving morning. Instead, she had set about making cornbread dressing with apples, onion, raisins, chopped pecans, evaporated milk, two pans of cornbread, seven slices of white sandwich bread, eggs, broth, poultry seasoning, sage, and salt and pepper. Like always, she'd put one of her own fat hens into the roasting pan and slid it into the stove. It had been Walt's job to feed the fire and keep us girls out of the kitchen.

Walt suggested, "Squirrel, Rabbit, c'mon with me into the living room. Macy's Thanksgiving Day Parade is about to begin. Rabbit, why don't you go turn on the television set?"

Walt's silver hair caught my attention. It had always been like a magnet to us girls, drawing our natural beauty-operator instincts toward him. I asked, "Can I comb your hair, Popo?" He looked at me, smiled, and opened his mouth as if to reply.

"No, I want to comb his hair," said Evangeline as she pulled the *on* button of the old RCA.

"Copycat!" I said. "When I get through, it'll be your turn. I called it first."

"But you always get to do everything first because you're oldest," she whined, coming toward me with her rabbit eyes squeezed into a glare and her determined jaw jutted out.

Walt waved his hands in exasperation. "Girls, stop fussing. I'll flip a quarter—that'll settle it." Walt reached into his overalls and pulled out a coin. "Okay, Squirrel, what do you call?"

"Heads I win, tails you lose, Evangeline."

"That don't sound fair to me. What are you trying to pull?"

"I just called it first," I replied innocently.

"Squirrel, Santa Claus is listening this time of year. Make it right with Rabbit."

"I call heads," I said, staring a hole through Evangeline's forehead.

"Tails," she said.

Walt flipped the quarter and said, "Tails, it is."

Just as soon as Walt turned his back and headed toward his favorite chair, Evangeline stuck out her tongue at me. I wrinkled up my nose at her and watched Walt ease himself down into his old squeaky office chair. Ruby had recently reupholstered it with the deerskin off the buck she'd shot through the kitchen window last fall. The chair had rollers so that Walt could scoot himself all across the living room's wood floor, change the television station, and snap back into his corner by the lamp and bookcase, all without having to stand up.

Evangeline plucked his black plastic comb off the bookcase and set to styling Walt's already perfectly groomed hair.

About the time the RCA warmed up, I could hear Itasca and Ruby heat up the kitchen. I walked over to the ottoman, plopped down, and, like a spy, peered around the doorway to take in what I knew would be more interesting than to watch Evangeline tease Walt's hair.

Itasca wore her Emily Dickinson outfit, which approximated the closest thing she owned to a Pilgrim's dress, never mind that it was centuries off cue. She'd also put on one of those Betty Crocker–like aprons that covered her all the way from her wrinkled, age-spot-covered neck down to her knees. Embroidered across the chest was *Queen Bee of the Whole Hive.*

"R-u-b-y," she said crossly, "just where in the devil is the roasting pan?"

"Being used in the wood stove," Ruby said, barely above a whisper, as she mixed a bag of miniature marshmallows into a bowl of heavenly hash.

"Well, I need one for the electric stove! A large one, if you please."

"I haven't got a large one." Ruby's voice may have been soft, but it had a steel foundation.

"Then this is a poorly stocked kitchen, if you ask me."

"Think what you like."

"R-u-b-y, get on the telephone and call that pretty blonde woman who works at that pathetic excuse of a store. Densesky's, isn't it? Have her deliver one to us."

Ruby set down a bowl of whipped cream that she was blending into the heavenly hash and looked up in disbelief. "You mean you want Selma to trot out here on Thanksgiving Day and deliver us a roasting pan?"

"Within the hour." Itasca's fiercely starched, somber Emily Dickinson outfit crinkled.

"I'm afraid you'll have to make do with what we have."

"Do not talk down to me. Call her!" said Itasca, shaking her finger at Ruby.

"That woman…has no business…in my house…today, or any other day," said Ruby, slowly enunciating her words with distaste like a toddler chewing boiled liver.

To punctuate her point, Itasca jerked off her Queen Bee apron and threw it on top of Ruby's wood-burning stove. Within seconds, it caught fire, but Itasca merely shrugged and stomped off toward her bedroom. Ruby grabbed a pair of long-handled tongs, stuffed the blazing cloth down in between the logs of the oven, and let it burn.

"Well, tutti-frutti!" said Ruby.

Word had it that Selma Davis had grown up in Sacramento, California, and had the same bittersweet sassiness of a grapefruit compared to, say, pears or bananas. A rumor had gone around Fireside that her folks had been truckers who hauled citrus fruit across the nation. Grapefruit, oranges, limes, and lemons—you name it. If it was citrus, they hauled it. I heard she'd even been born on the floorboard of her folks' Peterbilt rig while crossing the Brazos River in Waco. Selma claimed to remember the feel of the rubber floor mat against her tender backside as she slid out of her mother's body like an overripe banana.

Fortunately, it had been her daddy's turn at the wheel, as her mama was completely unaware of what was about to happen. Her mama had been filing her nails, and then leaned out the passenger window and, with a little gusto, blew the nail dust onto the river bridge. You can imagine her surprise when her baby girl emerged at the exact same moment. That explained a lot about what made Selma like she was, in my book.

No one knew exactly what it was she'd done for a living before coming to Fireside, but I had a strong possibility fixed in my mind. I thought she'd most likely been a go-go girl who'd danced half-naked for money in one of those cages. You've seen them on the TV wearing bikinis and strange tattoos painted on their bare skin. Words like *Groovy, Far Out, Peace, Dig it? Luv,* and *No Nam!* Once I'd seen a go-go girl for about a split second before Ruby snapped off the television, saying she didn't want us girls filling up our young minds with such trash.

While Selma might have been born on the floorboard of a citrus rig, it didn't mean she had nothing going on upstairs. She had a mind like a brain surgeon's: the ability to focus on business at hand and eat a sandwich at the same time, or at least remember having eaten one.

Over the summer, I'd cornered Selma by the stack of lime-green go-go boots she was organizing. I slipped some dangle bracelets over my skinny wrist and gave them a spin. Selma was watching me out of the corner of her eyes and I, her. She was wearing an orange psychedelic dress and matching boots, which led me to think of Orange Dreamsicles. This just naturally inspired me to start the quiz that had made her famous in Fireside.

"Say, Selma, what did you have for supper on May third of 1958 and where?"

"I had meatloaf, lima beans, and mashed potatoes at Mother's Little Truck Stop in Bakersfield, California."

I tried to get the best of her and asked, "How about on July seventh of 1960?"

"Brussels sprouts, macaroni and cheese, and Spam."

"Sure it wasn't, say, green beans instead of brussels sprouts?

"You sure how many eyes you got, Juliet?" she replied, pulling one green boot out of a box and setting it on top for display.

"Yes, Miss Selma."

"Then I'm sure it was brussels sprouts."

Word had it that Selma could do most anything she set her mind to doing. She could parallel park a big rig in front of Densesky's when burly, muscle-bound men couldn't. As if they were no bigger problem than selling Ruby's eggs, she ordered and sold G.E. appliances in such abundance that virtually every house in Fireside had a General Electric skillet, except ours, of course. She also sold fabric by the yard, cutting it on as straight a line as any surgeon. No telling how many patterns and notions she sold to young and old seamstresses alike, and was even looked up to as a fashion guru by Fireside teenagers.

"Just remember girls," she told her young customers. "This year, everything is big and short. Big sunglasses. Big teased, frosted hair. Big boots like Nancy Sinatra wears. Skirts so short you should not cross your legs at the knee, and short shorts. The big and the short of it will take you anywhere you want to go."

I might have really liked her if I hadn't believed her so dead set on winning Walt. Girls my age and up followed Selma like ducklings on a pond. If Selma wore Dreamsicle orange, lime green, or watermelon red, then the girls in Fireside High School rushed to buy fabric in those colors or, better yet, a ready-made dress from Densesky's that was an exact replica of hers. Whenever Selma drew her liquid eyeliner out long on the sides like a cat, little copy kittens sprang up in English class at school, underneath hair dryers at the salon, and at slumber parties.

Even the music that Selma selected to play over the dry goods system, one wall away from the grocery section at Densesky's, was a trendsetter. This was an issue between herself and Mr. Densesky who did not always have his finger on the pulse of young America. The grocery section of Densesky's played music by Lawrence Welk and Benny Goodman because that was what he liked. Selma, however, had control over the music in the dry goods and appliance areas, and she charmed us inside with the music of Petula Clark, Sonny and Cher, and the *one and only* Mr. Tom Jones.

There was exactly one virtue that kept Selma from being tarred and feathered by the mature women of Fireside who did not appreciate her ability to distract their husbands, and that was the fact that she never missed a Sunday service at Epiphany Methodist Church on Main Street. However, this virtue was tainted by the unnerving fact that she insisted upon wearing her way-too-short miniskirts to church, just like Sunday was a regular day of the week.

"She's too old to be wearing such," grumbled Ruby one Sunday, but that was purely conjecture on her part since nobody in Fireside had any idea what Selma's real age was. The men swore she wasn't a day over thirty, while women had it on good authority that she was at least forty-five and, like old lettuce, was headed for seed any minute.

Selma also managed the gift shop area in Densesky's that took up only two rows in the dry goods department. This was my favorite place to browse in Fireside because the possibilities were endless. It displayed cucumber-shaped pickle forks, temporary Batman tattoos, windup alarm clocks in the shape of Basset hounds with signs around their necks that said, *Just wind my tail, I'll howl and wail,* Silly Putty, ceramic dishes for banana splits, coconut-scented aftershave, and Betty's Bath Bubbles that smelled a little like Tootsie Rolls.

My new best friend at Fireside Elementary was sandy-haired Dixie Flagg who lived next door to Selma. Dixie claimed to have an incriminating file on Selma, filled to overflowing with verifiable truths about her moral character, boyfriend and husband history, strands from her last haircut confirming once and for all that she was not a natural blonde, a telephone bill that had blown out of the trash can into Dixie's hands, a magazine renewal card from *Vogue*, which proved she did not have an original fashion idea in her head, and six loose S&H Green Stamps that had fallen out of a grocery bag that *had not come from Densesky's*—the very fact of which could get her fired forever and ever, amen.

Selma set a sad example for the women of this country and was, by nature, a lone wolf. All of her family was long dead, and, furthermore, she had been made a widow due to the sudden, mysterious death of her unsuspecting husband.

"Wonder what killed him?" I asked Dixie as we took turns at the school water fountain in the main hall.

"Got hit by a bolt of lightning in the dumpster behind Densesky's." Dixie shoved up the sleeves of her yellow sweat shirt and held her ratty hair back with one hand while she took a drink from the fountain and then wiped her mouth on her upper arm.

"What in the thunder was he doing in there?"

"Selma got mad at Dave and threw her wedding ring away. Later, they kissed and made up," Dixie giggled. "Then when he went to fetch her ring, *bingo*, his number was called. Lightning struck and killed him before he knew what hit him."

"What a nasty way to go," I replied.

"Nasty, but fast," said Dixie. "They say that when the fire department hauled him outta there, her ring was clutched in his burned hand. Was Selma's fault he died the way he did. A crying shame, if you ask me. I think you can convict someone for that in a court of law."

"How do you know?" I asked.

"I been studying law since I turned five years old."

"Go on now," I said.

"No, I mean it." Dixie frowned at me. "We inherited my granddaddy's law library when he choked to death on his malted milk shake. Sucked it clean down the wrong pipe. I guarantee you somebody sued someone for that."

"On account of what?" I asked. She seemed sure of herself, but I'd never heard such talk before.

"On account of it was too cold for human consumption. Would have killed anyone but an Eskimo."

"I eat ice cream all the time, so does Evangeline, and it ain't never killed us."

"Maybe not yet, but don't you ever let that Selma Davis serve you anything real cold. You'll be dead before you can say *frosted*. She's as mean and evil as they come. I heard she had a whole litter of babies when she was married to Dave and ate them like a wild animal before they was dry behind the ears."

"Oh, she did not," I said. "She can't be that bad."

Selma lived in what stood for as the screen of a drive-in picture show. Her place was not what you'd call a palace, but the rent was reasonable. Instead of the screen being flat like most, it was the backside of a tall, narrow home. The Fireside Drive-In was most popular with smooching lovers and old bachelor ranchers who liked to pretend that if they stared at the screen long and hard enough, they might get to see Selma shave her shapely legs or dry off after a long, hot bath.

The most anyone ever saw, however, were her pink terry cloth towels hung out on the bushes to dry near the front of her home. I, myself, saw old man Ernest Boone pull one off a bush and smell of it like it was Chanel No. 5 on Marilyn Monroe's scarf. He momentarily put it back on the bush, then, after a second thought, jerked it up, stuffed it underneath his sweat-stained shirt, and spun out like a high school boy in his GMC truck.

Selma did have only one living relative so far as anybody knew. Her sister, Bernice, lived off in some big city where she'd earned a mint, making and selling expensive chocolate-covered tangerine candies to department stores like Nieman Marcus and Bloomingdale's. You've heard of Tango Tangerines, haven't you?

The reason I mention that Selma was not all alone in this world is so you don't get to feeling too terribly sorry for her. She had a sister, all right, and a whole trainload of men just waiting for her.

The drive-in was closed for the season on account of the folks in Fireside not wanting to freeze in their cars after October, and business dropping off like loose teeth in an apple. They were not a good fit for one another until springtime. Like a bunny in her nest, Selma stayed out of our sight unless we went looking for her.

Ten

On the Saturday following Thanksgiving, Itasca stopped up the only toilet we Cranbournes had that was inside the house. Take it from me, you cannot flush nasty undies and expect them to vanish from the earth. They will come back to haunt you in a bad way. I was crossing from the living room to the kitchen in search of Montgomery Ward's Christmas catalogue when a river of water gushed from underneath the bathroom door and dampened my tennis shoes.

"Mamaw, the river is up. We're all gonna drown in here!" I yelled.

Ruby had just come in from milking the cow, like she did every morning before breakfast, and said, "Hush that, Juliet."

She brushed past me toting the bucket of milk rich with butter, and I caught the scent of Noxzema still on her face from her morning rinse. I counted on the comforting familiarity of these morning rituals of hers like others count on air to breathe.

"But just look at what Grandmother Cranbourne went and done!" I put my hands on my hips and tapped my tennis shoe against the linoleum floor.

"What do you mean?"

I pointed in the direction of the bathroom. Ruby's face went red. "Oh thunder," she sighed. "Walt just threw away the plunger two days ago because the rubber was rotten."

"Want me to go and find him?"

"No, child. If you'll remember, he and Evangeline have hauled off a bunch of heifers to auction so we don't have to feed as many this winter. Cost of feed has gone sky high."

"Well, what in the world has Grandmother Cranbourne been doing in there?"

"I'd rather not know. Guess I'd better check on her." Ruby waded to the bathroom door and knocked. "You all right in there?"

"I'm fine. Just fine. Go away! Don't need an audience standing outside the door."

We could hear her moving around, shoving back the daffodil shower curtain, moving heavily into the shower tub, and turning on the faucet.

"Well, do you need any help?" asked Ruby, anxiously.

"No. Make that *hell no.*"

"Suit yourself." Ruby cleared her throat, threw up her hands, and shook her red head. "Guess Juliet and I'll be going to town in a bit."

"Good! Take your time."

After Ruby and I took turns mopping up the water, we piled into Walt's old ranch truck because the Thunderbird was still being repaired, thanks to Itasca's wild ride. His new going-to-town truck would have been fun, after all it smelled better, but not this old remnant from Noah's ark. Ruby's humor was not improved, and she shifted gears with a vengeance.

"Don't know how much I can take," she said. "I'd rather be at the picture show, stuffing myself with a bucket of buttered popcorn."

"Or maybe at the drugstore getting free handouts of candy," I said. "Ice cream too?" I looked at her from the corner of my eyes to see if she was getting in the spirit.

"Tutti-frutti," she said. "It's too cold for ice cream by itself. I'm thinking that a hot peach cobbler would have to go underneath it."

"That's fine," I said and smiled.

We barreled into town, backfiring a cloud of black smoke the whole way. Our first stop was the hardware store, but it was closed on account of the holiday weekend. The only choice left was to go to Densesky's.

Ruby was still wearing what she always wore to milk the cow on cool mornings: worn-out blue jeans and a red flannel shirt. Her hair was combed, but not styled so that she virtually became the Chore Girl pad that Walt teased her about being. She did not look at all like my fancy Ruby who went decked out like a department-store window whenever she went into town to sell eggs.

We walked into Densesky's quiet as mice. Ruby didn't want to attract any unnecessary attention, it was obvious to me. She whispered, "Now, Juliet, honey, you go on to the back of the store and get a plunger. I'll just wait here by the magazines." Ruby picked up an issue of *Better Homes and Gardens* and hid behind it.

I strolled back to the broom, mop, and plunger section of the store, wrinkling my nose at the stale smell of Mr. Densesky's cigar smoke coming from behind the meat counter. "Yallo," he called without looking up.

"Howdy, Mr. Densesky," I said and moved on.

When I arrived at my destination, I noticed right away that the store carried two different kinds of plungers: the traditional red rubber one on a vanilla stick and then a modern black one with a plastic handle. No one should tempt a child with two choices when it came to important necessities. I thought I'd better try the suction test. I took down both plungers from the display stand and whacked them down on the cement floor. They both suctioned down tightly, and then I yanked them up one at a time, making a loud, *pop!* when the seal broke. The traditional red one made far more noise and naturally got my vote.

Oh, it made me feel powerful. I was queen of something. Reigning Toilet Queen. No, that was no good. Queen of Bathroom Helpers. Nope. Her Royal Highness, Queen Juliet of the Universe and Serious Overflow Rescue Operations. Yes, that worked. I paraded my royal scepter all the way back down the aisle to where Ruby stood reading. *Whack, pop. Whack, pop. Whack, pop.* Amused customers pushed their carts to either side of the aisles and watched as I passed.

Just as I finished my musical solo with a resounding suctioned whale of a pop at Ruby's feet, Selma came running up in a short, tight black skirt and a pink sweater that bounced as she moved. She looked at me and smiled, then at Ruby, and then at the plunger. Ruby refused to lower the magazine.

"Well, Ms. Ruby, could I help you today?"

"No, thanks," Ruby said. "We've helped ourselves."

"Mother's little helpers are noisy, aren't they?" said Selma.

"I hadn't noticed," Ruby said, as she licked a finger to turn a page.

"Well, if you need anything, you can find me in dry goods stocking Christmas ribbon. We have quite a selection this year. Come look when you have the chance."

"Thank you, but we're overflowing with ribbon," Ruby said.

"And toilet water," I added helpfully.

"I see," Selma said. "Come by some morning and I'll buy you a cup of coffee."

"I appreciate the offer." Ruby managed to pay for the plunger and the magazine without showing her face to anyone. I was sure she'd been taught how to do that by some mail-order charm school.

"Juliet," Ruby said once we were headed back home. "You get to do the dishes alone tonight. I don't know when I've been more embarrassed."

"I'm sorry, Mamaw," I said and swallowed. "I didn't mean to. I was just having a good time."

"It'll be all right," she said, but pulled the truck over to the side of the road, put her head down, and wept. Eventually, she said, "I haven't ever raised two girls before. I know your parents could have done better than the job I'm doing."

I hated to see Ruby cry. It made me feel like the sorriest scoundrel on the earth. "No!" I said. "You're a blue ribbon, Mamaw. It's just me and Evangeline. We're messes."

"The good Lord doesn't make messes. You girls are lovelier than the flowers in May."

I thought of Mama way up there in New York, tap-dancing and wearing heaven knows what, sleeping past noon every day, and staying up until the wee hours of the morning. I made myself think of what it would be like to be ignored in person by her every day, and I realized that just being here with Walt and Ruby and Evangeline was better. I still missed her something awful, and I couldn't even say how much I missed my daddy, but I knew Ruby was solid. She was building a good foundation underneath us girls, better than the cement floor at Densesky's. The real vacuum in my life at present was worrying over whether Walt would leave Ruby for a woman who sold Christmas ribbon and plungers.

When we walked back into the house, the first thing Ruby did was check on Itasca. She was curled up in her room with the Venetian blinds turned to cut out the light.

"George, is that you?" she asked, rising up on one elbow. I could barely make her face out in the darkness, but I could smell her age—like on old books or garage sale clothing. Only the slivers of daylight that filtered in around the edges of the blinds helped me see the skin hanging loosely from her arms as she rubbed her forehead.

"No," Ruby said, "you know he can't be here." Ruby's voice was soft and velvety as cream on custard pie.

Itasca went on, "George, the boys need shoes for school. They've outgrown everything. And Walter has an earache. He needs to go to the doctor. Don't know where we're gonna get all the money for that."

I flat wasn't sure I could take in anymore and covered up my ears by cupping them with the sleeves of my stretched sweater. Ruby put her arm around me and kissed my forehead.

"Mother," she said. "Don't talk like that. I've got Juliet with me, and you're scaring her to death."

"I can't see Juliet because George is in the way. Right there in front." Itasca sat up straight and leaned against the headboard. "Come on over here, Georgie Porgie, and let me take a gander at you. It's been ages since you been to see me."

Ruby pulled me out of the bedroom and into the hall. I was shaking so bad my knees could barely hold me up. "Why's she talking so crazy?" I said.

"Well, she's either suffering from dementia, not getting enough oxygen, or is having a visit with George."

"Nuh uh!" I said. "She wouldn't even swap sandwiches with that man. He took a Greyhound bus to kingdom come and left them without a penny. She told me that."

"No, honey. Kingdom come is heaven. He died young from a heart attack."

"I thought she was just plumb mad at him all this time. But he couldn't help dying on her, could he?"

"The human heart doesn't always make good sense. Sometimes, those of us left behind get mad at the ones who've died before us."

"What will happen now?"

"I'm going to call the doctor and have him come take a look at her."

"No, that's not what I mean."

Ruby took in a good, deep breath. "She will go to be with George."

"And with my daddy?"

Ruby wrapped her arms around me and pressed her wet cheek against mine. "And your daddy."

I was beginning to figure out that understanding the human heart was a lot like untangling a whole fence line of mustang grapevines. It was nearly impossible.

Eleven

The days of the doldrums came creeping back to me and stayed like a three-legged tarantula that seemed to mostly go in circles. Like most kids, we thought time simply dragged by unless it was, of course, Christmas morning or our birthdays, in which case it bolted by like lightning toward metal.

My sister and I got up each morning, avoided Itasca any way we could, ate our breakfast, and then shot out of the house, heading toward the bus stop a mile or so down the road. Our breaths froze in the December air, and our lungs ached, but we hungered for more chilly weather. Cold days in Texas were always numbered and short in supply. When they finally arrived, our spirits soared.

At school, I studied about Lyndon Johnson and the recent election of Richard M. Nixon, and digested that all right. Learning about Comanche Indians, Pancho Villa, and horse latitudes rather excited me. But when I tried to work equations in arithmetic, it was about like trying to decipher hieroglyphics blindfolded.

As far as I could tell, there was no call to learn anything more than addition or subtraction unless you were going to be an engineer or scientist. I was far more interested in where Nancy Drew was headed in her next adventure or why Nelson Right stuck a cattail in the catsup at lunchtime than why multiplication tables were necessary for my mental growth.

Therefore, when Mrs. Clark worked problems on the chalkboard, my mind wandered toward what our Christmas tree would look like as soon as we decorated it, or what Selma Davis was up to at Densesky's. I thought about how good it would be to have a Milky Way chocolate bar and whether Ruby had any stashed away at home.

By the end of the week, I'd accumulated two red zeros on pop arithmetic tests, and a note to take home to Ruby and Walt for their signature. My heart fell into my go-go boots like a rock. When I handed the paper to Ruby, I could hardly bear to see her disappointment in me.

"Where's your mind been, honey?" said Ruby as she placed pecan cookies on a rack to cool.

"I dunno," I said and looked at the linoleum. I could hear the ticking of the rooster clock, and it was nearly as loud as my heart.

"You're too smart a girl for this. Guess you need more study time at home." Ruby looked back over her shoulder toward Itasca's bedroom. "She's sleeping. It's quiet in there; go get your makeup work done. I expect you in there every afternoon soon as you walk home from the bus. When I see your grades go up, we'll see about making a change, but not until then."

I felt as if I'd been sentenced to thirty years of hard labor that was somehow combined with solitary confinement. Just being in Itasca's presence usually felt like punishment anyway. After the toilet incident, Itasca had kept to herself, staying mainly in her room, and often taking her meals alone. The house had become quieter—even downright dull—so that until my sentencing, Evangeline and I roamed about outdoors in search of adventure.

In the midst of the front yard was a cement table where Ruby had served a barbecue buffet-style feast every October until our father died. Fifty or sixty friends would come in their best Sunday outfits, stuff themselves with Ruby's cooking, and drink sweet tea until dusk. It was the same cement table that, come November and December, Evangeline and I would tie peacock feathers to our arms and jump from, flapping wildly, pretending we could fly. In summer, there would be elephant ears to strap to our arms, but now only the skinny spines of long, beautiful feathers that couldn't even keep a peacock aloft.

We were told to stay in the yard the first Saturday in December while Walt and Ruby marked the sheep that were to be culled with a fat, red-ocher crayon. Walt would straddle the older ewes and hold them still while Ruby marked a stripe down the middle of their backs. Walt would quickly get off and grab another. When all this was done, they would be separated, and the marked ewes were loaded up into the livestock trailer and driven to auction. Evangeline and I had a good view of the process and could even hear our grandparents' conversations when the wind was right. But initially, it was my sister who captivated most of my attention.

"Watch me fly, Juliet! I can fly farther than any old John Glenn," she said.

"With cement blocks on his feet," I said. "Watch me. I can fly like Peter Pan."

We jumped, each landing with a plop on our rumps onto the muddy winter ground. On my last jump, I knocked the wind out of myself and rolled over on my side, my knees drawn up. It was then that I looked toward the pen for sympathy and found instead that Ruby and Walt were knee-high in Corriedale sheep and conversation.

"Might last another two months," Ruby said. She wore old denim pants, a faded University of Texas sweat shirt that had belonged to our father and was covered with stains. Fastened at her throat with a pink diaper pin was a cloth steeped to high heaven in Mentholatum. It served two purposes, to ward off a sore throat and as a deodorizer when the stench of the pen became too much. As always, Ruby's hair was done up, giving her an air of elegance, despite her surroundings. Ruby was a star, in my eyes. Stars just naturally look good all the time, don't they?

"Ruby…know this is bound to be hard on you. The way she is…" Walt pulled his earmuffs down from his head and let them rest around his neck. He leaned forward and pecked Ruby on the cheek.

"I'm doing it for you."

"Know you are, Ruby girl." He pulled one black work glove off his hand and wiped a speck off her cheek. "Couldn't do it without you. That's for sure."

Ruby smiled briefly and then folded her arms across her chest. "She doesn't make a whole lot of sense sometimes. Think maybe it's dementia?"

"Lord knows," he replied. "Might be the cortisone. Could be she's having ministrokes. Lack of oxygen. Doctor said yesterday there wasn't much to be done. Said to just give her anything she wants. Can't be made well—just comfortable if we're lucky."

Walt blew warm air onto his bare hand and then put the glove back on. He leaned forward and kissed Ruby square on the lips, and I do mean *kissed.* Furthermore, Ruby seemed *happy* about it. Why would they want to do that? I wondered. After all, Walt was no Elvis; he was just a granddad. Good-looking, but Geez Louise, he was ancient—a whopping fifty-something.

I shrugged and returned my attention to my sister as we stood poised to plummet. With tattered peacock feathers strapped to our arms, we jumped one final time. We slid in mud, rolled around, and made a general mess of ourselves and what was left of the yard. There were bare spots where carpet grass had been ruined in a circle around the base of the table. After picking ourselves up, we stiffly walked over to the antique boot scraper and began dragging our tennis shoes over it. Then we made a pass at trying to wipe the mud off our high-water corduroys.

We heard Walt's shrill whistle as he tried to signal Sport to help herd the remaining sheep into the chute. He was trying to train the new cocker spaniel that Ruby had rescued off the highway the week before, and the dog was doing fairly well. However, one ewe was trampled by another, fell, and was unable to rise.

"Juliet, they got a sick sheep?" asked Evangeline. "Is that what they was talking about?"

"Maybe," I replied, and let it go.

"Why do things get sick?" she asked. "Did our daddy get sick?"

"Not exactly," I replied.

"Did our mama get sick?"

"She might have gotten sick of things."

"Of us, Juliet?"

"Nope," I said, putting my arm around her shoulder. "We're way too cute." I could smell the nutty odor of Evangeline's snack still on her breath, which had been peanut butter heaped on a Ritz cracker and crowned with banana slices.

"Think so?" Evangeline looked doubtful as she surveyed our filthy clothes and shoes. Her hair was a puffball of frizz, dried grass, and mud.

"Well, *I* am, anyway."

"If you are, then *I* am too!"

That night, a miracle happened. When the dinner hour rolled around, Itasca wished to be served in her room. She wasn't "up to snuff," she said, and wanted just herself and her pal Eleanor Roosevelt to have a quiet visit over a bowl of potato soup.

"Suit yourself," Ruby said.

Before long, Ruby and I were up to our elbows in potato peels and the makings of grilled cheese and tomato sandwiches. While I dropped chunks of Irish potatoes into a boiling pot of water, Ruby slid her paring knife underneath the tomato skins. She always peeled tomatoes as though she were a chef. The skins were tough, and she did not think they helped the appeal of a meal.

"You do that so fast, Mamaw," I said, stepping back from the boiling water.

"If I dropped them in hot water first, they'd slide off slick as a whistle," she said.

"I'll bet that nobody in the entire universe can do that good as you."

"Well, likely there are a few who could, but not many." She winked at me and chuckled.

I doubted that our mother could have done that as tomatoes made her skin crawl. That got me to thinking about her and feeling empty. I tried to remember what she looked like the last day I saw her, but the image wouldn't come. That unsettled me, and so I resolved to get her picture out of my plastic daisy billfold and memorize it.

Just as soon as dinner was ready, Ruby let Evangeline and me put up TV trays in the living room and watch Ed Sullivan. Then she carried Itasca's dinner on a bed tray with extra helpings of everything, just in case she wanted them.

Ruby looked at the thermometer hanging outside the kitchen window, and said, "My Lord, it's twenty-seven degrees outside." After putting extra wood in Itasca's room heater and in the wood stove in the kitchen to heat the house, she and Walt ate supper and then disappeared into their room.

Evangeline and I got to watch the entire *Ed Sullivan Show* and then old reruns of *Gunsmoke* until our eyes grew heavy. We were never allowed to stay up past nine in the evening unless it was for some reason really special. Ruby did not emerge until after eleven o'clock to snap off the TV. As she passed by in her chenille housecoat, the scent of soap and lavender wafted behind. She looked so happy just then.

On Christmas Eve, Walt drove up to the house in Ruby's Thunderbird that had been painted Lucille Ball red, where it was once green. I watched him saunter up the sidewalk with a broad smile. He climbed up the steps, slipped inside the house, and removed his Stetson. I dropped the window blinds and ran to give him a hug. He patted my back with his rough hands. He had fingers the size of sausages and wore a size eleven wedding band. This I knew because he'd recently had it pounded back into shape at Fireside Jewels and Such, and word had gotten around. It was the largest men's ring in the Hill Country. He'd gotten it caught on the tractor and was lucky it hadn't ripped his finger plumb off.

Walt kissed the top of my head and whispered, "Where's Ruby?"

"In the kitchen making pecan cookies," I replied, taking in a good whiff of his Old Spice aftershave.

"All right, then," he said and disappeared into the next room. He crept up behind Ruby, gave her a kiss on the back of her neck, and then dropped his black Stetson on top of her head. It settled down over her eyes and ears, and she began to giggle like one of us. "Can you see?" he asked.

"Not a bit," she said.

"Good then," he said, satisfied. "Take hold of my hand, old girl, and follow me."

He led Ruby outside, guiding her gently down the porch steps and across the sidewalk. When they reached Ruby's Thunderbird, Walt guided her hand out to touch it. In her excitement, Ruby tossed off Walt's hat, which I caught like a bridesmaid would a bouquet.

"Red, Walt?" Ruby said, wide-eyed.

"Ruby darling, that's so it will match your red hair."

"I thought that green looked good with red."

"Red matches the fire in your heart better. Red is more of a go get 'em color, whereas green is more of a cedar-chopper's color."

"Oh," said Ruby.

Seeing that he might be fighting a losing battle, Walt reached out and kissed her twice. He gestured with his great beefy hands and said, "Take a look at the upholstery, would you? I had it changed to match the red paint. And no more hail dents on the hood, either. It's practically a brand new car, Ruby."

"Well, that was thoughtful of you, Walt, honey." Ruby ran her hands over the hood. "She does look pretty, doesn't she?"

"Elvis would be kickin' himself all the way home for not picking this color in the first place if he could see how pretty you look leaning up against this red Thunderbird. He would have to dump Priscilla for you right away."

"Think so?" Ruby reached up to tuck a wisp of hair behind one ear. She smiled flirtatiously at Walt.

"Sure do."

"Well," Ruby said, "I don't think I'd trade *you* even if he did."

Twelve

For a solid week after the Thunderbird came home, I tuned into Miss Alma Webster on station KOFF, expecting to hear that Elvis had died of heartache over a woman named Ruby.

On Christmas morning, Evangeline and I were surprised to find packages from our mama containing matching brown plaid jumpers, cream-colored turtlenecks, tights and Oxford shoes. We went into Walt and Ruby's room to change clothes right away.

"She's lonely for us," said Evangeline as she slid her new turtleneck over her head and wriggled into her jumper. "Don't you think?"

"Sure," I said. "Who wouldn't miss sweet girls like us?" I grinned and struck my best Count Dracula pose, but my dramatic efforts went unnoticed by my sister. She just stared at her new shoes lying sideways on the floor as if she saw straight through them.

"She probably cries herself to sleep in her blankie every night." Her chin quivered. Evangeline, herself, had done that very thing for months after our mother had disappeared.

"You're probably right. But Mama doesn't have a blankie so she has to use a handkerchief instead," I said.

"Oh, no blankie! Then she must be really sad."

"Evangeline, Mama might not miss me much, but I know she misses you."

"You sure?"

"Well, you're her baby. And I read in *National Geographic* that a mother gorilla will just naturally pine for her baby when it's taken from her."

Evangeline stood up tall, squared her shoulders, and held up her tiny fist inches from my nose. "I ain't no baby monkey, Juliet."

I dodged Evangeline's fist and ran around on the other side of our grandparents' oak bed. "You *are* hairy!"

"My hair has superpowers because my real mother is Wonder Woman. She has a crown, big poofy hair just like mine, and a powerful lasso. I can lasso airplanes and tall buildings, going all the way to New York in no time flat."

"Not me," I said. "I'm gonna be a flying nun like Sally Field. It is a more glamorous way to get there, and a lot less trouble."

"But not as groovy," she said. "That's your problem, Juliet. You're just not groovy."

Christmas night was the coldest I could remember. Everyone said so. Even Miss Alma Webster on KOFF said it was a "real doozy of a cold spell." Windowpanes frosted over. When we went outside to let the water faucets drip, our breaths hung suspended on the air, and the hairs in our noses grew stiff. I followed Ruby out to the chicken houses to make sure the brooder heaters were working, and within fifteen minutes, my hands were so cold I could barely feel them. I had gone with her to sing "We Wish You a Merry Christmas" to young white hens, but they were unappreciative of my efforts. Couldn't say I blamed them for being cheerless, since some would soon wind up in Ruby's freezer.

Come nightfall, Walt had built a roaring fire in the kitchen wood stove, in the bedroom cast-iron heater, and in the fireplace. I pulled on two pairs of socks and slept in my Yogi Bear pajamas and wore my blue jeans and turtleneck on top of that. Evangeline did much the same, but added her blue flannel housecoat on top of that.

When Ruby helped us pull out the sleeper sofa and make up our usual bed in the living room, she piled on an old wool army blanket that was probably left from the First World War. It had seven or eight moth holes, and the trim had been ripped halfway off the top. After that, she put a hot water bottle in between us.

Before long, Evangeline and I fell asleep only to be awakened at 2:00 a.m. by Itasca plopping heavily into bed with us. "Scoot over, you little scoundrels," she said. "Pipes burst under my floor, and the wood is already buckled up. My bed is rocking like a battleship during the Confederate War. Tilts every time

I draw in a good deep breath." But for all of her trials and tribulations, Itasca was asleep in no time.

On the other hand, Evangeline and I had to sleep on our sides and listen to Itasca snore. She smelled bad—like old rancid shoes and mothballs.

"Oh, dear Lord," I said. "Just kill me now."

"Hush up, Juliet," called Ruby from the other room. "I can hear you."

"Yes, ma'am."

When we awoke in the morning and went to investigate the disaster that had occurred in Itasca's room, we were dismayed beyond repair and yet, somehow, delighted too.

"The ice man rose up from the deep and smote Great-Grandmother," I said.

"Smote her good too!" Evangeline paused and said, "Juliet, what's *smote* mean?"

"Got even," I said.

"The ice man is our friend." Evangeline smiled wickedly.

"Maybe she'll have to go back and live in Arkansas."

"I can pack up her clothes."

And so we did. All of Itasca's costumes went into brown paper bags from Densesky's. We rolled the Emily Dickinson outfit into a ball and shoved it into one sack. Next went the Eleanor Roosevelt frock, followed by scuffed black shoes on top. They were shoes that had been beaten to death by time, odor, and the porch steps each time she'd climbed them. We threw in her yellowed, snagged socks, talcum powder, and an old partial denture plate with its shiny pink center.

It had once nested in the roof of her mouth loosely and caused her to click like a pecking hen when she ate. Walt had felt right sorry for her and had taken her to the dentist in Fireside not long after she'd arrived. But we weren't taking anything for granted and thought she might possibly need it in the future. Evangeline and I didn't want to give her a single excuse for coming back to live with us, if we could help it.

When Ruby came in and saw what we were up to, she said, "What in the tarnation are you girls, doing?"

We froze at the sight of Ruby's unhappy expression.

"Was Rabbit's idea," I said. "I thought I'd go along with it."

"That so? And what idea was that?" asked Ruby.

"To help her pack up. She can't live in here with the floor like that."

"Well, you are right about that, Squirrel."

"Thought she'd have to move on back to Arkansas, although I'm sure we'll all miss her."

Ruby looked away and tried to suppress a smile. She shook her head and cleared her throat and looked right back at the two of us. "Well, she can't go back to Arkansas. You girls can move her things on into the living room, where she'll be staying with you until the plumbing and the floor are fixed."

"You mean we got to share our bed with her?" said Evangeline. "Lordy, she can snore the ears off an elephant."

"Do not use the Lord's name that way," said Ruby. "It just isn't right."

"Well, dadburnit, I won't then," said Evangeline.

Ruby started to say something, and then changed her mind. She walked right on out of the house into the December cold and hid in the cellar with her transistor radio for the next hour. We could hear Elvis singing his gospel hits like "(There'll be) Peace in the Valley" or "Crying in the Chapel," when we popped open the back door to spy on her. When she finally emerged, she looked a good deal happier.

Three days later, as workman began to prize up boards from Itasca's bedroom floor, Ruby decided it was chicken-killing time. Walt scooted off into Fireside on some kind of mission that couldn't wait, while the rest of us were recruited to do the dirty work. Evangeline and I watched Ruby go out into the chicken yard from the kitchen window. We leaned so close to the glass that our breaths fogged it. Evangeline started to draw stick figures on the panes, but I wouldn't have it.

"Lean back," I told her.

"Quit bossing me around!" she replied, indignantly polishing her artwork off the pane with her sleeve.

"I have a hard time believing Ruby has got it in her," I said.

"You're right," said Evangeline. "She don't even whip us good."

One by one, Ruby grabbed a chicken by its legs, carried it to the old butcher tree stump, and amid a flurry of wings, cut off its head with an ax.

I looked at my sister and shook my head. "Don't take nothing for granted, Rabbit. Popo always said she could skin him alive, but I never believed it till now. I was flat-out wrong."

"Better not cross her no more," she said. "That could be us out there."

We had always loved Ruby, but on that day, we gained a new respect for her. She was stronger than either of us. Toughness was something Ruby carried in her, even if she looked as delicate as a dandelion. No wind would blow her away. She'd remain from season to season, bending in the wind to this force or that, but never breaking. Her roots ran deep, and her head was on tight.

When Ruby had finished with the chopping block, she brought the hens inside the kitchen. She singed the feathers over the wood stove, and the smell was unforgettable. After she'd finished with a chicken, she'd pass it along to Evangeline and myself and make us pluck.

"Get all the pin feathers, girls. Take your time and do a good job."

Let me just say that never in anyone's life have they done work that smells that nasty, feels that greasy, and makes them want to give up eating fried chicken forever, as fast as that.

Evangeline's face went completely white as we plucked the first bird. She threw up in the kitchen sink on top of the poor, scraggly chicken carcass she was plucking and lay down on the linoleum, as pasty as porcelain. After crossing her arms over her chest like an Egyptian mummy, she was immediately excused to go into the living room and lie on the sofa with a wet rag across her forehead. On top of that, she got to watch the *Porter Wagoner Show* with Dolly Parton dressed up in a costume you would not believe. I tried my best to throw up too, but luck was not with me.

"Mamaw, I think I'm 'bout to die," I said, weakly.

"No, Juliet, you stay. You're old enough to help," said Ruby when she caught on to what I was doing.

"All right, Mamaw," I replied glumly. "I may never grow up right though."

"You'll get over this before you get married, I suspect," Ruby said.

Thirteen

Itasca, who'd hardly been seen for days, emerged from her room with a white towel wrapped around her head like a turban. After the repairs had been made to the bedroom, she'd hardly wanted to leave it. She wore a one-piece swimming suit that had red and white stripes down one side, and stars down the other. She looked like the tattered remains of a battleship's flag.

Evangeline popped up off the sofa like she'd just been called to examine a UFO and ran into the kitchen. "Good gravy! Jeepers creepers, would you looka her!" she said, gaping at Itasca's outfit. "It ain't legal to do that to the flag. My teacher said so. She said—"

"Hush, Evangeline!" Ruby said, as she rinsed her hands in soapy water. She looked over her shoulder at Itasca and winced. "Mother Cranbourne, can I get anything for you?"

"Well, Ramona," replied Itasca, reaching up to twist the towel turban one more notch. "Maybe you could point me in the direction of the beach."

Ruby stood thoughtfully, obviously perplexed about what to answer. Finally, she dried her hands on a flour-sack cup towel and replied, "Come with me. I'll take you to the closest beach I know of in Central Texas." She led Itasca to the bathroom, turned on the tub faucet, and filled it with water. "You can swim here as long as you want."

"Well, I'll be needing a sand bucket," Itasca said, holding onto the towel bar and leaning over the running water.

"I'll fetch you one," Ruby said.

Ruby helped Itasca get into the tub and walked back into the kitchen. She lifted her old enamel milk bucket off the kitchen counter, rinsed it, got a large ladle from the utensil drawer, and took them to her mother-in-law.

"Bless your heart, Ramona. I'm 'bout up to my neck in sand and water. I need that pail desperately."

"I can see that."

"You are such a good sister," Itasca said.

Ruby smiled sadly at her and said, "You okay?"

"I don't know. I can't make up my mind about anything. Everything is so fuzzy. Except this beach, of course. I can see it plain as day. Take that sand dollar over there. Can you believe how perfectly it is shaped?"

"I see," Ruby said, wrinkling her forehead. "Maybe that prednisone the doctor prescribed is giving you fits. I'll give him a call. In the meantime, isn't there anything else I can do for you?"

"I'll let you know when I get through with all of this sand. Where do you want me to put it?"

"The sink would be a good place."

Itasca stood up and stepped out of the tub. She bailed water for a good twenty minutes while Evangeline peeked through the keyhole. I left the hallway, went into the kitchen, and kept a good safe distance from Itasca. I might be called upon to read to her to get her mind off going to the beach, and that was the last thing I wanted to do considering the condition her mind was in at present. Ruby walked over to the kitchen sink and began to run tap water over a chicken we'd processed that day.

She placed it on a cutting board and began to prize it apart with a butcher knife. Next she salt and peppered it and dredged it in flour. After what we'd been through with processing them earlier, I did not believe I would ever eat chicken again.

Walt came through the front door with a handful of mail and grocery store advertisements. He had just returned from a visit to the hardware store and post office and was dressed to the hilt in his khaki clothes and Stetson. After dropping the mail on the table, he walked toward the bedroom intending to change clothes. Right away, he spotted Evangeline on her knees spying on Itasca through the bathroom keyhole.

"Get away from there, Rabbit," he said. "You ought to know better than that."

"But, Popo, she's gone and poured every bit of water we've got down the sink." She put her hands on her tiny hips and stomped her foot. "You said we shouldn't waste water, that it is a thing that no animal or plant can live without."

Walt pulled Evangeline back from the door.

"We've got plenty of water," called Ruby from the kitchen. "It is to be used for necessity and emergency. This is both of those."

Walt led Evangeline into the kitchen and out of Itasca's earshot and said, "Have a seat, young lady." He motioned to the kitchen table covered with the week's mail, a bag of Cheetos, salt and pepper, and paper napkins in a ceramic rooster holder.

"Yes, sir."

"Listen, Rabbit. You are not to spy on your great-grandmother, now or ever. She deserves her privacy, same as you."

"But looks like to me her marbles have all fallen out."

"She is an old, sick woman, and we will be good to her anyway. If I catch you doing this again, I'll take you out to the pasture and have you bring in a stack of kindling high as my shoulder for the winter. Do you understand?"

"Yes, sir," said Evangeline, studying her shoes.

"Now you go over yonder and ask Ruby if you can help her set the table for dinner. A girl who has time to tend to her great-grandmother's business needs more chores. I'm going to roll up my sleeves and wash dishes after dinner. You can help dry."

"Okay, Popo."

When Itasca finally emerged from the *beach*, she was too tired to change from her swimming suit and required Ruby's help to do so and to get into bed. Walt tended the chicken Ruby had been frying, while I stirred a pan of creamed corn and checked on the biscuits in the oven.

"Juliet, you can go on in the bedroom and help your great-grandmother out," Ruby said when she reappeared in the kitchen. I slowly stirred the corn and avoided looking at her.

"I can't leave my job here, Mamaw. The corn might burn on the bottom, and then where'll we be?"

"Do as I say. Keep your great-grandmother company till she falls asleep. I'll bring you both a plate, and you can eat with her."

"You know I'm just getting the hang of cooking. I might turn out to be a real good cook someday if I stick to it. How 'bout sending Evangeline instead?"

"No, this is your job tonight. Walt has already given your sister her tasks. Great-Grandmother might want you to read Mark Twain or Nathaniel Hawthorne to her. Evangeline's a little on the young side for that."

"But Mamaw, do I have to?"

"Go on. Scat!"

As I dragged my feet going to Itasca's bedroom, I fantasized what it would be like if our father was alive and our mother home. Our daddy would be taking us to a drive-in picture show most likely. Us girls would be sitting in the backseat making ourselves sick on popcorn and Orange Crush. I'd be waving to my friends from school in the cars next to us until it got too dark to see.

We might go to the little playground just below the movie screen and sit on the teeter-totters awhile and see who could make the other fly the highest and hit the ground with the loudest thud. When we returned to the car, our parents would cover us with hugs and kisses and ask us what kind of a present they could give us when we got home for being such fabulous, perfect children.

After the movie, they would tell us stories about princesses and princes who married and lived happily ever after. We would not be made to do a lick of work and would be appreciated every day as though they were seeing us for the first time. Walt and Ruby had clearly grown tired of us and were taking us for granted. We were the only grandchildren they had, so why would they do that?

Ruby put her hands on her hips and gave me *that* look. I dragged the toes of my tennis shoes over the wood floor so that the squeak of them sticking became a fingernail on chalkboard kind of sound as I moved toward Itasca's room. I pretended I was the Hunchback of Notre Dame and arched my back as I moved toward the black widow spider's room. Out of fear of what might happen if I didn't, I shaped up as I knocked on her door.

"Come in, George," she called.

Oh, this isn't good, I thought. I haven't even been inside yet, and her mind has rolled plumb off her bed. I took a look back at Ruby and saw her watching me from the kitchen. I had no choice but to go inside.

Itasca wore a long, white flannel nightgown that bore rows of eyelet lace across her chest, at her throat, and on her cuffs. She rested in an upright position against two of Ruby's fattest feather pillows. The antique lamp on her night table had once been converted from kerosene to electricity by Ruby's father, our great-grandfather Gemburree. He had been a sharecropper all his life, growing cotton until it just didn't pay any longer to farm on such a small scale. Victorian cottage roses were painted on the lamp's side and cast a pink glow on Itasca's worn-out face. She was in the midst of conversation with someone I couldn't see.

"George, do you know who this girl is?" she said, smiling and looking at the wall. "You do? Well, I thought so." Then Itasca turned her acorn-colored eyes on me. "Well, what are you here for?"

"I thought I might keep you company, Grandmother Cranbourne."

"Do tell?" she said. "What do you have in mind to do?"

"I can read a little something if you like," I said.

"No, thank you, my little Shakespeare child."

"Well, I'll be going then," I said. My heart rose thinking I might slip out her back bedroom door, escape outside, and go hide out in the washhouse until the chicken business was over, though I might freeze from the cold and mildew from the damp.

"Hold on," said Itasca, giving me a toothy black-widow smile. "Let's have a visit."

My heart sank. "I'd be glad to come back later."

"No," she said. "There are things you ought to know so you can pass them on to your children."

"I haven't got any children on account of I am still a child myself. Popo says I am a young sprout."

"But you might someday," she said.

"Not me," I said. "That's Evangeline. I'm the one who's never going to marry. I'm the one who's going to achieve her destiny. Don't you remember?"

"I recollect that now."

"You want me to call in Evangeline so you can tell her instead?"

"No, Juliet. I want to talk to *you.*"

"Yes, ma'am."

I was stuck now. Plopping myself down in the cane-bottomed rocker by her bed, I was set to rock up a storm. I was preparing myself emotionally to be eaten. Black widows were known for eating their husbands, and perhaps even their great-grandchildren.

Fourteen

Itasca looked mildly perplexed at the commotion I was causing in the rocker, but started on what I feared would be a long-winded tale of her life's woes.

"When I was a young girl, I trained for years to become a ballerina. I practiced every day from the age of five onward when other girls were playing dolls. I devoted myself in every aspect to my dream of being on stage, performing in front of thousands. My teachers always said I had potential, that I had been born to dance. I had the slim body of a ballerina, and muscles and joints that obeyed my commands."

Itasca stretched out her arms and felt her sagging skin, dismayed. Then she curved her right wrist and lifted her hand as if to pose, and then let it fall against the bed.

"After all those years of devotion to the art of dance, I became just what I dreamed I would and went from playing minor roles in the ballet to the lead. I even played Clara in *The Nutcracker* in the Mariinsky Theatre in St. Petersburg, which was thrilling. Then I returned to the city to perform in *The Dying Swan,* my personal favorite. After that, I traveled all across Europe and the United States, performing role after role. I had an enchanted life during a magical period in the history of dance."

I slowed my rocking chair until it was stopped and silent on the wood floor. I leaned toward Itasca, not knowing whether to believe her, after her trip to the *beach* and all. I stared holes in her eyes, trying to discern whether she was telling the truth or lying her head off. Ruby had always told me that a person's eyes gave them away, but Itasca gave no indication of guilt.

"It was," she said, "the best time of my life."

"Oh," I said. "What went wrong? Why did you quit?"

"One day, I was playing Clara in Little Rock, Arkansas, and my life changed, completely. Close to the theater was a café where I often went between rehearsal and the performance. It was there that I met the handsomest man I'd ever seen. He was tall and lean and carried himself with such authority. I was completely swept away from the minute I laid eyes on him. The café was crowded, and it was pouring rain on that cold December day. He'd seen me trying to fold my umbrella and get inside, so he opened the door for me. Such a gentleman. Such a *gentle man.*"

"Goodness gracious," I said. "Is this the same George you've been talking about? He don't sound the same."

"Oh, indeed. He was such a good, good man," she said, nodding and smiling.

"What happened, then?" I said.

"One thing led to another, and before long, we were sharing a table. It became *our* table as we met there every day for lunch for a week. George was a law student at the University of Texas at Austin and was simply in town between semesters visiting his family."

"Then what?" I asked.

"We were married a month later. I left the ballet and then lived with him in Austin until he finished his education. After graduation, we returned to Little Rock where I soon had little Walter and then Melville. When Walter turned two, George disappeared from my life as suddenly as he'd come into it."

"Where in the world did he go?"

"Across the river."

"Why didn't you haul him back home?"

"He came back this morning and took me to the beach. I've wanted to go there for so long. We took a picnic and then hunted for shells."

I cocked my head and tried to think what on earth she was talking about, since she'd hardly left her bed. Then I remembered how she'd gone into the bathroom and bailed water for the longest time.

"Oh," I said finally.

"Says he's going to carry me across the river on his back to where he's been all this time. I'm so excited, I can hardly wait," she said.

In my mind, I could see an image of George carrying Itasca across his back like the fox in *The Gingerbread Man* fairy tale. Anyone who would leave any of my family, even old Itasca, had to be a mean old fox. He had left his wife and his own two boys who must have needed and missed him like I did my daddy.

Itasca's eyes began to droop, her jaw sagged open, and she snored to beat the band. I could hardly take the noise, even though I wasn't trying to sleep myself. But I knew better than to return to the kitchen where all that nasty chicken business was still going on. So I just laid low until I could hear that the ordeal was over and the mess cleaned up.

Soon as it was safe, I made a beeline to the living room and found Walt leaning back in his chair, precariously balancing on the wheels of the office chair he favored. He was watching *Perry Mason* and drinking hot cider. I wanted to talk to him straight out about his father. I thought maybe I had information he didn't know a thing about.

"Great-Grandmother told me your daddy is just yonder across the Pedernales River. You might want to go out and round him up. I'm sure he ought to be ready to come home by now."

"Cut off that television, would you, Squirrel?" he said and snapped his chair back down on all four wheels. He reached over to his bookcase and grabbed his knife and whetstone where he'd left it on top of the *Funk & Wagnalls* 1912 encyclopedias, the bindings of which were tattered and recently taped together. As he sharpened his knife, he looked up at me and smiled sadly.

"She's not talking about the Pedernales River," he said.

"The Colorado, or the Llano, then?"

"No, no river any of us have ever seen. In the old days when folks passed on, they said someone crossed the river or the flood. My father died when I was still in diapers."

"I thought he left her."

"People sometimes feel that way—even get mad about it."

"Was Great-Grandmother mad?"

"Yes, I 'spect so. After all, she was left nearly penniless to raise two ornery boys alone."

Another thought dawned on me that made my knees start to feel weak and my hands shake. "Are you and Mamaw mad because you got left with us?"

Walt put his knife and whetstone back on the bookcase and held out his arms to me. He gave me a hug and petted my head like I meant more to him than even a prized hunting dog might have.

"Not even the tiniest bit, Squirrel. You and Rabbit are the stars and the moon and the sun to us."

"Are we as good as the Big Dipper?"

"A million times better. Ruby and I would be lost without you."

"What will happen to us when you and Mamaw cross the river?"

"By that time you'll be grown up and out on your own."

"Are you and Mamaw old, Popo?"

"We are medium old. Like two steaks on the grill that still got a little pink left in them. That's us. We ain't cooked through and through, just yet."

His answer didn't satisfy my appetite to know for certain they weren't leaving anytime soon. I couldn't, for the life of me, imagine ever being grown up enough to be all right without Ruby and Walt. It made me cry, so I went to sit on the front steps and whistled for Sport to come let me pet him. When he came up, wagging his tail, I pulled him up close to me, and we both cried together. Well, I cried, and Sport howled. He had big chocolate-brown eyes and always seemed to understand what I was thinking.

Before long, I heard a gun go off around the back of the house by the kitchen. Sport and I raced toward the sound. Ruby was coming down the back steps with her Winchester, holding her shoulder.

"Shoot!" she said. "I hurt my shoulder getting even with that durned squirrel that keeps tearing up our wiring in the house." She put the gun on safety and went over to pick up the dead squirrel. It hurt her to reach out with her right arm, and she winced. "Don't know who won the battle, me or the squirrel."

She looked at me and laughed. "Tell you one thing, though, I'm gonna win the war. You can bet on that."

Except for her sore shoulder, Ruby looked pretty fit to me. There was still plenty of life in her, I decided. I dried my tears and teased Sport into chasing me back around the front of the yard where the swing sets were. I managed to pull him up into the swing with me, and he let me do it. We sat there until I got too cold to tolerate the seat's metal and heard Ruby calling me inside to take a bath.

The next morning, Ruby selected two of the chickens she'd killed, processed, and frozen; put them in a grocery bag; and set off for Mrs. Applewhite's house with both of us girls in tow.

Wintertime had peeled away the layers of ivy from Adah Mae's decaying house so that it resembled a dirty, hairless cat with black eyes that saw everything. When Evangeline and I ran up to sit in our customary seats on the porch swing, Ruby lifted the bag of frozen chickens from the trunk and walked up to us on her way to the front door. Evangeline and I shivered from the cold and damp.

"I'm sorry you're cold, girls. This won't take but a minute though. Why don't you do a few jumping jacks or play the hokey-pokey while I'm inside? You'll stay warmer that way."

"Okay, Mamaw," we said and then ducked out of sight as Ruby knocked on the door. We did not want to be turned into field mice or porcupines by the old witch inside.

Just as Ruby disappeared inside the house, we saw the curtains move and realized that Adah Mae had been watching us through her field glasses.

"Now, who's the spy?" called Evangeline and stuck out her tongue.

"Forevermore, Evangeline! Don't stick out your tongue at that old woman. She'll roast us like potatoes with the fire from her witch's breath, or throw us in a pot and boil us good."

"Will not," said Evangeline, tugging at her pink parka. "She can't run as fast as me."

"Of course she will," I said. "Or she might watch you through those binoculars of hers and catch you with her sticky tongue like a toad catching a fly. I'm telling you, she's got nothing better to do than set in front of that window and wait for you to let your guard down."

Voices came from inside the house. "No, Ruby, I don't want to leave this house. If I'd wanted to, I'd have left years ago. It's not safe out in the world."

"It's not safe in here either, when you are in serious need of medical attention and aren't getting any. You've got to see the doctor for your legs. You might lose them if you don't," said Ruby.

"Doesn't matter one whit to me. I ain't leaving for no reason."

"Suit yourself," said Ruby.

We could hear her footsteps and then saw her standing in the doorway. As she pushed it open, Adah Mae appeared behind her.

"Don't go, Ruby," Adah Mae said. "It's not safe out there for you either. You've got to watch that wicked creature who lives across the street from me."

"Who on earth are you talking about?" said Ruby.

"That Selma Davis. You wouldn't believe who all goes to her house at night. She's a siren, I tell you. Nobody can resist her."

Ruby's face turned crimson. "I'll keep that in mind, Mrs. Applewhite. Call when you need me."

Ruby's shoulders sagged as she walked down the porch steps and motioned for us girls to follow. She took a deep breath, blew it out into the frosty air, and looked across the street toward Selma Davis's tall, narrow drive-in picture show of a house.

"Just what I needed to hear," she said.

It seemed to me as if the whole world had it in for Selma, myself included. How could one person shake up so many folks in my small world? Like a stick in an ant bed, Selma had stirred us up something awful.

Fifteen

After that day at Adah Mae's house, Ruby seemed to grow antsy. Her preoccupation with reading seed catalogues, planning for her garden, and cooking for all of us Cranbournes seemed to fade.

She picked up her old fiddle from the closet shelf in her and Walt's bedroom and tuned it. Then she would sit on the cedar chest at the foot of their bed and fiddle and sing her heart out as long as the door stayed shut. We were not allowed to go in there.

Sometimes, she'd get on the black rotary phone, wait until the party line was clear, and then call her sisters, Pearl and Sapphire Gemburree, who lived in an Airstream travel trailer because they kept moving according to where their gigs were. Ruby had their tour schedule and could reach them on an office phone now and then.

"I just can't keep up with you girls," I overheard Ruby tell Sapphire one day. They were somewhere in Tennessee outside of Nashville playing for a corporate Christmas party.

"Yes, they was good old days, wasn't they?" Ruby paused for a moment and said, "Wouldn't take a million dollars for the nights we used to play in Longhorn Cavern. We was just girls then, of course. Don't guess anyone had more fun than the Gemburree sisters."

She listened for a while to what Sapphire was saying and then replied, "You know I can't go back on the road with you." She lowered her voice until it was just above a whisper, but I could hear every word. "Because I've got the girls and Walt's mother. I couldn't be away at night."

I became increasingly anxious over the next few days that Ruby would change her mind and want to leave us. Just the thought made me want to crawl underneath a bed and hide. I did not breathe a word of my concern to Evangeline, but told Sport everything based on the knowledge that he couldn't tell anyone. I opened the back door and let him inside the house when Ruby was out gathering eggs and Walt was asleep in his chair with his Stetson pulled low over his face.

Sport and I crawled underneath Ruby and Walt's bed and had ourselves a good quiet cry. Soon, I heard Walt stir from his nap and get out of his squeaky chair. He dialed the rotary telephone and asked for Miss Alma Webster at station KOFF. He wanted to know whether Ruby could go play her fiddle on the air sometime.

On Christmas Eve, Ruby and Walt made us put on the red-velvet dresses they'd recently bought us for an undisclosed special occasion. They tried to get Itasca to join us and to put on the outfit of her choice, but she refused, saying she'd already had enough of Christmas due to the incessant carols coming out of Walt's radio and didn't think she could take much more joy.

Evangeline and I were mystified about why we were going in the first place, but Walt said, "I thought it would be a treat for you ladies to witness a live Christmas Eve broadcast at the station. Besides that, I hear there's famous musicians gonna be there. Might be some fiddlin' going on too."

Ruby's ears perked up. "Who's that?" she said.

"Wild horses couldn't drag it out of me," said Walt. "But you'll recognize 'em when you see 'em."

Ruby speculated on whether one could be Elvis, but none of us could remember whether he played the fiddle. She smoothed her green satin dress over her knees as Walt shut the door and walked around to his side of the Thunderbird. We drove the five miles into town, and Walt pulled up in front of station KOFF, which was located just across the street from the courthouse.

Station KOFF broadcast from a two-story yellow cupcake of a house that had once been owned by an old widow woman. She used to serve iced tea and lemon squares to each newly convicted criminal and the deputy who escorted them from the courthouse to the jail across the street. She told all persons involved that she felt right sorry for them and hoped her refreshments would make them feel better.

The veranda stretched across the front of the house and wrapped around its sides like packaging around Little Debbie cakes. There was white wicker furniture including tables and chairs and an old black lab named Sal.

Just as Walt opened the door to station KOFF, out barreled a puffball of a white dog with glassy black eyes and tiny paws. He tried to catch her, but she seemed to vanish in thin air. Quickly, he went inside, knocked on the glass to the studio room, and called out, "Miss Alma, your dog just lit out for the hills."

Miss Alma pushed a button on the panel in front of her and emerged from the studio. At the age of eighty-two, she was tall and wiry and had been nicknamed Praying Mantis by the children at Fireside Elementary. Her stiff reputation had been helped considerably when she'd come to our school gymnasium/cafeteria and tossed little rubber footballs out to us during lunchtime. They wreaked havoc with our lunch trays of fish sticks, mashed potatoes, and peas and landed in bowls of tartar sauce.

"What were you saying, Walt? I can't hear a thing behind all that glass, don't you know," said Miss Alma.

Walt patiently repeated himself, "I said that little white dog lit out the door for somewhere when we came in."

Miss Alma was horrified. "You mean my Little Bit got out?"

"Yes, ma'am," he said.

She started shouting orders like the captain of a sinking ship. "Ruby, you go on in and start playing the fiddle. Play any Christmas tunes you want." Then she looked at Evangeline and said, "Hot Shot, you hit the red button when Ruby starts to play." She motioned to me take a pile of papers out of her hands. "Sunshine, you just start reading anytime Ruby quits playing. I don't want any dead air on my station. None. Zip. Nada."

Walt said, "Miss Alma, I'll go out and hunt for your pup."

"That dog won't come to anyone but me. My car won't start, though, so you can drive, if you will." She started to cry. "And if I don't find that dog before she gets run over, I'll have no reason to go on. She's all the family I've got left."

"Now, don't cry, Miss Alma. We'll comb every inch of Fireside in the Thunderbird until we find her."

Walt escorted Miss Alma to the car and then walked around the trunk and opened it. He pulled out Ruby's fiddle and brought it back inside the station where I stood wondering what in the world was going on. I was holding the stack of papers Miss Alma had thrust at me, trying to make sense of them. He walked past me and found Evangeline smiling at the instrument panel of the studio as if she were about to play Chinese checkers. Then there was Ruby near tears perched on a stool.

"You've got to play, Ruby," said Walt as he hugged her. But she just looked at him as if he had two heads.

"On the air? I thought we were coming to watch someone else play."

"No," he said. "I knew you wouldn't come if I'd told you right off. I put your fiddle in the trunk while you were getting ready."

"It's been so long since I played with Sapphire and Pearl."

"If there's one thing I know," said Walt, "it's that my girl can do it. Go on and seize the chance. Play every pretty Christmas tune you know."

"I don't even know where to start," said Ruby, ashen-faced.

"Start out with a little Elvis," he said. "How about 'Blue Christmas,' on account of Miss Alma's dog being gone?"

Then Walt took off down the sidewalk, climbed into the Thunderbird, and he and Miss Alma roared off. Now there was no one to save us but ourselves. In my opinion, there was nothing left to do except get with the program.

Ruby looked horrified, but I just said, "C'mon, Mamaw, I've been hearing you play. You'll do just fine."

Evangeline picked up Miss Alma's visor cap that advertised the Fireside Inn on its brim and pulled it down over her bushy hair. "I'm itching to hit the red button," she said. "And Miss Alma put me in charge of it. So what I say goes."

Ruby fumbled with her fiddle and bow trying to get it out of its black case. "Juliet, you go on and start. Just read the first paper you come to. I've got to tune up before I can play. Confound it." She quickly tuned her instrument, and then Evangeline counted to three and hit the red button.

I was so scared that my knees were knocking, but then Ruby gave me *that* look, and so I just opened up my mouth and talked into the microphone.

"Howdy, this is Sunshine Cranbourne talking, and I'm the newest voice of Fireside." I was feeling pretty good about my beginning, but my sister helped me get over that.

Evangeline butted me aside and said, "Her name ain't Sunshine nothing. It's Squirrel! She ain't been sunshiny a day of her life."

Ruby reached out and plucked Evangeline away from that microphone and gave her a glare as big and tough as any thrashing. "Go on, now," she coaxed me, smiling.

I nodded and said, "Miss Alma's dog, Little Bit, has run off into the streets of Fireside. That's right, she's a doggone pup. If you find her, would you please bring her to the station?"

Then I looked down and began reading from the top page of the stack. "Welcome to the Fireside Christmas Broadcast, brought to you by the Fireside Inn. For those of you becoming engaged during the holiday season, the folks at the Fireside Inn want you to know they have a reception kit for you. It includes a Bundt wedding cake with cream cheese or German chocolate icing, twenty-four matching paper plates and cups, two gallons of green sherbet punch, and a pound of birdseed.

"In addition, the lucky bride and groom will be entitled to VIP guest treatment. With this, you will receive fresh linens on even numbered days and hot sticky cinnamon buns and coffee on odd ones. We have bathrooms on every floor—always one located down the hall from you. To top this all off, Mona Gladbird has just graduated from a correspondence course on how to be a concierge extraordinaire, so she can attend to all your Fireside sightseeing whims. So when you have hotel or reception needs, *rest* assured that the Fireside Inn is equipped to serve!"

Ruby tucked her fiddle under her chin and began to play "Blue Christmas," then went right into "Merry Christmas Baby" and "White Christmas" for starters. After she played "Silent Night," she nodded at me and waved her bow.

I looked down at my papers, realized I had already read the one on top, slid it to the bottom and read, "Do you want to stop snoring in its tracks now? Milton's flesh-colored geckos are trained to sit on the nostrils of your loved one, exerting just the right amount of pressure to stop snoring. They are recyclable and serve as companions too. Known worldwide to improve the spirits and bring harmony to a disgruntled marriage. A one-year warranty comes with every gecko. Unable to visit Milton's Gecko Farm in person? No problem, just go by their distribution center on Main Street and say Milton sent you. Milton's Gecko Farm has been training geckos with pride since 1952!"

We heard a tap on the studio's glass window and looked up to see Selma Davis wearing a Santa Claus hat, red Christmas ball earrings, a tight white sweater, short black skirt, fishnet hose, and boots. As far as I knew, she was the only person in the entire town of Fireside who wore fishnet stockings. I had seen women gasp and cover their mouths when she'd worn them at Densesky's just after Thanksgiving. I kind of wished I had some and a pair of black go-go boots to go with them.

She was smiling broadly, her bright-red lipstick rimming her front teeth like a garland. One hand was behind her back, which made me wonder what on earth she was up to. Maybe she was hiding ribbon candy.

"Woo hoo!" she said, as I pushed open the studio door for her.

Ruby just looked at her and then picked up her bow and started to play "I'll Be Home for Christmas." She turned her back to us and kept right on playing and avoided the entire opportunity to give Selma one whit of her attention.

"Well, if it isn't Little Miss Sunshine Cranbourne, the new voice of Fireside? Look what I found," Selma whispered, pulling a small white dog from behind her back. It was Little Bit, shivering and slightly damp. She growled at me when I reached for her, but I paid her no mind. After she sniffed my hand, she let me take her from Selma.

"Oh, Little Bit, you cute little scamp," I mouthed. "Miss Alma's going to be so happy to see you."

I ushered Selma and Little Bit into the studio, out of earshot of station KOFF's listeners, and waited until Ruby put her bow down. Then I headed back over to the microphone and said, "Christmas has come to Fireside early. Miss Alma, if you're listening, come on back to the studio. Little Bit is here and full of vinegar and spit."

Ruby raised her eyebrows and then mouthed, "Juliet, don't say *spit* on the air."

"Sorry, folks, I meant to say *spirit*. Little Bit is just plumb full of Christmas spirit."

On account of us being busy with our jobs on KOFF, Selma didn't hang around for long. I held on to Little Bit while Selma opened the front door and headed down the sidewalk. Walt and Miss Alma had apparently heard my announcements and just rolled up in Ruby's Thunderbird. Selma sashayed down the sidewalk like she'd been practicing to do just that all her life. Walt walked around the car to open Miss Alma's car door and tipped his hat to Selma.

Selma waved and blew them kisses. I stared a hole into the back of Selma's upswept, ratted-to-the-sun hairdo. I was sure that at least one kiss had landed squarely on Walt's cheek. When he smiled at her, I lost all doubt.

Sixteen

Miss Alma went on and on about what a fine job we'd done in her absence at station KOFF. Turns out, she'd been listening to the broadcast in Ruby's Thunderbird the entire time that she and Walt had been patrolling the streets of Fireside looking for Little Bit. She tucked Little Bit under one arm and reached to pluck her Fireside Inn visor off Evangeline's head.

Miss Alma said, "I like to play Texas hold'em at Snooksie Stokes's house on Saturday afternoons. Ever since I played it at the Golden Nugget in Vegas last year, I've been on fire for the game. It's hard for me to get away from the station to play. I can't spin records, reach out to my fans, and hold a hand of cards at the same time. What do you girls think about coming on Saturday afternoons for a while so I can whip Snooksie? Course Laverne and Lucy May play too. I might need to whip all of them. What do you say? Are you in?"

Ruby was tucking her fiddle back into its black case. She appeared to consider it for a moment and smoothed her green satin dress. Despite the duress of the past few hours, every hair on her head was perfectly in place, and she looked happy. It was the first time I'd seen her look that chipper in a long while.

"Well," said Ruby, "I do have to come into town every Saturday afternoon to deliver eggs to my customers anyway. Wouldn't be a bit out of my way to drop by here and help out, Miss Alma. Guess the girls and I could do that for a spell. That is, if they want to."

Ruby suppressed a smile and raised her eyebrows. "Evangeline, Juliet, are you interested? More importantly, do you think you can mind your p's and q's when you are on the air?"

Evangeline and I looked at each other and hugged before we remembered that we were supposed to be enemies. "Yes, ma'am!" we said.

Ruby sighed contentedly and said, "Seeing you girls give each other a hug is the best Christmas gift I could have."

I felt a little ashamed when she said that, knowing full well that meant there were 364 other days in the year when we were a pain in her derriere. I managed to mind my manners throughout the rest of the entire day. It was bound to snow!

The next morning was Christmas, and after Evangeline and I had opened our presents, which consisted of clothing and roller skates that could only work on the uneven sidewalk that ran around the house, food preparations became serious.

Due to our foray into broadcasting, Ruby's cooking schedule was slightly behind. She told us that, with the right attitude and willingness to work, we could make up for lost time. Although she had managed to make cornbread the night before for the dressing, everything else still had to be done.

Evangeline dropped pecans into the glass dicing jar and pumped the plunger's dicer up and down until the nuts were in tiny bits. I chopped onions and celery with a dull knife. More celery and onion skittered across the floor than went into the bowl, but Ruby didn't say a word. She just kept working as fast as she could, first making a pumpkin pie and then a coconut cake with enough shavings to choke a horse. Next was her most important creation, a banana pudding with a mile-high meringue. She had to drop the oven racks down to their lowest possible position due to the extreme height of the meringue.

"I call this my reaching-for-the-stars meringue," she whispered excitedly. "Don't even breathe, Juliet, or it will fall. If you must breathe, go into the other room to do it." Ruby had meringue stuck to her widow's peak, but I didn't tell her. If I wasn't supposed to breathe, then I knew I shouldn't talk.

"Banana pudding," Ruby whispered, "is one cantankerous dish to prepare. Just a minute too long in the oven and the bananas will get tough. It's your job, Juliet, to watch the meringue brown. I want you to just tap me on the shoulder when it is a light golden color."

So I stood and studied the meringue for the next few minutes, wanting to do my best job. I felt Ruby's nearness as she stirred brown sugar, butter, and canned milk into the mashed sweet potatoes. She spread the mixture into a baking dish and decorated the top with marshmallows and cinnamon.

I thought there couldn't be a better feeling in the world than the warmth I felt flowing from her. I knew she and Walt loved us girls, and it helped to fill that hollow place inside where our parents should have been.

I managed to walk a straight line, behaviorwise, until school started again after the Christmas holidays ended and my fourth-grade classmates got to me. Fireside Elementary wasn't the easiest place for a young broadcast star to be, I supposed.

Mrs. Hedelmeyer, the school librarian, seemed to not mind the laughter at my expense, when it became apparent that I had achieved notoriety. She even had the nerve to ask that I give a report on my recent experience at station KOFF when recess was canceled due to cold January rain.

She had us sit cross-legged on the library floor and called me up to the front. "Juliet, why don't you come up and give us a talk on what it is like to be live on radio?"

I was turned around talking to Dixie Flagg who sat behind me writing her phone number on my hand and flat out hadn't heard my teacher call my name.

When I didn't respond, Tyrell Masterson's red head bobbed up. He stage-whispered with a hand in front of his mouth, "She ain't answering 'cause her name's Squirrel."

The entire fourth-grade class doubled over in laughter and taunted me. "Squirrel, here Squirrel." "Want to eat some acorns, Squirrel?" "You are a squirrel of a girl. Guess that means you drive folks nuts. Ha-Ha! Yeah, that's right, drive them out of their trees."

Encouraged to become bad to the core, Tyrell stood up, put one hand behind his head and the other on a hip, which he wiggled like a glamour girl. He said in a squeaky voice, "Hey, listeners, this here is Squirrel. You need me to knock you right out of your tree, I can do it!" Then he thrust one skinny hip out and pretended to knock his friend Dale to the ground.

I reflected on the fact that, thanks to Evangeline's interjection during my broadcast, I was now known as Squirrel, the voice of Fireside, not as Sunshine, the nickname I'd been given by Miss Alma.

By the time Evangeline and I got on the school bus, heading for home, I was seeing red. Everyone was calling me Squirrel over and over again. It was all too much, and I eventually started to cry.

Leroy Huggins chanted, "Squirrel is a crybaby, Squirrel is a crybaby."

Evangeline got up out of her seat and made her way down the aisle when the bus stopped to let Millie Jane off at her house. A gust of cold January air whipped through the aisle and made us shiver. She stood in front of Leroy and said, "Leave my sister alone."

"You gonna make me?" he asked. He puffed himself up into a seventh-grade bully stance with a raised fist that he brought in front of her little chin.

"No. I'm gonna let Mr. Roper make you," she said jerking her thumb toward the bus driver. "And I bet he's packing his paddle that has air holes in the side to make it whack harder."

Mr. Roper's ears picked up at the sound of his name. He closed the door to the school bus after Millie got off and came back to see what was going on. He didn't whack Leroy with the infamous paddle. He just moved him to the front of the bus where he could keep an eye on him. He said that Leroy would be spending the remainder of the school year in seat number one.

Evangeline and I were always the last on the bus in the morning and the last off in the afternoon. After we got out of the bus and began the long walk home, neither of us said a word. I had been surprised that Evangeline had stood up for me on the bus, and ashamed that I'd been crying and hadn't handled the situation myself. After all, I was twenty-two months older than Evangeline and should have shown Leroy how cows eat corn.

Instead, because I didn't know what to say, I just kept quiet. Once at the house, I raced inside to call my friend Dixie Flagg who'd given me her phone number.

Itasca and Ruby were huddled around the fireplace trying to keep warm. Ruby moved the log with a poker, stoked the fire, and added another piece of wood. Sparks popped and shot up the flue as she replaced the fire screen.

"Where's Popo?" I asked as I flew past them.

"He's in town. Picking up the mail and buying Reddi-wip for the fruitcake."

"Well, that cake is getting pretty dried out," said Itasca. "We've been eating off the same one for a solid week."

Itasca was poised for a good fight over having to eat fruitcake that was a bit dry, but Ruby just moved away from the fireplace and went into her and Walt's room. I soon heard the snap of her fiddle case as she opened it and then a few phrases of music. It soon stopped and then she opened her door.

"Rabbit," she called. "Would you come in here?"

Within a few moments, I heard the sounds coming from Ruby trying to teach Evangeline how to fiddle. I repeatedly lifted the receiver to dial Dixie. Hattie Lilly was on the party line, though, and she told me to "get off the phone, you heavy breather," every time I tried. It didn't pay to make a phone call anywhere on our party line when you had a stuffy nose from crying.

"You've got to grow thicker skin, Juliet," Walt told me that night at dinner. Just the fact that he steered clear of my pet name made me about half-sad and wanting to tear up again. "Especially, if you want to be on the radio now and again. One thing I want to tell you is that I'm right proud of the job you done. No more notice than you had, was a miracle you could come out sounding so professional."

He pushed my hair out of my right eye. I had recently started to comb it in the style of Barbra Streisand, parted to the side and looped a little low over one eye, but my hair was frizzy and big. It just wasn't working.

Ruby watched him brush back my hair as I tried to pull a piece of pork chop off the end of my fork with my front teeth. "A little Dippity-do gel and some Aquanet hair spray can work wonders with frizz," she said. "Why don't we have our own beauty shop here at the house tomorrow? I'll give you a manicure too, if you'd like."

The thought of getting to do that with Ruby felt warm and cozy. She touched my cheek and the world seemed like a friendlier place.

We had not been called into station KOFF to do the New Year's Eve program due to previous arrangements with a family who had bragging rights to four generations of continuous yodeling and alpenhorn expertise. I didn't blame Miss Alma one bit for not changing her program to accommodate her new crew.

While Evangeline was beginning to prove that at least one Cranbourne child had an ability to play the fiddle by ear, she was not ready, by any means, to play on the air. In just seven days, she could already play two short songs with minor squeaking. When Ruby handed the fiddle to me for a lesson, I stood there, looked at it, and handed it back to her.

"We're all better off," I said, "if I do not touch this. I'm a better talker than musician. I like to dance, but fiddling ain't in me."

"I understand that, Juliet," she said and put the fiddle back into its case. "Just thought I'd ask."

We washed and graded eggs to take to Densesky's and all Ruby's Saturday customers. When they had all been separated in cartons according to size, it was time for us to get ready to go to town to deliver them and then head to the station. After all us girls had taken baths, Ruby got out a tub of Dippity-do, put some on her hands, and then ran her fingers through my hair. She got a barrette out of the cabinet and clipped my over-eye swoop up out of my line of vision. As soon as the gel dried, my hair sealed into a sculpture that felt permanent like bronze. When she dabbed a little Vaseline on my chapped lips, I noted the way they shined in the mirror.

By the time we got to the station, I felt primed to perform, as if all station KOFF listeners could see me as well as hear me.

When I got up to the microphone, I said, "Welcome to Fireside, Texas, and to Saturday afternoon with the Cranbourne family. This is Juliet talking, and Mrs. Ruby and Miss Evangeline have got my back. Today's program is brought to you by Methuselah's Hair Meditation, whose motto is 'We think, therefore we hair!' Today only, order your 969-day virtual hair-meditation program right this minute for a ten percent discount off the regular price of four ninety-nine. Methuselah's guarantees that bald glare can be reduced by virtual hair, or your money back."

When I talked to an audience I couldn't see, it was easy to pretend they weren't there at all, and so my fear was little to piddling. Somehow, I just knew I had it in me.

Seventeen

Our calendar was punctuated by holidays and little celebrations when we could manage them. Valentine's day was celebrated throughout the town by way of chocolate, mysterious love notes, and dreams fulfilled. Yet some occasions may have left us feeling empty were it not for Walt and Ruby.

At the end of February, Walt picked Evangeline and me up from school in his truck and handed us a brown paper parcel. It was from our mama.

We ripped open the paper and found a Montgomery Ward's shoebox stuffed with shoelaces, hair ribbons galore, and two red Swiss Army pocket-knives. We were as puzzled as we were intrigued by the gift and did not quite know what to make of it.

"Popo, do they use knives like these in New York?" asked Evangeline.

"Well, don't know for sure, but most likely they do," he replied as we drove past Densesky's.

"What would they use them for?" she asked.

"Let's see. They might use them to open clams with in a restaurant. Or maybe if a bird puts his foot through a doughnut box or gets it tangled up in vines, they could free him by using this knife."

"Maybe even Wonder Woman uses these," offered Evangeline. "She lives there, I think."

"Wouldn't surprise me one whit," said Walt.

I felt along the bottom of the box and found the back of an envelope where our mama had written a short note to us. It read:

Dear Girls,

New York is jumping this time of year. I hope you get a lot of use out of these goodies.

Juliet, be kind to your sister. Both of you mind Ruby and Walt. Do not give them a hard time.

I miss you girls.

Love,
Mama

"Popo, if Mama misses us so much, how come she don't just come on home?" asked Evangeline.

"Well, Rabbit, maybe getting famous takes lots of hard work and time."

"Oh," she said, puffing her cheeks out with air.

Walt looked at us, sighed, and started up the engine. "Girls, let's go on down to Densesky's and have a vanilla cone."

When we arrived at Densesky's, also known as the Pride of Fireside, the first person I saw was my best friend. Dixie Flagg munched enthusiastically on a double-dipped chocolate cone. The evidence of her enjoyment was stuck to her nose and her lips. A few minutes later, Evangeline looked about the same, but I cautiously dabbed my mouth, lest I look like them. Walt just couldn't take it, so he went over to the jukebox, played Patsy Cline tunes and studied the music menu.

"My birthday is coming next week," said Dixie, adjusting her pink headband over her ridiculously teased sandy hairdo.

"I know," I replied, staring at her hair with an open mouth.

"Why'd you do that to your hair?" said Evangeline. "Looks like chickens been scratching…"

I elbowed her and said, "But I like it, Dixie. Can you show me how to get my hair to do thataway?"

Dixie smiled, pleased. "Did it myself!" she said. "Sure, I can help you do yours like this too!"

"Oh boy!" Evangeline said, returning her attention to her cone.

"How about you and Evangeline spending the night with me? My mama just bought a busload of old prom dresses from the Goodwill," Dixie said smugly. "We can all dress up and act like we're Diana Ross and the Supremes. I've got one of her forty-fives. We can sing until we get good."

"That'll be when we're about a hundred and fifty," said Evangeline as she bit a hole out of the bottom of her cone. Ice cream ran down her hot-pink blouse.

"Who gets to be Diana Ross?" I asked.

"Me. It's my birthday," said Dixie.

"Then I get to be Mary Wilson," I said.

"All right," Dixie said.

"I never even heard of those people," said Evangeline, perplexed.

"That's because you're still a little girl," Dixie said.

"Yes, but I'll grow up someday," said Evangeline. "When I do, I'll be the smartest girl in Maitlin County. There won't be anything I don't know. For instance, if you want to know who can make the best Jacob's ladder with yarn, just look to me. Anybody who needs a hole dug to China in her backyard before you can say lickety-split will call me. I can catch horny toads so fast they don't know what hit them. After I get a jar full, I will turn around and sell them for fifty cents a head. You name it, I can do it!"

Patsy Cline sang "Crazy," as Selma Davis hurried up to the counter to wait on us. "Need some ice cream for these sweet girls?" Walt looked up, nodded, and smiled. Selma smiled back, but appeared to be in a hurry and soon left the counter to cut yardage for a customer in dry goods.

Dixie's eyes lit up. "In that case," she whispered, "you two can help me toilet-paper Selma Davis's house. I been looking for just the right girls to help me out. Hers is the tallest and strangest house in Fireside, what with it being a movie screen too. It will take the smarts of girls like us to figure out how to do it up right."

By now, ice cream completely covered up one of Dixie's nostrils.

"Dixie, you might want to take care of that," I said. I handed her a napkin and pointed to her nose.

"Oh," she said, dabbing at her nose and smearing it around even more. "That better?"

"Lots," I replied, looking away and trying to remember why I counted her as my best friend in fourth grade. It didn't take me long to put my finger on it. She was an exciting person, a fearless fire-breather. I admired that quality, because it was a characteristic far removed from my own.

"Dixie, your face looks like the ice cream on the floor underneath your chair," said Evangeline.

"It does?" said Dixie.

"Here, lick my napkin, and I'll wipe it off you."

Evangeline worked diligently at Dixie's nose, the way I'd often seen Ruby clean my sister's. She cleaned the outside, but failed to get inside the nostril. "You need a plumber," she said. "I just can't help you."

"Girls, you need to bring about five fat rolls of toilet paper each," whispered Dixie as we parted. "Bring Scott brand because it goes farther. I've got plenty of experience in these matters."

"Okay!" we said.

So it was set in stone, or at least in ice cream, that Evangeline and I would spend the night of Dixie's birthday with her. It was to be our first night away from Ruby and Walt since we'd moved there.

When we arrived back at the ranch carrying our prized package of shoestrings, hair ribbons, and pocketknives, we walked around to the back door, on account of the front door being locked. As we rounded the corner of the house, we could see Ruby through the kitchen window.

She was wearing her striped pedal pushers and an old denim shirt of Walt's. She'd cranked up Elvis's "Blue Suede Shoes" on the record player about as loud as it would go and was dancing as hard as Mitzi Gaynor on the smooth blue linoleum with a spatula in her hand.

Walt pushed through the kitchen door and said, "Go, baby, go!" He slid up to Ruby, tossed her spatula on the counter, took her hand, and began to dance right along with her. Since Walt towered above Ruby, he had to bend over quite a bit just so they could make eye contact.

Evangeline and I backed right out of the house and sat on the kitchen steps. We giggled and rolled our eyes and mimicked them.

"You never know what a grown-up will do next, do you, Evangeline?" I said.

"Naw," she said. "This just ain't normal behavior for old people."

"I think you're right. I don't know many other grandparents who still act goo-goo eyed."

"Way they got their bottoms stuck out and shaking while they dance make me think Great-Grandmother zapped them with the cattle prod."

"Wouldn't put it past her," I said and put my arm around Evangeline's shoulder. It was one of the few times that we had ever been in agreement about much of anything. As sisters, it had been our job to argue about anything and everything whenever possible. It was a job we had taken to heart and worked toward with great efficiency, until lately. I thought we were slipping a tad in that regard.

After a dinner of fried venison sausage, black-eyed peas, mashed potatoes made with plenty of evaporated milk and butter, and wedges of iceberg lettuce with a dollop of mayonnaise, our household formed into two distinct troops. Ruby and I went into the living room and settled down on the sofa. Walt, Evangeline, and Itasca settled into her bedroom, telling stories.

Tales of fact and fiction drifted through the bedroom's open door. Walt recounted riding cattle cars all the way to Kansas City and back and claimed to have shoveled more manure than any Texas politician ever had on the campaign trail. Evangeline told about how she'd once dug a hole so deep in our backyard in Austin that a small Chinese explorer girl had climbed out. Naturally, she had shared a peanut-butter-and-jelly sandwich with the girl and sent along a bottle of grape Nehi for her trip back home.

Predictably, Itasca went on about George, how he'd missed this or that event with the boys and with her, but that she had found it in her heart to forgive him since he hadn't really meant to leave them in the first place.

All the while, Ruby and I remained on the sofa and thumbed through seed catalogues looking for the most appealing Beefmaster tomatoes on the market.

"How about this one?" I asked.

"Looks good," she said.

"You gonna order it?"

"I don't know. I'm trying to imagine myself holding one of those and a blue ribbon from the county fair as well." Ruby pushed back the sleeves of Walt's old shirt and said, "Sure would like to win this year."

"You can, Mamaw. I have faith in you."

"The biggest thing I've got to worry about is keeping the hornworms and deer away while the tomatoes are growing."

"I'll help you," I said, smiling.

"You will, Juliet? You'd do that for me?"

"Sure I would."

"You are sweeter than flowers in May."

"I know," I said, confidently.

"You do?"

"Yes, you've told me before."

Later that night, Evangeline and I lay in the hideaway sofa bed in the living room, counting the ceiling tiles by the light of the flickering fire. Though late March, there was still a chill in the air on some evenings, and Walt had put two sticks of wood on to burn in the fireplace before Evangeline and I crawled into bed.

"Why in the world does Dixie want to go and waste all that toilet paper on Selma Davis's house?" she asked.

"I've never heard of doing that either, but Dixie knows about all kinds of interesting things," I said.

"Like what else?" said Evangeline.

"Like how to act and sing and dress like a Supreme."

"Oh," she said.

"I think we'll make great Supremes, don't you?" I asked.

"I don't know," she muttered. "Right now, I don't much care. I got this stupid old spring sticking me in the back again. When I grow up, my back's gonna look like a coil from all these nights of sleeping on this durned old bed."

"I'll sleep on it tonight, Evangeline."

"You will?"

"If…"

"If what?"

"You'll swear on a stack of Bibles, cross your heart, and hope your eyeballs drop out if you break your promise not to tell."

"About what?"

"About planning to toilet-paper Selma's house."

"Oh, all right," she replied.

"One thing we don't need is for Mamaw and Popo to find out. This is our very first sleepover since we moved here, and we don't want to spoil it."

Eighteen

The next morning, Walt had an announcement to make. We were seated around the kitchen table, stuffing ourselves with Ruby's scratch waffles smothered in Log Cabin syrup and surrounded by bacon.

"Rabbit, Squirrel—I'm going on a trip. Come next week, I'm going to fly to the East Coast to visit a friend."

"You are? Why?" I asked. Suddenly, I was filled with sadness and fear at the thought of Walt leaving town.

"Well," he said, "because this visit is way overdue." Walt reached for another piece of bacon.

Itasca poured cream into her coffee and said, "Does your friend come from a good family?"

"Sure, Mother. The very best."

"It will be good for Walt to see some country that he doesn't have to ranch," said Ruby as she poured more coffee into his cup.

"I want to go," said Evangeline.

"Me too," I said.

"Sorry, girls. I need for you two to watch after Ruby and Mother. I won't be gone more than a week."

Apparently, it had already been set in stone that the most important man in the world to us would be leaving for a while. Ordinarily, I would have moped around a good bit just dreading the moment when Walt would leave, but not this time. Evangeline and I were not without something to look forward to ourselves. Within just a few days, we would become the Supremes.

On Saturday morning, we dug out Ruby's old stage costumes she'd remade to fit us. Evangeline's dress was blue satin with what seemed like miles of netting that gathered at the waist and flowed down its skirt. Mine was similar, but in red with a crocheted red rose at the waist and spaghetti straps, underneath which I wore a sweat shirt.

We put on her old elbow-length white gloves, which went up to our armpits. I wore a black-velvet headband with matching veil, which went to my chin. Evangeline wore a hat covered with a zillion fake daisies and white netting. We decided we wanted to practice being Supremes before we unveiled ourselves in front of Dixie.

"Mamaw, would you come be a Supreme with us?" we asked, while Ruby was bent over the kitchen sink, scrubbing eggs for our Saturday trip to Densesky's and station KOFF.

"A supreme what?" she asked.

"A Supreme like 'Stop in the Name of Love.'"

Ruby looked puzzled for a minute, and then it dawned on her. "Oh, of course. I know who you mean. Well, all right, just let me dry my hands. I'm ready."

"Oh no, Mamaw. You've got to get all dressed up and beautified like us," said Evangeline, modeling her arm-length gloves.

"Let me see what I can do," said Ruby.

She disappeared into her bedroom and emerged in a 1940s green-sequined floor-length dress from her Gemburree days with Pearl and Sapphire—and long white gloves.

"You look like a movie star, Mamaw," I said.

"Thank you, Sugar Foot. I can't even tell you how happy it has made me to learn that I can still fit in this thing," Ruby said.

"Do you want to be Diana Ross, Mamaw?"

"Who wouldn't?" she said, as she placed an album on our daddy's old turntable. "Girls, hold on. I am about to present to you, the one and only, Miss Diana Ross."

Ruby knew all the hand motions, the hip rotations, the way to hold her head, and the dance steps. She was a vision to us of all that was fun and fancy in a classy, nutty sort of way.

Just when we were all in the middle of dancing and singing to "Baby-Baby," along came Itasca in her white nightgown. We all froze dead in our tracks as if we'd just been sprayed by insecticide.

Itasca crept over to Walt's office chair on rollers and sat down heavily. Then she proceeded to roll on over to the middle of our dance floor. Copying Ruby's hand motions, Itasca joined us in our performance and began having a big old time.

It was obvious to me, right then and there, that an alien had kidnapped our old great-grandmother, replacing what was crusty, moldy, and bizarre, with someone we could possibly even like.

The four of us, Supremes every one, danced for the entire length of the album. If I could have shellacked the five best hours of my life so far and pressed them in memory for eternity, this would have been one. A girl might not remember that all her clothes had been starched just so and hung in her closet or that anyone could have eaten off a spotless kitchen floor, but she would preserve in her heart forever the fact that grown-ups had danced with her.

While Itasca had always been one to wear costumes, even if she hadn't seen them as such, she also had a stern opinion of what was appropriate and proper. It was all right for her to dress like Eleanor Roosevelt or Emily Dickinson, but it wasn't all right to use the wrong fork or have just plain old chicken on Thanksgiving Day. She was a queen in exile, without crown or wealth, but blue-blooded for sure.

Somebody had turned on the *nice* switch inside of Itasca. It was true that she hadn't felt well for most of the time I'd known her, and that must have contributed to her behavior, but, over the next few days, she was easier to be around. The days of suffering us to eat her scorched oatmeal were gone. It had been a while since she'd wanted to cook. This was just one change that made her feel safer to be around.

If she didn't get her way about what channel the television was on, or what the menu for dinner was, she just said, "All right, Ruby. Suit yourself."

When I was helping Ruby shell pecans for a pie, one flew out of my nutcracker and smacked Itasca on the chin. She neither glared at nor threatened me. She just plucked the fallen nut out of her lap, cracked it, and ate it. That pretty well summed up her lifelong philosophy: if something offends you, eat it!

Itasca was not only serious about eating, but also had principles about etiquette and entertaining. That evening, she held forth on the art of proper napkin folding for dinner.

She was wearing a 1920s flapper dress made of white satin, a tiara, black feather boa, and bright-red lipstick. Evangeline and I could not take our eyes off her and this latest costume.

It was Friday lunch and the last big meal before Walt's departure to visit with his friend. We were seated around Ruby's table, enjoying a farewell dinner of fried pork chops, mashed potatoes with cream gravy, stewed tomatoes canned from Ruby's garden, early June peas frozen right off the vine, iced tea with enough sugar to please even Evangeline, and icebox cookies drowned in peaches and syrup for dessert.

"The key is in the starch," said Itasca. "Soak the napkins in it for at least an hour, let them get partially dry, and then iron them into oblivion. *Then* you fold them."

"That's quite a trick," I said. "I didn't know you could do that with paper."

"Not paper, dear. One uses linen napkins for proper entertaining."

The only entertaining I knew of was the kind we'd just done in the living room, the type you might find on *The Ed Sullivan Show.* I had never seen anyone folding napkins on his "really big show."

Just like he always did at the noon meal, Walt arose during dessert, tuned in his old radio to station KOFF, but this time Selma's twangy voice came on, advertising for Densesky's. I watched his face for signs of overattention as he sat back down and poured coffee into his saucer to cool it. Did he enjoy her talk of yard goods and bubble bath for sale a tad too much? Did his heart leap a smidgen at the mention of Kleenex or sunflower birdseed available for the first time at that unheard-of low, low price?

Walt simply picked up his saucer without splashing a drop of coffee, blew into it, and then slurped it like a boy.

"Walter Scott Cranbourne, for heaven's sake!" said Itasca.

"I'm not five, Mother," he replied quietly.

"Then don't act like it," she said.

Station KOFF moved to the Fireside Feed & Mill commercial, "And we've got thirty-three piglets for sale, all good lookers, waiting to grow up and become bacon!"

"No!" wailed Evangeline. "Nobody should eat those little piggies!"

"It *is* the way of life, Rabbit," said Walt gently patting her on the head.

"The food chain," said Ruby. "One animal feeds off another. It is the way of life."

"Then who will eat us?" I asked.

"The IRS," said Ruby.

"Oh," I said, wondering how big the teeth of the IRS were.

After lunch, we saw Walt off as he got in his truck to drive to the Austin airport. Evangeline clung to him and cried so hard that his khaki shirt was wet through to his undershirt.

"I'll be back directly, Rabbit," he told her. "I'm just taking a short little trip. I'll bring you and Squirrel back a little surprise. Maybe root beer barrels or some such."

That didn't pacify Evangeline, however. Since we'd lost both parents, neither of us wanted to contemplate the possibility of another one, even if it were temporary. In Evangeline's mind, a trip translated into, *he's certain to be killed or might just plain run away.*

Ruby picked Evangeline up, all fifty-four pounds of her, and patted her like a baby. "He'll be back before you know it. Won't be gone long. Let's dry those tears and go have a piece of peppermint. Isn't that what Popo gives you on afternoons when you're supposed to be taking a nap? I'll give it to you early today. Then let's go have us a rest before we head into town. Then we'll see what mischief we can get into when we deliver eggs. Here's an idea, maybe we'll have a soda at Densesky's fountain before we head on over to KOFF."

"Okay, Mamaw," said Evangeline, but she was still bawling. Then tears started running down my own face. Guess I couldn't help but cry along too.

Walt sat in his truck and stared at the sorry shape we were in with a horrified expression on his face. Up to her eyeballs in crying girls, Ruby called out, "Walt, time to get a move on, now, if you know what I mean. It doesn't help these girls one whit when you dillydally."

"See you all next Sunday," said Walt, mournfully, as he shifted gears and backed away from the house. When he drove off, he took off his Stetson and waved it out the truck window at us. Ruby shooed us inside the house, gave us peppermint, and got out her fiddle.

"Girls, if we're gonna wallow in it. Let's wallow good. In the meantime, I'm gonna teach you to yodel." She started to play a piece by Hank Williams called "Lone Gone Lonesome Blues," and changed the words to fit our situation.

I interrupted her by saying, "Oh, Mamaw. I don't think that's a good idea. It might break a windowpane or something. Or maybe give Great-Grandmother a heart attack."

"Nonsense," she said. "You don't have to have a good voice to work out the blues through music."

That was how we passed the afternoon. The nap had been forgotten while we yodeled like sick, heartbroken coyotes singing into a hairbrush microphone. Not Ruby, though. She sounded good. Real good. By the end of the instruction, I thought I heard that Evangeline was beginning to catch on. Doggone it. That could only mean one thing, which was that I was the only one in the room who had no talent.

The following day, I opened the Cranbourne Variety Hour at Station KOFF with Fireside news.

"Congratulations to all my Fireside school friends about to start spring break. Happy birthday to all you kiddos celebrating birthdays during this time. Coming up is the day we celebrate as the Annunciation to the Virgin Mary by the Archangel Gabriel that she would give birth to the Baby Jesus in about nine months. I was born on the day of the Annunciation and say thank you to my mother, wherever she is, for delivering me here, safe and sound."

Then I went on to read the Fireside news that Miss Alma had left me. I had begun to modify the news, changing the parts that bothered me. If someone in Fireside got killed in an automobile accident, I didn't say it like that. Instead, I said, "Mr. So and So changed his address to the Sweet Bye and Bye and is now playing checkers with St. Peter." Or "Mrs. This or That took up knitting on Thursday and is now making a sweater for her new friend, St. Michael."

I always tried to make my listeners happy. Even if the deceased were what Ruby calls "no count" and did nothing other than laze around on the sofa watching soaps and eating Little Debbies all day, I would say that she had been a motion study expert, a concept I'd learned from having read *Cheaper by the Dozen.* Can you see how much happier the relatives of those folks might have felt with just the right slant on things?

While we never have violence or theft in Fireside, there might be an occasional grease fire, which I would report like this: "The temperature has been extra warm and toasty in the Fireside Café, so you might want to check on Vivian and Jim Bob and give them a hug." Or if a tornado knocked down a barn, I'd say, "A prevailing southerly wind swept through the Miller place last week." I'd heard that *prevailing* word quite often on TV when Walt watched the weather on CBS.

I am no dummy, despite how I might look sometimes. I have been told that many of the things I report are about acts of God. I just wouldn't want to give His handiwork a bad name, so I try to put a pretty spin on it. That way nobody goes around blaming Him. Everybody needs someone to watch his or her back now and then, at least I do.

Nineteen

Since this marked the beginning of spring break, our days without Walt seemed to stretch out endlessly before us. The one gem on the horizon was the coming Friday night at Dixie's house, but that seemed forever away.

Ruby kept us as busy as she could. We helped to prepare her garden for spring planting. By that I mean, we practiced being scarecrows for later, kept our eyes open for snakes, rabbits, squirrels, and even armadillos, all of which loved to dig or occupy holes. Ruby made us go into the house while she got out her shotgun and dispatched two armadillos in the corner of her garden. She carried both by their tails and pitched them into the chicken yard for her pullets to peck at. I, for one, didn't know whether I really wanted to eat eggs laid by dodgy little birds that had dined on dead armadillo. Ruby said it was going to be her blue-ribbon garden, and she didn't want pests moving in before she'd even planted.

Lambs and calves were being born left and right. It was highly unusual that Walt would have left during springtime for this reason. Often, Ruby would have to get up during the night to check on a young heifer she thought might have a tough labor, or even a ewe suspected of carrying twins. It was important, she said, not to get her scent on any newborn, or its mother might reject it.

Whenever this was unavoidable due to a tough delivery, Ruby would make the calf or lamb her pet, and we would help feed it out of giant Dr. Pepper bottles with black rubber nipples pulled over the ends. The chalky powdered milk we mixed with water from the garden hose came in large double-papered bags from the feed store. It didn't look all that appetizing to me, but the lambs loved it, wagged their tails, and nibbled our fingers as they drank.

On Tuesday morning, one ewe butted Ruby so hard she fell onto a rock in the sheep pen, which caused a severe bruise down one hip and the back of her thigh. She cried a little and then disappeared into the bathroom to take a long, hot bath. However, just as soon as she got into the tub, Itasca set to hollering for us all to come into her bedroom to say hello to George.

I went first, knowing Ruby couldn't. Peering around the corner of her bedroom door, I said, "I'm here, Great-Grandmother."

"C'mon in, child. I want George to see how big you've grown."

I walked into plain view, noting Itasca seated upright in her bed, but that her skin was nearly colorless now. Phlegm plagued her voice, and I was surprised to see her joyful smile.

"Yes, ma'am?"

"Well, what do you think?" she asked, pointing to the foot of her bed.

I looked to where her feet rose underneath the chenille bedspread, creating two little hills with a valley in between. About four feet above that was a sliver of pulsating, brilliant light that reminded me of the glare cast off Ruby's Thunderbird windshield in August, only brighter.

"Why, I don't know what to say. Great-Grandfather sure don't look like I thought he would."

"That's all right, Juliet. George, what's that?" Itasca looked at the light and nodded. She never took her eyes off it as she spoke. "He says he has a message for you."

I wasn't sure I wanted to hear it, but said, "What is it?"

"It's from your father. He sends his love and says to think really hard about consequences before you act. Also, when you look at the Big Dipper, think of him and he'll blow you a kiss."

You may not believe this, but what I'm about to say is absolutely true. That light moved right on into me and filled me to overflowing with love. It made me feel as if I were cherished by everybody in the universe *and* their brother. Then the light disappeared but left its warmth inside me for days. I wasn't certain what to make of it, but it sure did feel good. I didn't want to change clothes or take baths for a good while for fear that I would accidentally lose that euphoric feeling.

Being filled with such good from above didn't stop me, however, from jabbing Evangeline in the shoulder in the middle of the night when she kicked me in her sleep.

"For crying out loud, Evangeline. Would you stop kicking me and talking in your sleep?"

"I'm gonna tell Mama on you!" she whined after I poked her in the shoulder with my pointer finger.

"Go ahead, if you can find her," I retorted.

In the moonlight, she looked like a much younger child than one who had turned eight last Memorial Day. Her pillow was wet with drool, and the annoying odor of old waffle syrup lingered on her pajama sleeve. Evangeline would wear the same sleepwear for a solid year if Ruby didn't occasionally root it out of her drawer and wash it.

Come Thursday, I thought God was coming to take me out of this world for poking my sister as I had. I stood at Ruby's kitchen sink, helping her dry the supper dishes, and was whistling the *Sound of Music* theme song we'd been rehearsing for a school production when I saw *the end of the world* mushrooming on the northwestern horizon. Billowy, angry clouds of brilliant reds, blues, oranges, and grayish whites suddenly erupted in the distant sky. Due to great-grandfather George's admonition to think about the consequences of my actions beforehand, I was certain that those massive, consuming clouds were coming to erase me like a mistake on a Big Chief tablet.

"Mamaw, the end of the world is upon us," I said, terrified. "I think that Jesus must be coming on the clouds."

"What on earth?" Ruby said, raising her eyebrows. Then her eyes looked where I pointed with that same wicked little pointer finger that had poked Evangeline.

"Well, I'll swanee," she said, leaning into the window. She removed her rubber latex gloves and cranked open the window to get a better look. "No, Juliet. That's not the end of the world. That's White Sands way out yonder in New Mexico. They're testing bombs again."

"How do you know?" I said.

"Heard it on the television."

"Oh. You sure?"

"Sure as I'm standing here."

"Well, if you're that sure."

Ruby wrapped her arms around me and kissed my sweaty forehead. "You and Evangeline are our pride and joy. Walt and I wouldn't let anything hurt either of you. No bomb is gonna bother our two wonderful girls. The end of the world is not coming anytime soon. You've been through an awful lot over the past few years. Now it's time for good things to happen. You have nothing to fear, sweet baby."

On Friday night, Evangeline and I spent all the livelong evening preparing our red vinyl suitcases and a duffel bag for the anticipated Saturday sleepover at Dixie's. We were to go there the minute our broadcast at station KOFF was over. We packed Ruby's old stage costumes, long white gloves, and old velvet hats covered with netting. Evangeline threw in a jar of peanut butter and a loaf of Mrs. Baird's White Bread in case she didn't like Dixie's mother's cooking. I threw in pink sponge rollers, a pair of skates, twelve pairs of underwear in case Ruby had been all wrong about a disaster not coming, and my diary so I could record everything we did, saw, and ate for eternity.

Last, but not least, was Dixie's birthday present. It was a two-part gift, the first of which was a box of Mr. Bubble, and the second was two sparrow eggs Evangeline had found and placed in a Band-Aid box surrounded by cotton balls. Finally, we packed ten rolls of toilet paper, which constituted all of Ruby's supply, snapped the locks of our suitcases shut, and pulled the drawstring of the duffel bag closed.

"You think we're gonna get our hides tanned for this?" asked Evangeline.

"No," I replied confidently. "Ruby told me the other day she wouldn't let nothing in the world harm us."

"Well, if you're sure," said Evangeline.

"I'm as sure as the flowers in May," I said, repeating Ruby's phrase.

We fell asleep on the living room floor that night, watching Topo Gigio on *The Ed Sullivan Show.* He seemed like a cross between a mouse and Jerry Lewis with an Italian accent. Evangeline said she wanted to marry him when she grew up.

I said, "Don't be silly. Save yourself for someone real like Greg Brady or Marshal Matt Dillon. You can't marry someone who is three inches tall."

"You can in *The Borrowers,"* she said.

"That's a book. It isn't real like television."

"It is more realer than TV," she said. "Much more realer."

Sometime in the night, Ruby covered us up with quilts and let us sleep on the floor where we pleased. When we arose with the howling March wind, we could hear the windmill outside near the tank turn and the metallic clanging that went with it.

Because it was the morning of our slumber party at Dixie's house, we just wanted the day to pass faster. We annoyed Ruby with so many questions about what we could do to make the time pass faster. She first had us wash and grade eggs, but after we'd cracked four in our nervous excitement by dropping them in the dishpan, she sent us to the kitchen table to cut buttons off old shirts she intended to turn into dust rags. We dropped each button into the old cookie tin and marveled at their different colors and shapes.

By the time we went into town to distribute the eggs and then on down to station KOFF, the March wind was whirling bits of trash, old leaves, and grass through the air. Ruby had to hang onto the hem of her dress with one hand to keep it from flying up about her waist and hold onto her fiddle case with the other.

After Ruby played her opening number, "Down by the Riverside," I launched into reading the local announcements: "The Southern Dames of Fireside are hosting this year's diaper-folding contest in the town square pavilion next Wednesday at 3:00 p.m. Entry fee is five dollars. Club president, Mary Clarice Farnsworth, would like to remind all those interested to please practice folding ahead of time. Last year's winner, Magda Prouski, mother of twelve cherubs (from San Saba), folded six hundred diapers in under an hour. Mary Clarice doesn't want our chapter embarrassed by poor performances. Irene, you may want to go ahead and start today. All proceeds benefit the Dames' charity choice, Dapper Diapers for Soggy Tots."

Evangeline handed me a piece of paper that had just been delivered to the station by a woman in double-knit pants, matching tunic, and a bright orange corsage, huffing and puffing.

I said, "We have an announcement from the Fireside Ladies' Club that meets the second Tuesday of each month at 7:00 p.m. at the library. This month's program will be given by Earlene Pickett and is called 'The Dangers of Collapsible Nylon Zippers, Fact and Fiction.'"

Evangeline started making faces at me while I was on air, but I only giggled a little before I scowled at her and gave her my best mad face. She was acting like a baboon when Ruby handed her the fiddle and made her play "Itsy Bitsy Spider."

We had more pent-up energy than we usually had on the program and continued to egg one another on toward worse misbehavior that got both of us sent to a corner of the studio while Ruby fiddled her head off. She gave us that look that said, *You are about to be grounded and might not get to go over to spend the night at Dixie's if you do not watch out.*

We shaped up after that, knowing that our immediate happiness hung in the balance. By the time Ruby dropped us off at Dixie's house around 5:00 p.m., she seemed thrilled to be relieved of the plagues we had been.

Dixie's folks came to the front door when we knocked. Wilford and Delta Mae Flagg worked at the Fireside Meat Processing Plant where they ground hamburger meat, made venison sausage, and sliced T-bones five days a week. Delta Mae's skin was thin, pig pink, and covered with spidery veins. Wilford was beefy, no pun intended, and sported the biggest belly of any man in town. I did not understand, for the life of me, how he could reach around it to work. When he picked up our heavy red suitcase, however, I noted his long, hairy gorilla-like arms.

"Come on upstairs, girls," said Delta Mae. "Dixie is up there doing God knows what."

Evangeline and I entered into the Flagg kitchen, as we trailed behind Dixie's mother toward the stairs. On the kitchen floor was one cracked egg glued to the edge of the baseboard near the kitchen sink. Beside it was a nest of coffee grounds and an onion peel.

Delta Mae noted my concerned stare. "Oh, don't pay no mind to that. Wilford was on his way outside to dump a load of compost into the garden and spilled a little. I'll clean it up, eventually."

I wondered whether it had been weeks since the spill because it looked and smelled quite old. The Flagg family tolerance for disorder must have been quite broad because everywhere we looked spelled chaos. Newspapers were stacked in ragged piles throughout the house—on the cracked linoleum of the hallways, underneath ladder chairs, and even in a pile on their sagging gold sofa.

"Good fire starters," said Delta Mae. "Someday, we're going to convert the garage into a family room and build a fireplace in it. We'll be glad we saved all them papers when that happens."

She led us up the stairs, each step flanked by scores of empty egg cartons. Trying to sound cheerful and to act as if nothing was out of the ordinary, I said, "Our grandmother would envy you those egg cartons."

"Oh, would she like to buy them?" asked Delta Mae, hopefully.

"Well, I couldn't speak for her." I swallowed thickly, knowing Ruby would definitely not want to buy musty old egg cartons from the Flaggs.

When we finally emerged into Dixie's bedroom, we found her perched on her window seat, spying on something next door through her paper-towel-cylinder telescope. "Cotton-picking communist!" she muttered.

Delta Mae stood behind us, watching out the window with an interested expression on her puffy face. She seemed unfazed by her daughter's assessment of their next-door neighbor, Selma Davis, but was concerned about her daughter's behavior as our host. "Dixie, aren't you going to say hey to your guests?"

Evangeline scowled and said, "What's a cotton-pickin' communist?"

"Well, I don't know exactly," replied Dixie, lowering her cardboard telescope, "but she ain't like us. That's all I *need* to know."

Delta Mae said, "Well, I'll be leaving you girls to start your slumber party now. Just don't get too rambunctious in here, all right, Dixie?"

"We won't get any rowdier in here than our mission requires," said Dixie, mysteriously.

Delta Mae rolled her eyes and said, "Spare me." She soon disappeared, and we heard her heavy footsteps going down the stairs.

"In Mississippi," said Dixie, "we didn't have communists. We just had good old people like you and me. But in Texas, we got these here weirdos." She jerked her thumb toward Selma's house and smirked.

"Miss Selma isn't weird," said Evangeline softly.

"Then how come she ain't remarried?"

"Maybe she hasn't met Mr. Right," said Evangeline.

"Shows what you know," said Dixie. "She's been keeping company with a man I think is a communist spy because she only sees him in the evening. By morning, he's gone, slick as a whistle. I found a whole bunch of shredded paper in her garbage can the other day. I know she spends her nights transcribing secret information for that scroungy old spy she's been seeing."

"How can you tell all that by shredded paper?" I asked.

"Because I've got a lot going on upstairs," replied Dixie, tapping her round head. "You'd be amazed by what I've learned by going through communist Davis's trash."

"Like what?"

"Like she made enough five-bean salad to choke an army and then threw it all out. What do you make of that, huh?"

She had me there. "Maybe she didn't read the recipe right?" I offered weakly.

"No. You're dead wrong. It's a conspiracy. I'm sure of it."

"A five-bean salad conspiracy?" asked Evangeline.

"Communists are tricky," said Dixie, "but I have lots more evidence against her than bean salad."

"Like what?" I said.

"Like a rolled-up pair of stockings without any runs or even a trace of fingernail polish on them. And then there was a hairnet."

"Selma wouldn't get caught dead in a hairnet," I said. "Anybody who lives in Fireside knows that."

"Well, that's the devious ways of communists and spies. They always do what nobody on earth thinks they would. They live to fool people."

"Who taught you all this stuff?" I asked.

"Watched it on the TV like any smart person would," said Dixie.

She reached down to the windowsill behind her orange flower-power curtains and produced two more cylinders wrapped in aluminum foil with our names on them. She had cut out the letters of our names from Montgomery Ward's catalogue, which lay on the floor in pieces, and had glued them to each roll. She said, "Look-a-here. I made you and Evangeline telescopes too."

We took them from her, marveling about her ingenuity, and were pleased that she had been thinking of us before our arrival.

"Let's start a club," said Dixie.

"What kind?" I said.

"The Fireside spy club."

We posted ourselves at Dixie's bedroom window, watching Selma's house until dinnertime. Each of us came up with our own theories about Selma's true nature and that of her mysterious male friend. They disappointed us and increased our suspicion by the lack of their appearance. Our interest only grew through their absence.

Delta Mae carried TV dinners up to Dixie's nest. There was soggy fried chicken, some gray mashed potatoes, watery carrots and peas, and a little bit of gummy apple dessert.

Dixie attacked the tin tray of food as if it were the best meal she'd ever eaten. "Does your grandma cook this good?" asked Dixie, rubbing her full belly.

"Her cooking is way better than this," said Evangeline, as she pulled out her bag of smashed bread and peanut butter from our red suitcase.

"Well, let's just say it is different from what we've had tonight. But this was really tasty," I said, with my fingers crossed behind my back. I didn't, though, say what it tasted like.

Dixie's mind had jumped to another subject. "If we're gonna be the Supremes tonight, we'd best get to it."

"What are we waiting for?" asked Evangeline, jumping up and flinging our suitcase open for the hundredth time.

We put on our old stage dresses, slid the long white gloves over our hands and up to our armpits, and slipped on our rickety plastic high heels. Dixie put on a black satin dress that bunched around her belly like an inner tube. That didn't bother her; she just pulled on pink ballet tights to cover her behind. Her belly stuck out anyway, but she was apparently used to the problem. I knew she couldn't help the way her belly quivered and shook when she moved. She had inherited the Flagg family abdomen, which was their trademark as far as I could tell.

Dixie went over to her purple-and-white record player, turned it on, and began to play "Hang On Sloopy." Unfortunately, just as we posed for our first dance moves, we heard a car drive up next door.

"Man your battle stations, troops," said Dixie.

We ran to our post at Dixie's window and watched Selma emerge from her car. Her glittering silver dress swayed in the March lion's wind, catching the last of dusk's light. Her partner was tall, wore a straw Stetson, and walked her up to the door. Though we couldn't see his face, there was something horribly familiar about him. I couldn't identify what attribute of his other than his height made my heart sink, but I believed I knew who he was. Judging by the look of things, he was bound to be our Walt.

Twenty

There were no words to describe the depth of my fury when we saw the lean khaki back of our beloved Walt standing on Selma's porch, but Mother Nature painted a pretty good picture of it. Huge thunderstorm clouds gathered overhead as if to say, *Now, see here. We won't be having any more of this nonsense. You folks are old enough to know better.*

I soon thought about the ten rolls of toilet paper stowed away in our suitcase. Seeing Selma pack Walt a wet one on the kisser made me want to get even. Whereas earlier, I had struggled with whether to paper or not to paper, I now knew it was my duty as Ruby's granddaughter.

When he and Selma disappeared into her movie-screen home, I turned to Dixie and Evangeline and said, "Girls, what are we waiting for?"

"You thinking what I'm thinking?" asked Dixie in her bizarre Supremes outfit.

"Right," I said. "Ten rolls won't be near enough."

Evangeline started to whine. "I'm gonna tell."

"Go ahead, you tattle-telling bawl baby," I said.

"I'm gonna tell about what you just called me too."

"Fine by me. I'll just get another sister," I said, nonchalantly.

"What are you talking about?" she said with round eyes. Evangeline had bright-red lipstick smeared up nearly to her nostrils. Dixie had teased her hair to high heaven, but hadn't smoothed down the top layer.

"Never mind," I said. "Evangeline, you look like Frankenstein's bride. You can't go out in public like that, even in the dark. Mamaw would die of embarrassment if the word ever got out. Go on, wipe your face. Then you can follow Dixie and me."

"Leave me alone, you old buzzard butt," she said, fuming and fidgeting.

"Juliet don't have no buzzard butt," said Dixie defensively. "A buzzard don't have no butt."

"How would you know? You old rhino rear!" said Evangeline.

I started to defend Dixie, but my sister was right. Saying Dixie didn't have a rhino butt was like saying Jimmy Durante didn't have a nose. So I thought I'd shift the blame. "Evangeline, what's gotten into you?"

"Two stupid girls. That's what."

Dixie put her hands on her hips and frowned. "I never once figured you for a scaredy-cat, Evangeline."

"Well, that's 'cause I'm brave like a March lion," she replied.

"If that were so, you'd come help us," I said, knowing it would seal the deal.

"Oh, all right," she said, pouting and rubbing her eyes.

Dixie and I flew into action while Evangeline sat on the edge of the bed and picked at a scab on her elbow. Dixie stuffed three additional rolls of toilet tissue down her blouse for good measure. After all, a job worth doing, was worth doing well. That made thirteen rolls of toilet paper. We figured we could make quite an impression with that many streamers.

The three of us crept down the stairs and froze when we spotted Dixie's folks in the kitchen playing forty-two and drinking extra-sweet iced tea from greasy Tupperware tumblers. Marinara fingerprints that had come from a pepperoni pizza kit also decorated dominoes and tableware. Johnny Horton was going *North to Alaska*, according to station KOFF, which was loud enough to cause deafness. Nobody in that room could have heard our footsteps even if we'd been wearing tap shoes.

We realized that toilet-papering Selma's front yard during the peak of the Saturday drive-in movie *True Grit* was going to be a challenge. Huge images of John Wayne and Kim Darby moved across the back of Selma's house as we sneaked around the back and counted thirty cars attached to speaker boxes.

"I've been watching that movie from the living room window for the past week," said Dixie. "We've got at least an hour before Rooster Cogburn moves on. There's a lot of work to be done to straighten out communist Davis, so let's get moving."

Dixie impersonated John Wayne and motioned us forward like a posse. We rounded the house and returned to the front yard. Six pecan trees stood waiting for their adornment like canvas for a paint brush.

We all grabbed our rolls of toilet paper and began to heave them as high as we could manage, given the wind. The paper streamers began to look like ribbons of moonlight as we tried to hurl the rolls up and over the pecan trees in Selma's yard. Nearly all of our efforts fell short of our aim, and the lower half of tree branches were mainly what was decorated. Straining with all our might, we heaved until our arms were tired and heavy.

By the time we'd run out of toilet paper, Selma's yard looked like a giant exhibit of contemporary art. We congratulated ourselves for our athletic abilities and our artwork.

But Dixie was not satisfied. "This just ain't finished," she said.

"Well, what are we going to do? We're out of paper," I said, breathlessly.

"No, that's not what I mean," said Dixie. "We've got to wet it down.

"What for?" I said. "Looks like it might rain anyway."

"We can't depend on Mother Nature to finish our work," replied Dixie.

"You want me to spit on it?" asked Evangeline. "'Cause you know I'm not that tall."

"No, doofus. Get the garden hose and spray it down. That way it will be nearly impossible for communist Davis to get it out. We'll mark this place as the hideout of a spy, forevermore," said Dixie, pulling up her pink tights and letting the elastic band snap against her rotund belly. "This way she's gonna spend years climbing trees and bending over bushes to pick it off. Then you'll be able to call *her* buzzard butt."

Evangeline got so tickled at the thought that she bent over laughing and became weak-kneed. Dixie rounded up Selma's garden hose and was delighted to find it had one of those super-duper spraying nozzles.

"Evangeline, you can spray all the way to San Angelo with this hose," said Dixie.

"I'll bet I can spray all the way to the moon, if I want," said Evangeline, who had developed a swagger with all that newfound confidence. She turned on the faucet and sprayed the pecan branch above her, but most of the water splashed back on her. Her Supremes costume was soaked through and through. All that netting and satin now weighed about a million pounds, to look at her. Then her pink eyelet bloomers fell to her ankles, which only made her laugh harder. She pulled them back up, but they only fell again.

"Tarnation, be thataway!" she said, stepping out of them and hurling them onto a bush.

Before all was said and done, we'd taken a turn wetting down the toilet paper. Our paper artwork was no longer all that attractive. The yard looked haunted in the moonlight, the vision of which began to give us the creeps.

"I believe I'm done, now," I said, thinking about going to bed, safe from being found out and distanced from the spooky vision that hung before us.

"Yeah, me too," said Dixie.

"Me three," said Evangeline.

We all crept back into Dixie's darkened house. Her parents had long tired of playing forty-two and gorging themselves on greasy pizza. Most likely, they had waddled off to a bed with sour-smelling sheets. Or perhaps they were perched on piles of newspapers left from the 1940s, or even in giant sandboxes like huge, ancient cats.

Upstairs in Dixie's bedroom, the three of us slept on a smelly pallet made up of an old stained quilt and sofa cushions we'd pulled up from downstairs.

"This quilt belong to some dog?" I asked.

"Used to, till he died on it," said Dixie, matter-of-factly.

"Died! From what?" Evangeline asked.

"To this day, no one really knows, but I think he choked on a fur ball."

"Dogs don't choke on fur balls," I said. "Just cats."

"Well, I think Helmut choked on a cat's fur ball. He liked them."

"Eeew," I said.

"It's the only spare quilt I got," said Dixie. "Take it or leave it."

We eventually fell asleep anyway, lulled by fatigue and the sounds of cars slowly leaving the movie grounds. Tires crunched monotonously and became white noise to tired ears.

At 4:00 a.m., thunder and lightning commenced, and a torrential downpour followed. The noise awakened me briefly as I realized that my weather forecast had come true. Just as I'd told Dixie, we needn't have bothered with the water hose; the rain would have done the job anyway.

Twenty-One

In the end, we could have gotten away with our toilet-paper escapade if only we'd remembered to retrieve Evangeline's pink eyelet bloomers from the shrub in Selma's yard. It didn't take a rocket scientist to figure out that Evangeline's tiny drawers didn't belong to Dixie. To make matters worse, Selma had sold them to Ruby in the first place and had a pretty good idea whose they were.

Selma didn't bother to confront us directly; she had the early morning Methodist service to attend. She just called Ruby and told her what she suspected before she left the house.

Ruby arrived at the Flagg residence dressed to the hilt for church. She decided, however, that our punishment should not be delayed when the futures of potential juvenile delinquents were at stake. Her sword of judgment was as mighty as it was swift. She put her misleadingly delicate hands on her hips, looked us squarely in the eyes, and sentenced us right on the spot.

"Clean up every scrap of that paper, and I mean every scrap. You two are grounded for a month. No watching Ed Sullivan on top of that. So that means no Topo Gigio! If I hear one peep of complaint or orneriness out of you two, you'll be shoveling manure in the barnyard. Take my word for it, you won't like it."

She folded her arms across her chest. "When Walt gets home, he may have more to add to this. Do I make myself perfectly clear?"

"Yes, ma'am," we said.

Ruby was boiling like a pan of popping grits. "Furthermore, I don't want to hear any excuses for this behavior. There is no acceptable excuse. By the time I'm finished with you, you'll by gosh wish you'd behaved yourselves."

She handed me a rake and Evangeline a burlap bag. "I want every piece of this tissue picked out of the grass and trees and put in this sack."

"Why doesn't Dixie have to help us?" said Evangeline. "This was her idea."

"That's between Dixie and her folks. I'm not raising that child. I am just responsible for you two. Life isn't always fair," Ruby said.

"Mamaw, could we please eat first?" I asked, feeling my stomach start to growl.

"No. No food until you've cleaned up this mess."

Ruby and food just naturally went together. I'd never figured her to be one to deprive us. "Just a biscuit?" I asked.

"No. Now get to work."

Dixie's family let her off scot-free. By their attitudes, it was obvious they believed that Evangeline and I had led their darling astray. They even took her to San Antonio to go bowling while we were pulling bits and pieces of paper out of an area that seemed the size of Maitlin County.

New wrinkles seemed to have formed around Ruby's eyes. I noted fine lines running above her lips, into which a tiny bit of lipstick had settled. Her shoulders slumped and the skin on her neck sagged a little. She looked tired to me. This surprised me as I realized for the first time that she would someday grow truly old and that she would die. My conscience began to gnaw at me, and guilt over our most recent escapade settled like oil underneath vinegar into my spirit. The thought of losing my grandmother scared me so badly I could hardly breathe.

There was work to be done, and Ruby wasn't going to cave in even if I turned purple and died. Evangeline and I began the long, nitpicking task of cleaning up the mess we'd made. What fools we'd been to not only wrap the place, but to wet it down. And then, Mother Nature had made it worse by soaking any pieces that Evangeline had missed with the hose. We bent over picking it up and raking until our backs hurt and we were faint from hunger. The hardest part was getting it out of the trees with the rake that was too long for us to manage easily. By the time we'd finished, it was three o'clock in the afternoon, and we *hated* Dixie.

After Ruby had inspected our cleanup, she opened the door to her Thunderbird wordlessly, no doubt worn to the bone by our shenanigans. She was wearing her green Sunday dress, and her ruby hair was pinned up with mother-of-pearl combs. I felt further shame when I realized she'd been dressed up to go to church, only to be deprived of it by the likes of us.

I thought she'd change back into her old striped pedal pushers and white blouse when we returned home, but she didn't. I realized she was keeping herself beautiful for Walt's return, which saddened me. He did not deserve such longing, such trust on her behalf. No telling what hoochy-smoochy thing he and Selma were up to now.

After feeding us ham sandwiches, apples, and Cheetos, Ruby settled onto the living room sofa and began to read to us out loud from the Bible. Evangeline and I were stationed next to one another like criminals in a courtroom. Thunderclouds were rolling in again, and the late afternoon sky turned dark. The air grew still as death and made us wonder aloud whether tornados would form and come our direction.

Itasca slowly wandered in and out of the living room, looking for her suitcase. She was wearing her white nightgown and faded pink slippers.

"Why do you need your suitcase?" Ruby asked her as she looked up in the middle of the tenth commandment.

"Going on a trip," Itasca said, faintly. As she was already dressed for bed, I could not imagine she was going anywhere.

"Oh. Where to?"

"Going to see George. Call you when I get there, if I can."

Like a nitwit, I rolled my eyes and sighed in exasperation.

"That's enough from you, Juliet," said Ruby. "You've used up today's quota of misbehavior."

"Yes, ma'am," I said.

"Now, back to the commandments. Let's see. The eleventh commandment, which you girls might not yet have learned in Sunday School is THOU SHALT NOT MAKE A MESS OF THY NEIGHBOR'S YARD."

"Selma's not our neighbor," said Evangeline, cocking one eyebrow. "She lives all the way in Fireside."

"In God's eyes, Selma most certainly is your neighbor, Evangeline."

"Is there a commandment in there about not stealing your neighbor's husband?" asked Evangeline.

"What has gotten into you girls? Why do you have it in for Ms. Davis?"

That was when Evangeline let the cat out of the bag. "Mamaw, Popo was with that Selma woman last night. No wonder he ain't home yet."

"Rabbit, what are you talking about?"

"They was kissin' and huggin' all over one another on her front porch!"

"Evangeline!" I said sternly. "Mamaw, don't pay no mind to her. She went and dreamed it all up last night on account of that awful chicken TV dinner we ate at Dixie's."

"Girls, you ever say such a thing again, I'll tan your hides."

"She's sorry. Aren't you, Evangeline?" I leaned over and whispered into my sister's burning ear, "See what you done? Now we'll have to go live in the orphans' home, thanks to you. Mamaw will dump us out on the sidewalk in Fireside, and we'll deserve it."

Ruby put the Bible back on the coffee table, still open to the commandments, and said, "You girls are so wrong. Your Popo has not been with Miss Davis. He'll be home any minute. If not, then I'm sure there's a reasonable explanation like he's missed his plane, or something." Thunder and lightning began as soon as she said that.

"I'll say," said Evangeline. "Missed it going and coming."

"What in the devil has gotten into you? Who took the sweetness out of you girls?"

We never answered, because we had no idea of what to say. The day had been too much for Ruby who started weeping right then and there on the sofa in front of God's eleventh commandment and us.

"Mamaw, don't take it so hard," I advised. "If Popo doesn't ever come back, you can find yourself another husband without even trying."

Well that opened the floodgates to the dam. Ruby started crying harder and harder. I was afraid to sit in the room with her in that condition. Mainly, I just didn't know how to comfort her.

Eventually, she got ahold of herself and then a miracle happened. The telephone rang, startling all of us. I hopped up out of my chair and made a beeline to the rotary phone in the kitchen, scared silly it would be bad news about Walt being run over by a milk truck, or something like it.

If voices could be the color and texture of honey, the man who called had one like that. "Is Ruby there?" he asked.

"Hold on, sir, I'll get her. Would it be all right to ask who's calling?"

"Just tell her that it's Thunderbird Man," he replied.

"Elvis!" I had shrieked into the phone, but quickly composed myself. "Oh, excuse me, sir. I'll see if she's available."

Ruby had already heard who it was and nearly floated to the phone on a blue velvet cloud.

"Yes?" she asked when I handed her the receiver. "Elvis? Oh, it *is* you. You'd like me to make you another cake, but leave out the pecans this time? Just the regular recipe? No, a new Thunderbird won't be necessary. The old one works just fine. You'd like to take me to lunch where?" Ruby hung up the receiver and nearly floated back into the living room, smiling broadly.

Just then, lightning struck a tree in the field out southwest of the house. We could see the strike from the living room. The chickens could be heard squawking all the way from their pen, and Sport began barking his head off. A fierce wind began to blow, and perfectly green leaves were ripped off the trees and flew with bits of grass and dirt against the house. But Ruby's face was filled with joy.

"That really was Elvis, wasn't it?" I said.

"I think maybe it was an angel that God sent to me when I needed him most," replied Ruby.

"I don't know, Mamaw. He sounded pretty real to me," I said. "And I didn't see any feathers falling out of the telephone."

"Well, it could have been an angel," insisted Ruby. "I've heard they can sound or look like anyone they've a mind to."

"Do angels ask ladies to lunch?" I said.

"Anyway you want to look at it, my Elvis is an angel," said Ruby, kissing the velvet painting of Elvis on his cheek.

"Well, just everybody kissing everybody these days," Evangeline said.

"That's enough from you, young lady," said Ruby.

"Why didn't Elvis call me? I can cook tapioca pudding." Evangeline pushed her frizzy hair behind her ears and scraped at muddy paw prints that Sport had left on her blue jeans.

"'Cause you're too durned mean," I said. "And you smell bad."

"He didn't call you either, Juliet. So I guess you must be mean and stink too."

Lightning struck again, this time sending us all scurrying to the window to peer outside. Rain poured in a solid sheet like water from a giant pail. Walt's truck was nowhere in sight, which was just as well since the caliche roads leading to the house were a sea of mud. He might get stuck out there in all that mess and have to get his truck pulled out by the tractor. Soon, it grew pitch dark outside without a star to be seen.

The telephone gave a half ring, was interrupted by another bolt of lightning, and went dead. Ruby frowned and shook her head, but recovered quickly. "Don't worry, he'll be home, directly," she said with conviction. "Why don't you girls play a game of checkers?"

"Okay, Mamaw," I replied, hugging her. "I'm so sorry for what Evangeline and I done to Selma and to you."

"I don't like what you did, but I do love you girls. Now play checkers and think about what you might do to make it up to Ms. Davis. I need to go and check on your great-grandmother."

Ruby disappeared toward Itasca's room, where seconds later we heard her knocking and calling out, "Mother Cranbourne, will you please let me in?"

A few moments later Ruby returned, frustrated. "I tried to open her door, but it was locked, and she didn't answer. I'm gonna have to take it off its hinges. Tried to pick the lock with a hairpin, but couldn't."

"What in the world's wrong?" asked Evangeline, nervously. "I'd just let her be, if I was you. She'll be a rattler when she comes out, shaking and wagging her tail. I'll bet she's got fangs a foot long. They say the older the rattler, the longer…"

"That's enough out of you, Rabbit," said Ruby. "That's no way to talk about a sick old woman. What if she was to hear you?"

"You'd be in a whale of a mess," I said. "But that'd be nothing new to you, Rabbit."

"I just want to make sure she's all right, that's all," said Ruby.

I followed Ruby out to the utility porch where she kept the deep freeze, her bonnets, cattle syringes, whetstones, and various tools. She picked up the wooden box of hammers, nails, pliers, and screwdrivers.

Ruby had Itasca's door pried open within ten minutes, just as if she'd done it a thousand times before. "Your daddy used to lock himself in the bathroom at least once a week when he was about three," she explained, reading our surprised expressions.

"You've got worlds of untold talents," I told her in admiration.

"This isn't the first time I've been told that," said Ruby, as we rushed into Itasca's room. The room was thick with a wet silence. We were soaked in it to the skin.

"Why don't she answer?" asked Evangeline.

"Lord have mercy," said Ruby as she snapped on the bedside lamp, illuminating Itasca's form. She had changed from her white nightgown and now lay across her bed in a black dress, skin pale as a ghost. Her suitcase was spread out on the floor, partially packed for her journey.

"Great-Grandmother has passed," said Ruby. "Please go on back to the living room and wait until I call you."

For the first time in a long while, we did not argue a word. We did not want to remain in the room one second longer than we had to.

Twenty-Two

Waiting in the living room for Ruby to call us was a frightful experience in itself. Another bolt of lightning struck, and suddenly we were enveloped in cave-like darkness. My heart hammered against my chest, and Evangeline whimpered like a pup. Soon we heard Ruby moving about in the kitchen. She felt above the wood stove for the ceramic cache of matches, found one inside, struck it, and managed to light the coal-oil lamp kept in the kitchen for just such occasions. Finally, we were illuminated in the amber glow of the antique lantern.

Following Ruby back into Itasca's room now seemed like the lesser of two evils, but she turned around and said sternly, "You girls, go back into the living room. Don't make me tell you again."

We meant to mind her, but then lightning struck again, bathing the house in an eerie glow for a split second. We couldn't stand the thought of being more than an arm's length away and stuck to her like grass burs.

Ruby just threw in the towel and said, "All right then, if you must."

Her lantern washed over Itasca's ashen face and her sagging jaw. One arm trailed off the bed and a turned-over water glass lay in a pool on the floor. We saw her more clearly than we had during our brief glimpse a few moments earlier. She wore the same black traveling outfit in which she'd arrived the day Mel had brought her. She had been in the midst of travel preparations and had somehow been swept up and carried out of herself. On the bed beside her was an open jar of Vicks VapoRub and several crumpled tissues.

"Too bad she didn't get to the Vicks in time," said Evangeline. "Whenever I get the sniffles, I feel like I might die too."

"She didn't die from catching a cold, honey. It was just her time to go. She was all worn out from heart trouble."

"And she missed her George," I said.

"That's right, she did. Long as I've known her." Ruby rubbed her hands over her eyes. The crow's feet underneath them were punctuated by fatigue and shock. Noticing them made me remember how frightened I'd been just hours ago when I'd first realized that Ruby and Walt would not last forever. I was scared anew.

The familiar odor of ammonia greeted our nostrils. "She wet her britches again," said Evangeline.

"She couldn't help it," said Ruby. "It's just natural. I'm going to light some candles in the living room on the mantel. I want you girls to get ready to go into town. I'll be with you in a minute. I want to put a little lipstick on her and comb her hair. She'd die if anyone was to see her like this. Us girls have to stick together in such matters."

I tried to figure out why lipstick was important. Who cared what a dead woman looked like? She was still dead. But then I thought about how Ruby had hidden herself behind magazines the day we'd gone into Densesky's to buy a plumber's helper. She hadn't planned on going just then and hadn't fixed her face. This was one woman looking out for another, even if they had fought on occasion. In the end, they were still a pair. Evangeline and I were like that no matter how much we squabbled.

Furthermore, it was obvious that tough times were much harder to bear without lipstick. I made a mental note to never spend a moment of my adult life without makeup. Maybe disasters could even be prevented by proper adornment. I tried hard to remember whether Ruby had been made-up the night we learned that our daddy had been killed.

Evangeline and I returned to the living room and worked each other up into a crying fit. Even though we'd lost our daddy to death, we had never really *seen* what it looked like. Itasca no longer looked much like the woman we'd come to know. Her body reminded me of an empty locust shell left behind while the real occupant had turned into something else. There was no question but that she was no longer inside herself and had gone off somewhere. All that was left behind was a worn-out body.

Ruby appeared presently and kissed the tops of our heads. "Everything is going to be all right," she said. "There's nothing to be afraid of."

After we calmed down, we followed behind her as she went to the kitchen and washed her hands with Lava. "Since the phone is out, guess we'll need to go into Fireside to fetch the sheriff."

"You think somebody killed her when we was in the living room?" asked Evangeline. "You don't believe maybe somebody would think you done it, do you?" she asked with round eyes.

"I'll vouch for you, Mamaw," I said. "You was with us all day long. She died on her own."

"You girls have big imaginations, and I think you've watched *Perry Mason* one too many times. I've got to get the sheriff because she died at home."

"Oh," we said.

"What a day for the phone to be out," said Ruby. "First it rains and then it pours."

By the time we'd gotten the sheriff, and after he'd filled out his reports, and Itasca's body had been wheeled away by the funeral home, it was two o'clock in the morning. Finally, it was time to get to bed.

"I can't sleep a wink in this haunted house," whined Evangeline.

"Honey, this house isn't haunted. But I understand how you might feel about now," said Ruby. "Guess we could all use a change of scenery, in any case. Let's go check into the Fireside Inn."

"Where they have all those beautiful weddings?" I said.

"Yes, Sugar Foot."

"Mamaw, I'm Squirrel, she's Rabbit. I'm not sure who Sugar Foot is."

Ruby smiled at me though her face was pale with fatigue. "I thought you were growing tired of the name Squirrel?"

"Just at school. Home is fine."

Ruby wrote Walt a short note telling him our whereabouts and to come find us before he talked to anyone in town. She didn't want him to find out about his mother from "some Joe on the street," she said. We threw a few things into Ruby's train case and my little red vinyl weekend bag and drove into Fireside.

Our room at the Fireside Inn had yellow rose wallpaper and white chenille spreads on its double beds. There was a fireplace in the corner and an overstuffed armchair and Victorian lamp beside it. By the time we'd taken our baths and slid between cool sheets, it was nearly sunrise.

For at least an hour, Ruby had talked about Itasca and how hard her life had been after the sudden death of George. Somehow, Itasca's passing had stirred up our father's death in all three of us. We mourned him all over again. Even Ruby cried. He had been her boy after all, the only one she would ever have.

"Do you think our daddy is rolling out the red carpet for her, Mamaw?" I asked, sniffling and grabbing onto my pillow. I listened to the gentle breathing coming from Evangeline right beside me. She'd fallen asleep first, her dark hair still damp and matted from her shower.

"Yes, Squirrel. I think he's giving her a tour of heaven about now too."

"Will he do that for us when we get there?"

"Right after he gives you girls a great big hug."

"Will he remember us?"

"He could never forget you. Your daddy loves you. Love is eternal."

"Even now, after what we did to Miss Davis?"

"Especially now."

When I finally feel asleep, I dreamed we were all in the funeral home selecting a casket. Gray fog surrounded us all as Ruby pondered the situation.

"How about this one?" a voice asked. I didn't see anyone, just heard the question.

"No, not that one. Walt wouldn't want wood for his mother. He'd pick metal," said Ruby in the dream.

"Excellent choice," said the voice.

"On second thought, wood just feels more friendly than metal. We'll take the mahogany one."

"Wood it will be. Excellent choice."

"Just tie it onto the roof of the Thunderbird so Elvis can sing us a hymn as we pass by."

When we awoke around noon at the Fireside Inn, I felt confused on many fronts. Confused to awaken at the inn rather than on the sofa bed at the ranch. Confused as to whether my dream had been a dream at all, or had really happened. Confused as to my role in helping to clean up this whole mess with Itasca dying and Walt being heaven only knew where.

Ruby was seated in the overstuffed chair, reading her Bible and sipping coffee she'd gotten from downstairs. I stretched, got out of bed, and then climbed into her lap and laid my head against her bony shoulder, shifting until I found a place to rest comfortably. I had grown so that I was almost as tall as Ruby, and covered her almost completely in that chair. I lifted her left hand and held my palm up to hers. My fingers were longer and thinner, which made me feel both powerful and yet somehow disappointed. I wanted to be just like her, in every way.

"Will you always be my Mamaw?" I asked.

"On one condition." She kissed my forehead and pressed her cheek against mine. I could smell coffee on her breath and Noxzema on her skin.

"What's that?"

"That you'll always be my sweet granddaughter."

"I will, Mamaw."

"You and Evangeline are my favorite girls in the whole world. Did you know that?" I leaned back and looked at her. Tears were welling up in her eyes.

"Oh sure. I know that."

She hugged me, wiped her eyes, and said, "Well then, we'd best get about our day."

"Okay."

"First thing is I'd better contact Mel and Nadine and their boy, Ralph. They've got a long drive ahead of them to get here from Arkansas. Second, we need to go to Densesky's and pick out a decent dress for Itasca. I don't want to bury her in one of those costumes she liked to wear. Walt always was embarrassed by her getups. Hopefully, he'll be home soon."

"Sure he will, Mamaw."

Evangeline sat up in bed, looking like a fright. Her unruly hair had been frozen into a spiked puffball. She squinted and scratched her arm, looking around wild-eyed. "Where are we? Hawaii?"

"Fireside, Hawaii," I said and laughed. "Home of the Texas luau."

"Really?"

"Guess if you don't know where you are, you could be anywhere."

"You're poking fun at me," she said and pouted.

"Just a little. Go take a peek in the mirror. There's an orangutan hiding in there."

"Stop it, you're the ape."

Just then, I caught a reflection of myself in the bedroom window. My hair looked just as bad as Evangeline's, yet Ruby hadn't said a word.

"You're right. We're both apes."

We dressed, went downstairs to eat in the Fireside Inn dining room, and then walked down the street to Densesky's. I was not particularly looking forward to going to Densesky's for many reasons, most of them having to do with Selma Davis. Sure, I loved to browse over the store's tapioca-scented lotions and coconut body powders, and to count the gumballs in the great red dispenser. I liked to hear the sound of baseball games erupting from the TV sets in the appliance division, and the snip, snip of Selma's shears cutting off calico yardage from the bolt in the dry goods department. I did not, however, relish seeing Selma after our toilet-paper escapade and Walt's disappearance.

We rounded the wall that divided Densesky's groceries from Densesky's dry goods and appliances and saw Selma unpacking boxes of new women's apparel, but her back was to us. She wore a pink headband and the signature hairdo that was teased to kingdom come. Big, white plastic bracelets clinked on her wrists and complemented dangling matching balls that hung from each straining lobe. The earrings swung and clinked wildly as she turned this way and that. Her pink high-waisted, double-knit dress barely covered her behind as she lifted her arms around to shake out a blue-plaid housedress.

It was her white knee-high go-go boots that caught my eye, however. They were made of patent leather and squeaked slightly as she moved. Even though I already had a pair, hers were much fancier and made me want them.

"Oh, Mamaw," I whispered, "those are the most beautiful boots I have ever seen. We should buy some to bury Great-Grandmother in, I think."

"I don't think so. Her feet won't show in the casket, you know."

"Oh. Well, maybe I could have some then."

"What in the thunder for?" Evangeline said. "You've got some already."

"Not like that."

"That's too durned bad. You're flat out of luck, Juliet. It's my turn to get something new." Evangeline stamped her foot, but I just rolled my eyes at her.

"Girls, we are not here to shop for either one of you," Ruby said.

Selma heard us, stood up, and turned around. "You ladies need anything?" she said, flashing us a great frosted lipstick smile.

Ruby drew a deep breath and began. "We need to purchase one of those housedresses. Maybe something like that one with the green and blue flowers on it."

"Oh, you mean our new flower-power model?" said Selma. "In an extra small?"

"No, it's not for me. We'll need a medium one, please."

"Then it must be for the senior Mrs. Cranbourne. Tell her if it doesn't fit, she can return it."

"She won't give a flying flip if it don't fit," said Evangeline.

"Oh, that doesn't sound like her," said Selma. "She's a woman who knows what she wants."

"She might used to care, but she don't anymore on account of she's dead."

"Evangeline, would you please mind your manners?" said Ruby, close to tears from embarrassment. "One more word from you, and I'll have you waxing all the floors in the house, do you understand?"

"Yes, Mamaw," she said glumly.

Selma cupped her hand over her mouth and said, "Oh, Ruby, I'm so sorry to hear about your mother-in-law. When did she pass on?"

"Yesterday evening."

"Aw, that's so sad."

"It was just her time to go."

Selma looked at Evangeline and me and said, "Would some Necco Wafers, jelly bean bunnies, and Red Hots help make you girls feel better?"

Somehow, Selma offering to give us candy after all we'd done to her and the bad things we'd said made us ashamed of ourselves. "No, thank you, Miss Davis," we said.

"You girls have a fever?" asked Ruby.

"No Mamaw," I replied. "We just don't have an appetite for candy today."

"Not even some bright-red waxed lips left over from last Halloween?" asked Selma.

"No, ma'am," I said. "Thanks just the same."

"They simply do not make children the way they used to," said Selma, rolling her eyes in mock exasperation to Ruby.

"Oh yes they do. They're just as wonderful," said Ruby, rubbing Evangeline's head.

She paid for Itasca's flower-power burial shroud and was about to leave when Selma stopped her.

"You know, I'm also a licensed beautician. I could fix Itasca's hair and makeup for the funeral, if that would help you any."

"You could?" said Ruby.

"Sure! I can make her look fifteen years younger by applying a little Scotch tape in strategic places around the hairline. Just tape and pull."

"Is there *anything* you can't do?" Ruby said in exasperation.

Selma reached out and took Ruby's hand. "I can't raise two girls, take care of a dying mother-in-law, husband, garden, play the fiddle on station KOFF, and heaven only knows what else. I can do the other things in this world I need to, in order to get along. But I cannot do what you do, Ruby."

"Don't feel so bad about yourself," said Evangeline. "I know one thing you can do real well."

"What's that?" said Selma, smiling.

"Quick, what did you have to eat on your seventh birthday?"

"Just milk toast because I had the measles," said Selma, giving her a wink. "Girl, how'd you know I could do that?"

I answered ahead of Evangeline. "Everybody in Fireside knows all about you." I looked at Selma, waiting for her to crack wide open like a watermelon on the sidewalk about our Walt. But no, she was one cool cucumber.

"Well, if you live in a fishbowl, it pays to swim in the same direction as the majority," said Selma, her earrings jangling as she talked. She looked back at Ruby and released her hand. "Ruby, call me if you need me. Ya'll excuse me. I've got to finish unpacking this carton before the crowd hits." Selma waved good-bye and went about her business.

Twenty-Three

After leaving Densesky's, we walked past the Fireside Elementary and took a right toward the Fireside Inn. When we arrived, Ruby paid our bill and thanked Mona for our delayed checkout time. We climbed into the Thunderbird and started toward the Fireside Funeral Home to deliver Itasca's new flower-power housedress. Ruby said she also needed to sign some papers there and make some decisions about arrangements. She talked about how sad it was that they couldn't reach Walt to let him know about his mother. Who knew why he hadn't returned the previous day when he should? Had his flight been canceled due to the storm?

Shortly thereafter, we drove past Adah Mae Applewhite's rotting cottage. Somehow, amid the general decay, Ruby noticed that her front door was ajar.

"That doesn't look right to me," said Ruby as she turned the car into the driveway.

"Naw, Mamaw, please don't stop here. This day has already gone sour enough," said Evangeline.

"How about let's just drop her a line in the mail?" I said, hopefully.

"Yeah, we could use one of those postcards they gave us at the Fireside Inn and mail it to her," said Evangeline.

"It wouldn't arrive soon enough," said Ruby. "Furthermore, why would she want to read a postcard from Fireside, Texas, when she has lived here all her life? You girls beat all I ever saw. Just sit on the front porch like you always do and behave yourselves."

Ruby put the Thunderbird into park, dropped her keys into her purse, which she slid over her arm, and opened the car door.

"Hold on, Mamaw, I feel a fainting spell coming on," moaned Evangeline, rubbing the back of her hand across her forehead like she'd seen in old Hollywood golden-era movies.

"You don't suffer from fainting spells, Evangeline. Tell me another story." By this time, Ruby was fast losing patience. She'd been tried and tested something awful for the past day or two. Anyone could see that the end of her rope was in tugging distance.

"Good-bye cruel world!" Evangeline swooned as she draped herself across the backseat of the Thunderbird in a mock faint.

"When we get ourselves completely dug out of this mess, I'm gonna see to it that both of you have something to think about other than mischief." Ruby got out of the car, slammed the door, and then reopened it. She stuck her head inside and made eye contact with both of us. "Ya'll have got thirty seconds to get out of this car and plant yourselves on the porch swing where I can keep an ear to your goings on. Do I make myself clear?"

"Yes, ma'am," we said, flying into action.

We were almost upon Ruby when her heel got stuck in a weak spot on Adah Mae's top step. She tried to free herself, wobbled, and fell backward down the steps. Her head cracked against the sidewalk and her eyes closed.

"She busted her head!" I said.

Evangeline and I could think of nothing to do but scream and jump up and down. When Adah Mae's oily head appeared at the door, we screamed all the louder.

"What's going on out there? Somebody trying to rob me?" Then Adah Mae caught sight of Ruby lying flat on the ground with blood trickling out of her skull. "Good Lord," she said. "That my Ruby?"

"I think she done killed herself," cried Evangeline, horror-struck.

"No! Wake up, Mamaw," I said as I knelt and wiped off her oozing head with my sweater. Evangeline dropped down and placed her head on Ruby's chest to listen.

Adah Mae's voice was tight. "Got to call for help, but haven't got a telephone."

Then all at once, a miracle happened.

She emerged from her rotting cottage and walked toward the street as quickly as her swollen legs could carry her. Within seconds, she'd flagged down old Ernest Boone who probably would have stopped anyway in shock at seeing her out in public. Few folks had seen the old woman for many years, except Ruby and us girls.

Ruby, small as she was, presented no problem when Ernest hefted her into his truck. Her jade-green sweater with pink orchids spread across it was thick with blood down her left shoulder. Had Ruby known that Ernest placed her bleeding head upon his lap, she would have had a conniption.

Ernest turned on his truck's flashers and sped away toward the Fireside Hospital. Evangeline and I had wanted to get in the truck and go with them, but neither he nor Adah Mae would let us.

Evangeline and I were beside ourselves and having a pretty good fit in the driveway when Selma Davis came home from work at Densesky's. I watched her as she pulled in front of her house across the street. When she emerged from her car, the first thing she did was shield her eyes from the afternoon sun and squint and stare at us.

Ruby's blood decorated my white sweater, and Evangeline lay limp on the ground, crying her poor eyes out. Adah Mae lifted her wings like a bird in flight trying to catch a lift on the spring breeze. Then she whistled like a man and successfully attracted Selma's horrified attention.

Selma hurried toward us, half running in white go-go boots. "Afternoon, Mrs. Applewhite," she said. Then she looked at us girls. "What in the world is going on here?"

Evangeline's face was beet red from the effects of torrential crying. I felt dizzy and like Chicken Little. "The sky is falling, Miss Selma," I said.

"And so it is," said Adah Mae. Then she told Selma all that had happened in the last thirty minutes. In the telling, it dawned on me that the same strange woman I'd believed to be a certified witch had just helped our grandmother.

Then she concluded by saying, "Almost as bad as the day I lost my daughter. Not as bad, but purt near. Ruby has still got some fight in her. Only the good Lord knows for sure."

The fact that Adah Mae had not retreated into the safety of her house made me realize that a miracle was still in the making. After thirty or forty years of hiding from the world, she now stood squarely in it. Through Ruby's fall, she had somehow been saved.

Selma thanked Adah Mae and then turned her attention toward us. She managed to smile broadly with frosted-to-perfection lips. "Ya'll come on home with me." Then she took off her go-go boots, handed them to me, and said, "Darlin', would you carry them please?"

I nodded as she picked up Evangeline and hoisted her onto her hip. Evangeline wrapped her legs around Selma like a monkey hanging on for dear life. Selma reached out, grabbed my free hand, and led me across the street to her house like she might a small child.

Selma set Evangeline down on her porch. She returned to her car and lifted her purse off the front seat. After rummaging through her handbag for the key, she hurried to the front door and opened it. Momentarily, she picked my sister up off the porch and walked to the sofa, setting her upon it like a mother cat dropping a kitten.

Her house was not at all what I'd expected. It was a maze of cornflower blue and pink. Scents of rose potpourri wafted across the room and filled me with its sweetness. An iron cross made from railroad spikes hung on the wall behind Evangeline, and a tattered Methodist hymnal lay on the coffee table. There was a copy of *Ladies Home Journal*, but no copy of *Vogue.*

"This doesn't look like a go-go girl pad," I said.

"Well, a go-go girl doesn't live here," she said, combing through Evangeline's tousled hair with her fingers. Evangeline had stopped crying and was just staring through Selma as if she hadn't seen her.

"I am confounded by all this," I said. "Mamaw is in the hospital by now, Great-Grandmother is dead, and we have no idea where our Popo is. What have you done with him?"

Selma stopped messing with Evangeline's hair and stared straight at me. "Done with him? I haven't done anything with him, silly goose."

"Do you know where he is?"

"I think I might, but I'm not certain."

"What do you mean you're not certain? Evangeline and I seen him on your front porch smacking you on the lips!"

"What?"

"You know…the night Evangeline and I toilet-papered your house."

"Good heavens. Is that what you thought? Is that why you wrapped my house?"

"I've got two good eyes, haven't I?"

"Tell me, Juliet, did you ever see his face?"

"I can't recall."

"If you had, you'd a recognized Mr. Densesky. He's been my boyfriend since not long after my husband died."

"Are you sure?"

"Of course I am. Think about it, Juliet. Those two are about the same height and age. They do favor their khakis too."

"But I saw Popo giving you a package outside of the store one afternoon when Evangeline and I were playing at recess. I know my grandpa, and he doesn't give gifts for the heck of it."

"You're right about that, Juliet. He gives them for a reason. But you'll have to ask him about that when he returns home."

Something about Selma, her tone and her lack of defensiveness or guilt, made me believe her. I realized I had been wrong, and shame from our toilet-papering caper burned my cheek like a hot rock.

"We shouldn't have papered your house. I'm so sorry."

"Well then, if you're sorry, you are forgiven." She smiled at me, stood up from her kneeling position by the sofa and straightened her skirt.

That she had forgiven me so easily made me feel even worse. "You can come paper our place, and Evangeline and I can pick up that mess too. It would serve us right. We'd be even."

"Don't you think I've made a few mistakes in my day?" Selma said.

"I don't know."

"Juliet, I can tell you this—you don't get to be forty-four and not ever have made a mistake here and there."

"You're forty-four?"

"Yes, but that's our little secret." Selma winked.

"Wait till I tell Mamaw. If she lives, that is."

"Oh, Ruby will be just fine. God takes care of His own."

Twenty-Four

Best as I could tell, Ruby had been admitted into the Fireside Community Hospital as fast as Ernest Boone was able to drive her there in his truck. He then called Selma's house and reported that due to the seriousness of her head trauma, she had not yet "waked up."

Selma asked him on her white princess telephone whether Evangeline and I could get in to see Ruby.

"No sirree, Bob," said Ernest. His voice boomed through the receiver. He always talked too loud on account of his poor hearing. Selma held the phone away from her ear until he finished telling what sorry shape Ruby was in. "You know they ain't gonna let no kiddos still wet behind the ears in to see her. Guess they ought to let 'em in anyhow, case she dies. I would, if it was up to me."

Evangeline heard him, same as me, and came out of her stupor to start bawling anew. We felt orphaned all over again. Were it not for Selma, we'd have had no one on earth to turn to during our hour of need. No telling whether our beloved Ruby would recover, Walt was mysteriously MIA, and Itasca was in limbo at the funeral parlor, waiting for heavenly beautification from the very woman who was helping us girls.

The only person in the entire county willing to care for us was this pink-dipped woman with palatial hair, who wasn't at all the person we'd believed her to be. I couldn't understand how I could have been so wrong. All of the signs had pointed to her stealing Walt from underneath Ruby's nose. All the while, she'd been in love with crusty Mr. Densesky, although I couldn't see why.

We lolled about on Selma's living room sofa, bursting into tears every so often. She tried desperately to find our missing grandfather who could make us feel better and who needed to know about not only the death of his mother, but also the serious condition of Ruby. He was unreachable, but she kept on trying.

Selma dialed our number at the ranch to see whether, by some miracle, it had been repaired. She only got a busy signal. "Was worth a try, I guess," she said. "It's still out of order, girls. In light of that fact, I think I'd better take you home to spend the night in case your grandpa shows up. He'll need to be told about the goings on in his family and won't know where on earth you've all gone off to, if we don't wait for him to come back. I'll stay with you until he arrives, and you all are safe as bugs in rugs."

"We can't go home," whined Evangeline. "Itasca is a ghost now."

"Right," I agreed. "She was crazy in this world. She'll be crazy out of it too."

"Nonsense!" replied Selma. "She was a sweet old woman, just different, that's all. If I was to discount all my folks on account of being eccentric, I'd have *nobody*. She loved you. Wouldn't bother a hair on your heads, even if she is a ghost."

Selma turned toward her bedroom and called out, "I'm going to pack an overnight bag. You girls put your feet up." Evangeline lifted her legs over the coffee table, and Selma shook her head. "But not on the furniture. That's just an expression."

When Selma was out of earshot, my wheels began to turn. "Evangeline," I said, "we've been as wrong as can be about her. I'll bet her patience with us is about wore out. We'd better put on our Sunday manners and behave ourselves or we'll be homeless. We could end up living in somebody's crashed up Buick in the junkyard."

"We could live with Elvis," she said.

"Elvis don't want us," I said. "He just wants Ruby and her cakes."

"Well, he can't have her," she said, sullenly. "She's ours!"

"And Walt's."

It wasn't long before Selma emerged from her bedroom with her overnight bag. She shooed us outside, locked the door, and told us to get in her car. She soon backed out of her driveway the way six-year-old girls navigate flying pigs at the county fair. You never saw anything like the way she sailed around the street corners of Fireside, clipping them as though they had the shape of cuticles. Every time we made a right turn to the highway, a county road, or private road, I repented of all my sins just in case it was the last turn we'd ever make.

Selma was wearing a white scarf around her piled-up hairdo. "Accelerate around the curves," she said. "Anytime you feel out of control, accelerate. Centrifugal force; it's a gas!"

"Can you buy that kind of gas in Fireside?" asked Evangeline. "I don't think our Mamaw shops there."

Selma looked in my direction and laughed, but her joy was short-lived. Apparently, Evangeline didn't take much to centrifugal force and soon got sick all over Selma's backseat.

"Evangeline!" I said. "I told you to behave yourself."

"I can't help it, durn your hide."

My spirits fell completely apart. This was about all I could take from the world and started bawling my head off.

"What's wrong, Juliet?" asked Selma, peering at me through her great white sunglasses.

"My nerves is bad," I managed to say. "And ain't nobody called me Squirrel for a while. I used to hate it, but now I'm lonely for the sound of it. And I'm up to my eyeballs in a stew of a mess. I don't think I can make it."

Selma raised her sunglasses and perched them on her head. With her white scarf flapping in the wind and those glasses raised like that, she looked like an aviator from an old picture show, but with a touch of glamour.

"Well, no wonder then. Look at what you girls have been through. Things will get better, though. Like after my husband died, for instance. I thought I'd never love anyone again, but along came Mr. Densesky. Or like the time I was jobless when I first moved here from California. I was down to my last can of Spam and lima beans. Wouldn't you know that very next day I landed my job at the store? The rest is history."

"Now can you eat Spam and lima beans and maybe even drink chocolate milk whenever you want?" I asked.

"Whenever I want," said Selma.

"Don't say nothing else about food, dummy!" yelled Evangeline from the backseat.

"Okay, fathead!" I said.

So much for our resolve to be good. My guess was that it just wasn't in us.

When we arrived at the house, Walt was standing at the front door, turning his key in the lock. I realized from the back, he truly didn't look all that different from Mr. Densesky, even in the broad daylight. From the front, however, he was a thousand times more handsome and, heaven forgive me, far more intelligent.

We parked around the front of the house, which was something I wasn't used to. That area was normally reserved for company. Even Walt had parked his truck around to the side and walked to the front door; whereas, he usually went into the side. That door had obviously been locked, and the only one the house key could open was the front one.

"Squirrel, Rabbit. Selma? What are you up to?" Walt reached down and patted Evangeline on the head. He looked at her soiled shirt and spoke tenderly. "You look a sight, honey. Feeling poorly?"

"Uh huh," she said.

"Sorry about that," he said. He looked over and around us like he'd lost something. "Where's Ruby?"

"In the hospital with a broken head," said Evangeline as she held her encrusted shirt away from her belly.

"In the hospital?" Walt's expression fell. "What in the world?"

Then Selma took over telling Walt all that had happened in his absence. About how his mother had passed ever so easily, like cream from a pitcher. How she believed Ruby would be okay, but that nobody knew much yet. Walt just nodded, looked down at his shoes, and then reached for me. I realized he hugged me on account of my not being the stinky one. He squeezed me tightly and then reached out and patted Evangeline on the back where it was safe to pat her.

She said, "How come it took you so durned long to come home?"

"Watch your language, young lady," he said softly, brushing a tear away with his sleeve. "I went to visit a friend just like I told you, Rabbit. I ran into a complication during my departure from the East Coast. I tried and tried to call, but the phone's been busy for a long spell. Must be off the hook."

"It's dead," I said, as Walt pushed open the front door.

When we went inside the house, Selma came in behind us. The late afternoon sun had become a ribbon of light streaming across the eggplant-covered sofa that had been left unmade due to the wee-hour departure we had made to Fireside the night before. I felt unmade too. Itasca was dead. Ruby was in the hospital. What was left of us fell into the shadows of the room like tumbled dice.

"I'll stay with you girls," said Selma, "while your grandfather goes to the hospital."

Right away, she led Evangeline to the bathroom and instructed her to bathe and use extra Dove soap. While she was bathing, Selma slipped out into the hallway and disappeared into the kitchen. I walked into Itasca's room half wondering whether she would be there hovering over the bed.

I could hear Walt and Selma talking softly in the kitchen, thinking we were out of earshot.

"Did you find Marguerite in New York?" she asked.

"Yes, I most certainly did. I had her packed up and ready to come home to the girls. Then we got checked in at the airport and were about to get on the plane, but things fell apart. She took off running and left her suitcase and all. I shouted for her to come back, but she never even slowed down. I missed my plane so I could try to catch up with her, try to talk some sense into her. I caught a taxi and went back to her apartment to hand her the suitcase. I sat on the landing outside her door for the better part of twenty-four hours, but she never showed up. Just vanished into thin air."

"How could she do that to these sweet girls?"

"Durned if I know. I told her how much the girls missed her the minute I laid eyes on her. Took me some doing to find her in that big old city. New York ain't for a country boy like me. Then I told her that James had been killed in Vietnam. She cried for a spell. I let her know that Juliet and Evangeline were getting along okay, but could be much better if they could just see her. She acted right ashamed of herself and like she wanted to do right by them, but somehow just couldn't. I'm glad I never told them why I was going up yonder. It would have made them feel worse than they did to begin with."

"Would you like for me to make another gift package to send the girls via my sister? Some kind of something they'd associate with her that would lift their spirits in the midst of all this mess?"

"That would be fine, Selma. Ruby and I would sure appreciate it. I'll write them a letter and drop it by the store so you can slip it in the package."

"You go ahead on down to the hospital and take care of your sweetheart, Walt. The next twenty-four hours will be the tell-all as far as Ruby is concerned. Don't worry about the girls."

"Selma, there's bound to be an extra jewel in your crown in heaven. Thanks for all you've already done, but I want to take the girls with me. That's why I didn't light out for the hospital the minute I heard. Soon as Evangeline gets out of the tub, we're heading out."

"All right then, suit yourself. I'm not much on crowns, anyway; they crush a good hairdo. Now, on the other hand, a good set of bodacious earrings in heaven, well, that's another story."

I slid down to the hardwood floor in Itasca's room and leaned over, pretending to be asleep when Walt came looking for me. I did not want to talk to anyone while I tried to digest what I'd just heard. I couldn't because I didn't have it in me.

When I'd been told, at the age of six, that Santa Claus wasn't real, I went right on believing in him anyway. I desperately needed to know that our mother loved us, despite the obvious. Furthermore, I didn't want Evangeline to know that Walt and Selma had been sending us the gifts all along. Evangeline would never get over it if she knew the truth. After all, she was and always would be my little sister, and it was my duty to protect her.

Walt picked me up in his arms and carried me to the living room sofa. When Evangeline got out of the tub, dried off, and dressed herself, he brought her into where I lay, still feigning sleep. He seated her at the end of the couch, right next to my feet. I did not open my eyes, but could feel her.

It was then that she whacked me on the souls of my feet and said, "Scoot over, Juliet. You're taking up all the room."

I just didn't feel like fighting her at the moment and sat up like I was told. Evangeline's eyes opened wide in surprise. She shook her head wondering what this world was coming to.

Walt sat down between us and, like lambs in the field, gathered us to him. He kissed us on our foreheads and apologized for having been away so long. After we'd hugged awhile, he gave us one peppermint drop each and then drove us in his pickup truck to the Fireside Community Hospital. While we'd spent no more than thirty minutes at the house, we were all champing at the bit to see Ruby. We were warned that we might have to stay in the waiting room and be denied the privilege of seeing her due to our ages, but Walt vowed to try to sneak us in, if need be.

We just walked in like we owned the place and went past each room looking for her. Finding her took all of a jackrabbit minute. There were only ten beds stretched down one hallway, and half of them were empty.

Ernest Boone was standing in her doorway with his ball cap cocked to one side. He was cleaning his fingernails with his pocketknife blade, which I was pretty sure was against the law in a hospital. He looked up at us and jerked his head toward the room as if we hadn't figured out where she was. Walt thanked him, stuck out his hand to shake Ernest's, but thought better of it when he noticed the open pocketknife. Ernest just smiled that fool grin of his, moved away from the doorway, and let us pass.

Ruby lay flat on her back in an old metal hand-cranked bed. She was still as death. Her chalky complexion painted quite a contrast against her red hair, like blood against snow. A bandage was taped against the front and top of her head where hair had been cut away. The sun was starting to set and sent streaks of orange light through the open window blinds. The room smelled like disinfectant spray and soap.

"She's not gonna like that when she wakes up," I said, pointing to Ruby's bald, bandaged spot.

"Neither will Elvis," said Evangeline. "Is she dead?"

"No, Rabbit," said Walt, as he leaned over to kiss Ruby on the cheek. "She looks delicate like that netting women used to wear on hats, but she's really strong as high-grade steel. She can throw a fifty-pound sack of feed fifteen feet."

"Why don't she wake up then?" asked Evangeline.

"She's just resting. Her brain's trying to heal itself."

"I've got an idea about how to wake her up," I said. "'Heartbreak Hotel' always gets Mamaw's blood pumping. She's told me that a hundred times."

"Can't none of us sing pretty," said Walt, "but why don't we give it a try?"

All three of us began to sing Elvis's song, even though you could hardly recognize the tune by the way we sang off-key and out of rhythm. Sure enough, Ruby's eyes began to flutter, probably from sheer aggravation. I knew she was about to tell us to quit ruining her favorite song.

"Am I in purgatory?" asked Ruby, her lips dry like cotton. "I thought I was going to be going to heaven one day. She just told me I would."

"Who just told you what, Ruby?" asked Walt, leaning toward her to hear better. Her voice was barely above a whisper.

"Itasca. She just told me she'd see me later. That I was not to follow her just now."

"You must be dreaming, honey."

"Oh, it was no dream. She was standing here so real that I could have touched her if I'd thought to."

"What else did she say?" asked Walt.

"That you would never love any other woman but me. That you never had and never would."

"She was right, Ruby darlin'."

"And she said to thank you for helping to take care of her during the tough times. Best of all, she said our boy was with her, and that he was happy and whole." Ruby smiled tearfully. "Can you believe it, Walt?"

"I can, if you're doing the telling."

Twenty-Five

Itasca's service was postponed to give Ruby time to recover in the hospital. No one could imagine that she wouldn't be there, and Walt's brother, Mel, needed time to drive down from Arkansas.

Evangeline and I returned to school, though we didn't much feel like it. Walt got us up early in the morning and fixed us each a poached egg over toast. This both impressed and mystified us since we did not believe he knew how to cook.

He did Ruby's chores without so much as one iota of complaint, and even milked the cow at six in the morning as though he'd done it every day of his life.

Of course, Walt knew how to do a good many things, but he did not know how to help us with our hair. He couldn't make himself stick his fingers in a jar of Dippity-do or help us snap the plastic clip over our pink sponge rollers. Therefore, we suffered from puffy-hair syndrome every day that Ruby was gone.

On Saturday, Evangeline and I got up, gathered eggs like we did every day, and washed and dried them. We helped Walt to grade and place them into cartons. As usual, we went into town, made the rounds of Ruby's customers, and then went to do our job at station KOFF.

I felt shaky about not having Ruby smiling at me in the studio, and just flat wasn't sure I could get through it. Normally, I looked forward to Saturday afternoons, but now it felt like a big fat test for which I hadn't studied. I could feel a pullet-size lump form in my throat, and the muscles in my shoulders knotted into wads.

Just when I thought I couldn't say a word on air, Walt tapped on the glass and smiled big as daylight. He was flanked by two women who looked familiar, but whom I just couldn't place. One was a tall, raven-haired woman carrying a banjo, and the other one was of medium height and had wiggly blonde hair, some might call naturally marcelled. She was holding a black guitar case like it was her pride and joy.

I knew these women, but it took me a minute to place them. Then I remembered. Ruby had an old parade photograph of the three of them playing their instruments on a farm trailer pulled by an old Chevy truck. They were wearing blue jeans and matching gingham shirts and huge smiles as they sat on bales of hay and played for all of Fireside along Main Street.

Ruby's sisters, Pearl and Sapphire, had come into town to be with Ruby during her time of need. Wordlessly, they got out their instruments, tuned them, and began to play "I'm So Lonesome I Could Cry," a Hank Williams tune. I hardly had to say a word on the show. Their evident love of Ruby, and kindness and concern for us, lifted and carried us through the program.

A little over a week later, Itasca's funeral was held in the Methodist church. Ruby was allowed to leave the hospital to attend the service, provided that she stayed in her wheelchair. The doctor expected her to make a full recovery in time, though she still suffered from a ripping headache and dizziness. Selma had procured a red wig for her, but her face was still swollen. Evangeline and I winced every time we looked at her.

There were just a few dozen people in attendance, mainly because Itasca had only lived in Fireside for a short while. Selma had made Itasca's face up to play to a crowd, however. She did not look like herself, but she did look a sight. How she would have loved that. Bedecked in a flower-power housedress, hair that was teased to kingdom come, *Dragnet*-green eye shadow, and the frosted pink lipstick that was Selma's trademark shade, she was the talk of the town.

"You ought to take her picture," said Hadley King, the only one of my classmates who attended the funeral. She and her mother had come early, mainly because they had just come from Hadley's dental appointment and had nothing else to do with their time. Evangeline and I were floating between the fellowship hall where the food committee was busily putting together small trays of sandwiches and cookies.

Hadley added, "She could become a poster woman for what a fashionable dead person ought to look like. Only I would have put red lipstick on her, if it was me."

"You think so?" I said.

"Uh huh. It would look groovy. Far out, even."

I looked at Hadley's long walnut-colored hair and envied its shine and straightness. She wore a purple miniskirt and matching sweater. She was a brunette Selma Davis in the making, I decided. That no longer seemed like such a bad thing.

"You want to come over and spend the night sometime?" I said. "Our Mamaw's a lot of fun. We could eat till we're sick, dance till we're dizzy, and sing and make fools out of ourselves."

"Do you have any grape Nehi?" asked Hadley.

"Loads of the stuff."

"Okay, then. I'll ask my folks."

Walt's brother, Melville, and his wife, Nadine, came into the narthex with fearful, huge eyes. They were a nervous pair who worried about odd things like whether giant earthworms were causing damage to our nation's highways or if we were about to be invaded by aliens from other countries and planets. Nadine often wore white gloves to occasions such as this, just so she didn't have direct skin contact with others.

Melville probably just felt guilty about foisting Itasca on us when she was at her worst. He did not make eye contact with his own brother, whenever Walt came up to shake his hand.

"Where's Ralph?" asked Walt, as he patted his brother on the shoulder.

"Gone to work for the CIA," said Mel. "He's got a spotless record. No speeding tickets. Ain't never been in no trouble. He's a good boy."

"How old is he now, thirty?"

"Just as of last week."

"Well, your boy can blend into a crowd. He'll make a good spook."

"Thank you."

We all filed into the sanctuary as soon as the organ music started up and sat in the front pew where family always sits on such an occasion.

Itasca's funeral consisted of the basic traditional Methodist service, and then there were poetry readings by Walt and Mel. In her own way, Emily Dickinson attended the funeral, and excerpts from Eleanor Roosevelt's speeches inspired even us children. Intermittently, we sang "When the Roll Is Called up Yonder," "Mansion over the Hilltop," "How Great Thou Art," and "Amazing Grace."

After her oak casket was wheeled down the aisle, we stood up to leave the front pew. As we faced the back of the church and began our recession, I saw Adah Mae Applewhite standing near the narthex. She was wearing a dress covered in a violet and ivy print and a big green hat to match. She waited as the casket passed and then, as Walt wheeled Ruby toward the open sanctuary doors, reached out and took her hand. She told her how sorry she was about Itasca's passing and that she was glad to see Ruby still among the living, despite her accident.

After we drove the short distance to the cemetery, we walked to our seats in the front row of the folding chairs that were draped with moss-green covers underneath a tent that was a darker shade of green.

Evangeline and I were about to have a full-fledged conniption fit, but Selma hurried to sit by us, which took our minds off things. Evangeline and I smiled at her and then hung on to Ruby and Walt just as we had for years. What I saw then was that the attendees of the funeral, most of whom were from Fireside, stared in amazement as the Methodist minister spoke over Itasca's casket.

They took in the gossip-worthy facts that Ruby was fractured in body and spirit, but not dead as rumored, that Selma had been somehow allowed to join our family even in a black miniskirt, and that Mrs. Applewhite, the infamous hermit, had come out of her shell and was seated near the front. Ruby's sisters, Sapphire and Pearl, who had been roaming around the fifty nifty US of A for longer than I'd been alive, had come home and become like gems in a heavenly crown.

We painted quite a picture that amounted to more than I'd understood at the time. We were not the typical family portrait taken in a Sears and Roebuck studio featuring a mother and father plus two perfect children.

As though a camera lens has been brought into focus through years of experience, I can see us more vividly. My memory now has more definition. This is what I know: One eccentric ballerina-grandmother had danced again near the end of her life and died. Two girls had been orphaned twice and claimed by grandparents. A marriage had been tested and polished to a sheen. A Spam-and-lima-bean-loving salesclerk had found true love. And an old lady who'd had nothing to live for except mold and mildew had been reborn.

Twenty-Six

Shaking off my childhood memories, I prepared to drive into Fireside where Christmas ruled the entire month of December. Once there, I always had plenty to keep myself busy during the holiday season. Climbing into my black Chevy Avalanche that was parked out in the shed next to the tractor, I drove the five miles between home and my House of Cranbourne store.

When I opened the door to the tune of twinkling sleigh bells, my manager, Hadley King Hammerschmidt, was wrapping a goody basket she had filled with crafty homemakers' delights and complimenting her customer on the fine choices she'd made. Hadley and I had become good friends the day of Itasca's funeral, and we'd been working together for years.

"Your mother will love these edible tiaras, top hats, and Santas. Just poke them into cherry tomatoes or cucumbers to dress up any holiday salad," Hadley said.

"Well, they're certainly *different,*" said the customer, as though it wasn't an entirely good thing. She was an out-of-towner who was dressed regally in a cashmere coat, gloves, and scarf. "Tell me again what one does with these velvet items?"

"Oh, you are not from here, are you, honey?" Hadley placed the scissors on the counter just long enough to unwind green ribbon from behind the counter. "These spectacular velvet cuties are the talk of the town. They are stick-on animal parts to dress up those dull milk cartons and naked eggs in your refrigerator. In twenty seconds flat, you can turn those ho-hum containers into a cow, complete with udder and neck bell. And the eggs turn into ducklings with these stick-on feathers and duckbills."

"Oh, yes. Now I remember. Well, at least I can be assured that my mother doesn't already have them."

"And I'll bet that she has never had jars of homemade pumpkin soup as tasty as these. Tell her that after she heats it up, just add a little dab of sour cream and parsley in the center. No one would guess she didn't make it herself. You know we roast pumpkins, skins and all, in the oven for going on two hours before we even start making the soup. A lot goes into this, I can tell you for sure. And these original spices you've chosen are de-lish! Just look, Butternut Squash Enchilada spice and Tapioca Heaven!"

Hadley smiled at me and then passed the finished basket to the customer. "Merry Christmas, honey. Come back and see us!"

The woman smiled briefly and then fled, probably overjoyed to get away from Hadley's running commercials for our products.

"Hey, Hadley. How are things going around here?" I asked.

"Brisk, girl. Business is strong. Lots of folks buying, not just looking."

"Music to my ears. Good job, Hadley!"

I looked around my fragrant and imaginative business with a mixture of pride and delight. Not only was the store filled with Christmas cheer on the inside—what with all of my crafty homemakers' helpers—but it was decorated to the hilt on the outside as well. It had become a major attraction through the past ten years for both locals and tourists alike. If one were not in the Christmas spirit upon arrival, one would be by the time one left Cranbourne's.

It is located on the corner of Persimmon Street and Third Avenue, the exact location where Christmas Glǘhwein is passed out to folks who come into town to see the Fireside Light Festival that lasts from the day after Thanksgiving until January second.

We stay open until nine o'clock during the holiday season as do many of the other stores along the parade circuit. The building that I've leased since not long after Marshal Matt Dillon won Miss Kitty for the final time was constructed in the early 1900s and has a false Old West front like those in *Gunsmoke*. The floor squeaks when you walk over to the shelves to take a good look at the merchandise.

Right now, I have a small fir tree decorated with gingerbread cookies shaped like Texas boots, the Lone Star flag, the State Capitol, and Elvis during various stages of weight gain and loss. Each child who comes into my store is invited to untie one cookie from the tree and to eat it on the spot with a cup of wassail on the side.

Rows of garland trim the entire store, all segments secured into place by a bouquet of pinecones I will recycle into fire starters by covering them with wax. Scents of pine, cinnamon, and mulled spices linger in the air, making all our customers think that perhaps Mrs. Claus has just left.

The whole burg of Fireside comes to life at Thanksgiving when the Christmas lights are turned on for the season. The courthouse square, just four blocks away, is turned into a giant nativity scene made by millions of twinkling lights. In its center are Joseph, Mary, and Baby Jesus riding in a Conestoga wagon, dressed in Western apparel. The three wise men wear chaps and cowboy hats. Oxen, sheep, and donkeys are all participants in what might be mistaken for a cattle-driving scene.

The mayor gets credit for the nativity, which is fine with me. All I can say is thank heavens I can't be blamed for it. He felt that Fireside citizens needed to do something to distinguish our little town from all the others on the Festival of South by Southwest Lights Trail throughout Central Texas. As you can see, being different is not always a good idea.

Inside the House of Cranbourne, however, rest assured that good taste abounds. The minute the cashmere-clad customer left, Hadley whipped out her compact mirror and tube of lipstick. With painstaking perfection, she applied a fresh coat of Mary Kay's Ravishing Red.

Hadley's good looks shamed me. Her black hair, with occasional streaks of gray, was perfectly coiffed and then shellacked into permanency. It was a modern sculpture that was up to the eye of the beholder to interpret. She snapped the compact shut and then beamed broadly at me.

"Guess who came in here this morning, asking for you?"

"The pest control company I called?"

"No, it wasn't a company. Guess again."

"The president, asking for my advice on how to jump-start the nation's economy?"

Hadley rolled her eyes. "No. But out of curiosity, what would you tell him?"

"That the key is to mass produce butter beans, can them with jalapeños and bacon, and have cute kindergartners sell them to their grandmothers." I looked at Hadley and asked straight up, "Well if it wasn't the president, then who?"

"William Bartlett."

"Forevermore."

Hadley raised her eyebrows and grinned. "Well, do you want to know how he looks? It's been years since you've seen him."

"Not particularly," I replied.

"I'll tell you anyway. He looks like Clark Gable with regular-sized ears, only better. He's moving back to Fireside. Says he can run his Internet architecture business from anywhere in the world these days, so he decided to come home. He sells his original house designs to folks in Australia, Europe, Argentina, Canada, and the United States, of course."

"Imagine that," I said flatly. Hadley shook her head in frustration, so I tried to spread a little lanolin on the situation. "I'm happy for him, Hadley. Really. What has this got to do with me?"

"He wanted to know your phone number, that's what!"

I had mixed emotions about hearing that William wanted my phone number. It was sort of like having butterflies and heartburn at the same time. I looked around the House of Cranbourne and thought about my work at station KOFF and my plans to see Evangeline.

"My life is pretty full, Hadley. I don't have room for much else. Anyway, this is my destiny."

"Well, honey, I'd wipe off my calendar to make space for this guy, if I were you. Furthermore, he's a good customer. He bought one of nearly every item in this store for his home, just hoping I'd tell you. Not to say that these aren't wonderful products, mind you! Anybody in his right mind would want them."

"You're a great salesperson," I said, smiling. "Did he say anything else?"

"That he moved back into the family estate next to the library. Just imagine him roaming around that huge plantation-style home with all those columns and that ivy. He's bound to be like a single pill in a bottle, just rattling around in there."

"Well, if I remember anything about him, it's that he is a pill. He'll get used to being lonely. But I guess it might be nice if Fireside made him feel wanted. Remind me to welcome our latest resident to Fireside on the air, will you? I always need some fill. No dead air on my watch."

"That's it? That's all you've got to say, Juliet?" When I ignored Hadley's prodding, she shrugged her shoulders and murmured, "If that don't beat all."

Hadley sighed, turned her back to me, and refilled the wassail Crock-Pot. She had been my very best friend since sixth grade. Because she'd been happily married for the past twenty-four years, she thought my life was fractured due to my single status. She had tried to fix everything with the same old glue each time: eligible men.

To add to her sense of familial satisfaction, Hadley's grown twin sons had recently graduated from Tarleton State University with matching business degrees. They now worked with her husband, Wesley, over at his Chevrolet dealership.

I could tell by Hadley's posture that she was put out with me, so I threw her a bone to gnaw on rather than William.

"Evangeline will be home soon."

She turned from the Crock-Pot and faced me. "Now that's news!"

"Nothing's been the same since she's been gone." I felt a lump rise up in my throat.

"Well, honey, these family matters can be so complicated."

"You'd think that something that happened over thirty years ago wouldn't amount to a hill of beans by now, wouldn't you?"

"Hills of beans have shaped the universe one bean at a time," said Hadley. "Get out your hoe and make a new row. Things are bound to grow."

Twenty-Seven

When I left the House of Cranbourne that day, the signs of Christmas provided a good distraction from worrying about Evangeline and William. Apparently, Santa's cowboy boots were hard to fill, as there were at least fifty empty cutout versions within two blocks of my store. There was a giant candy cane wonderland in the town park and a gingerbread house big enough for high school seniors to walk through.

Next, I saw Selma Davis Densesky, who was seventy-something, climb out of her fire red Camaro that was parked in front of her store. She wore the same puffy blonde hairdo she'd had during my childhood. In the spirit of Christmas, I rolled down my Avalanche window and shouted out, "Hey, Selma, how're you?"

Selma's hearing and eyesight were failing, and all she did was turn and squint, trying to recognize just who I was. She shook her head and then headed into the store like she couldn't quite make me out.

I headed back to the ranch, keeping an eye out for darting white-tailed deer and listening to Christmas carols on the radio. I couldn't quit thinking about the fact that William Bartlett was trying to locate me. He had been to my store, gotten my phone number, and all for what reason? The last time I'd seen him wasn't pretty. That day played over and over in my mind like a scratched Tiny Tim recording, annoying yet part of my past.

My thoughts returned to the day before high school graduation. We were rehearsing in the gymnasium, sweating like chicks in the brooder house. I was neither valedictorian nor salutatorian, but was third in the class and expected to give the opening prayer for the whole shebang.

Due to the years I'd spent broadcasting on station KOFF, there was nothing that particularly frightened me about public speaking. But that day, I'd been overcome with sentimentality in missing my parents. To comfort myself, I'd worn my mother's ratty cast-off slip, the straps of which were held together by two large safety pins. The entire yellowed mess was hidden underneath my apricot double-knit wonder dress I'd made in home economics. It had a temperamental nylon zipper in the back.

Mr. Zentner, our high school principal, was saying, "And now, to lead us in prayer…," but my mind was elsewhere. I was thinking about all the disasters I'd heard about happening on graduation day: Ruby had drowned, nearly for good; two distant cousins had died in a car accident; a senior girl from the previous graduating class had dyed her hair green by mistake. You name it, and it was an imminent possibility in my own life.

"Go on, Juliet. What are you waiting on?" Eighteen-year-old Hadley tugged on my sleeve to get my attention. I noticed her hip-hugger, bell-bottom jeans with variegated purple and pink butterflies embroidered on the legs. Her black hair was parted down the middle and tied up in two puppy-dog tails. It was her silver peace-sign necklace suspended on black leather that mesmerized me, however.

Peace was exactly what I needed. I had no tranquility myself, although I was trying to absorb some by rereading the words to the Prayer of St. Francis, which I held in my hand. I was, though, unable to memorize all of the words, which only fed my panic.

"I can't do this," I said, but Hadley made me move forward. She grabbed hold of one sleeve and pulled me toward the podium causing my nylon zipper to split down the back. As she let go, I felt the entire dress fall down to my ankles, exposing my mother's ratty, hole-infested slip.

William Williams Bartlett, my boyfriend and the class valedictorian, groaned dramatically. "Lord, have mercy! The coachmen are rats again and it's Cinderella after midnight. Send in the fairy godmother!"

I quickly pulled my dress back up over my shoulders and held it together behind me with shaking fingers. "Willy Billy Bartlett, you are a six-and-a-half-foot rat, yourself!"

"Don't ever call me Willy Billy!" He flushed in indignation. "You know I hate that."

I ran off the stage, out the gym door, drove home, and hid out in Ruby's cellar, ashamed to the hilt. I decided then and there not to return to school for my own graduation. Somebody else would have to pray the ceremony open besides myself. I tore my copy of the prayer into tiny bits and set fire to them in a tin can.

No amount of begging or pleading by Walt, Ruby, or Evangeline could get me to change my mind. I have always regretted it too. I know now that you've got to finish things for the better in this life or they will haunt you forever.

I couldn't help but wonder whether my focus on disaster had attracted it to me like a magnet. You know what I mean. Like when you're thinking about how nervous you are about baking a coconut cake for the county fair and within five minutes the whole thing falls into a heap in the oven.

Oh, I got my diploma all right. I had earned it. I just didn't get to shake hands with Mr. Zentner, and, most importantly, I didn't get to feel Walt's, Ruby's, and Evangeline's pride. I just felt their sad eyes upon me boring holes into my heart.

The following Monday, however, I started summer school at the University of Texas at Austin, and William Williams Bartlett went off to school at Texas A&M in College Station. Perhaps we should have known all along that we were not meant to be together by virtue of our choices of rival universities. We did not talk again. I thought he owed me an apology and ought to have made the first move, but I guess he was waiting for hell to freeze over first.

Hearing that Willy Billy Bartlett was back in town was a little bit like hearing I was going to have to have those bunions cut out after all. Just when I thought I was shed of him for life, there he was like a toadstool after the rain. What I wouldn't give to cry on Ruby's shoulder one more time.

Just then, Elvis's velvety voice came over the radio, singing "Blue Christmas" and "Silver Bells." Elvis had been Ruby's favorite man in the world, except for Walt. The fact that Elvis's music started to play at the exact moment I was missing Ruby meant I was supposed to know she had her ear to my heart. My Ruby was with me, whether I could see her or not.

"Mamaw, tell me what William wants with me," I said into the December air as I got out of the Avalanche. The passenger seat dimpled and then returned to normal, just as if she had gotten out too. "You know how I can be dense as a turnip sometimes."

Ruby's words, "More like a tree stump…Sugar," popped into my mind.

Like a dandelion on the breeze, she was gone again. I wondered whether living alone was going to be my undoing. I closed my eyes and concentrated on Ruby coming back to talk to me, but she did not.

I went inside the house and tried to pretend that I did not feel abandoned by her. Let me just say this about that: when two parents have vanished from your life like mine, with no good-byes, no nothing, you cannot help but feel tossed out with the dishwater.

Inside Ruby's chilly kitchen, I set my purse on the counter and shivered. I stuffed some kindling and old KOFF copy into the wood stove, lit a match, and watched the fire eat up the personal column I had read on air the week before: "Ms. J is seeking a Mr. ? to join her in Flamenco lessons. You don't have to be tall, good-looking, or rich. You just have to be able to clap your hands and stomp your feet."

There weren't many available bachelors in Fireside that I had anything in common with or that I hadn't already crossed off my list. I'd have to admit that I was picky. Thomas Sonic primped in the mirror every time we'd passed one on a date. I didn't much like a man who spent more time at the beauty parlor than I did. Then there was Matthew Morris whose breath smelled of that morning's oatmeal and brown sugar at seven in the evening. Clayton Weatherall spent all his time souping up old cars and making them run lickety-split down the highway. He had a collection of speeding tickets that he'd framed like trophies.

"I got this baby doing a hundred and twenty on a Saturday night. Wouldn't have gotten caught, except I had the bad fortune to lose a headlight due to a parrot knocking it out and slowing me down," Clayton said.

"A parrot?" I said.

"Somebody's pet got loose, I imagine. Cost me over five hundred to replace the headlight and pay the ticket. That was way back when. Would have cost a sight more nowadays."

As you can see, there's not a lot to choose from in this town. Most of the good ones have moved away, gotten jobs in cities, or gotten married. So can you blame me for advertising on the radio? I have always loved to dance.

I washed my hands and made myself a fried egg, tomato, and mayonnaise sandwich, the best in the world by my standards. I chased it down with a cup of hot apple cinnamon tea poured into a glass cup Ruby once let me dig out of a new box of Crystal Wedding Oats.

After I tidied the kitchen, I went to work trying to figure out what on earth to do with Ruby's treasures. Our four-room house had only two closets, one of which was stacked to the ceiling with things I never could bear to throw or give away. Every item reminded me of her, which meant that each time I'd attempted to clean it, I'd merely taken a trip down memory lane and cast off nothing. Now, however, Evangeline was soon due in from Portland, and I needed to clear the space for her clothing.

I half expected Ruby to swat me on the behind when I began digging out boxes and old hanging clothes from the spare bedroom closet. It was the same bedroom Evangeline and I had shared at one time and where Itasca had died. I pulled out hanger after hanger of old empire-waist dresses with shell buttons, black and blue velvet hats with veils, and platform shoes from the 1940s.

Decaying boxes left scraps of cardboard across the linoleum floor as I dragged them out. They contained everything you'd ever want to know about the twentieth century: old pairs of round eyeglasses with broken arms and scratched lenses, metal hair combs with missing teeth, and a cookie tin of odd buttons we'd cut off discarded garments.

Then I found a small wooden box containing some of Walt's childhood things: an iron pull-toy horse the size of my foot, a top minus its string, and an old framed photograph of Walt and his brother, Melville, as youngsters, each dressed in drab woolen sailor outfits that had likely been borrowed from the photographer. Their expressions had been solemn; even so, I could see the light behind Walt's eyes. He knew his Ruby lay ahead of him even then, I figured.

As I placed the photograph of them aside, I spotted a picture of my father as a three-year-old. His hair was blonde and long and curly as a girl's. He was feeding an orphaned lamb some milk from an old Dr. Pepper bottle with a black rubber nipple stretched over the end. I got to thinking about Daddy and how much I missed him, even after all these years.

I was beginning to get sadder than I could bear, so I stopped work on the closet and sat down to organize my notes for my next broadcast from station KOFF. It always made me feel better to lift other folks' spirits, so I wrote a vegetable horoscope for the *Fireside Farmer's Almanac* portion of my show:

I dedicate this afternoon's vegetable horoscope to my father, James Cranbourne, who gave his life during the Vietnam War. He was a capricorn and planted the pomegranate tree near our cellar. Here's to you, Dad, wherever you are.

Aries: Did your spouse call you a "tyrannical despot" this morning? Eat lots of miniature peas for a sweet disposition; do not even look at a beet or all will be lost.

Taurus: Raging, humorless bulls can be turned into gentle, smiling calves by the consumption of tender white corn.

Gemini: To counteract extreme loneliness, eat two radishes and carrots. Then call your mom who will be thrilled that you are eating vegetables, finally.

Cancer: For those of you who woke up on the mean side, try some tasty butternut squash. It might soften the angry redness of your cheeks and add just a touch of yellow where needed.

Leo: For a reduction in the excessive courage you might be feeling about now, consume three helpings of pinto beans and attend the Blue Moon Dance.

Virgo: Raspberries with a touch of mint might be just what you need to restore your virtue. Don't call Mom. She doesn't need to know.

Libra: Finding your balance askew? Take a big old bite out of a raw turnip and then hang upside down on your child's swing set. Your perspective will be shocked back to normal!

Scorpio: Feeling too nice, lately? Chomp down on a serrano pepper and refuse water until you've cleaned your house. This will work wonders for the disposition.

Sagittarius: For ye with an anxious heart, eat a raw red onion. This will ward off ailments, enemies, and bad nerves.

Capricorn: As a cure for excessive stubbornness, eat a pomegranate, one seed at a time. Then clean up the mess whether you want to or not.

Aquarius: O cucumbers, wherefore art thou? To enhance creativity and achieve artistic sensibility, consume a cucumber salad while listening to Mozart and reading Shakespeare.

Pisces: A bowl of watercress is the perfect antidote for those feeling dry around the gills.

That wraps it up for today's vegetable horoscope. Just remember to avoid beets, as we do not eat them in Fireside. Anyone who would, just cannot be from here!

Twenty-Eight

Thinking about Evangeline's upcoming visit made me anxious. I knew how hard I'd tried to protect her from what I'd believed to be the truth when we were children. Now, after looking back, I began to wonder who it had been that I was really protecting, my sister or myself.

I had not wanted to believe the worst about Walt, wondering just exactly what it was that Selma had meant to him. After all, he had been a larger-than-life hero to me, greater than any John Wayne or Jimmy Stewart.

I had just finished watching an old Bing Crosby and Rosemary Clooney rerun on television and sat down at the kitchen table to work on my next broadcast for station KOFF when who should call but a flash from the past. Specifically, I had started writing my Welcome to Fireside copy, which was my version of a Welcome Wagon for the newest arrivals in town.

I plucked the old black rotary receiver off the wall and could tell right away that it was William Bartlett by his Dan Rather–like voice.

William's voice was strained. "Juliet…is it…really you?"

"Didn't you just dial my number?" I asked, just halfway teasing.

"Well, yes."

"Then, it's me."

"You sound good."

"You too. What's going on?" I asked as I bit on a hangnail.

Dead silence ensued as I could practically hear the wheels in his head spin. He had never been known to use an excessive amount of vocabulary unless he was really angry or had drunk too many Mountain Dews. "I'm buying your building, Juliet."

"What?" I asked, feeling a certain meltdown coming on. "I told Emil I wanted to buy it myself if it ever came up for sale. I've paid rent for so long, I could have bought it three times over. Now he's gone and sold it to you?"

"I'm sorry, Juliet. I didn't have any idea you wanted it. The reason I called was not to bring you apparently bad news, I was just wondering if I may crawl up into your store attic and take a look at the wiring? I need to see what condition it's in."

"You can give Hadley a call. I'll make it a point not to be there."

"Juliet, after all these years, couldn't we just..." he began.

"No sir. No sir, we most certainly could not," I said abruptly, and added, "Willy Billy."

I could not tell who hung up first or the hardest. It was a draw. Reaching down to pick up the unfinished station KOFF copy, I crumpled it up and stuffed it down Ruby's wood stove.

When the twenty-second of December rolled around, so did Evangeline. I'd had the premonition that something would be different about the day when I realized that the kitchen clock had lost three hours. I couldn't figure out why that had happened. The electricity hadn't gone out, and I certainly hadn't unplugged it. Later, the scent of Ruby's fried chicken wafted over me as if she were turning batter-dipped wings and drumsticks in popping grease, same as she always had.

You know how you can feel a person's presence before you see him or her, all that electrical energy and heat oozing out? That's the way it was when Ruby came around. I don't know whether I could explain how real that scent of frying chicken was, except to say that it made me both hungry and a little sad. If it hadn't been for the smell that I identified only with Ruby, I might have mistaken her for Walt, or maybe even my daddy.

The odor of Ruby's pan-fried chicken stayed with me all morning and afternoon until Evangeline's roly-poly Volkswagen Beetle pulled up to the side gate and into the sacred parking spot heretofore used only by Ruby's Thunderbird. I had parked the Thunderbird in the garage, due to the possibility of sleet in the forecast.

"You *drove* all the way from Oregon?" I said in disbelief as I pushed open the screen door. "I thought you were going to fly this time."

"Well, I just couldn't make myself. You know how I hate airplanes."

"Uh huh, but I can't remember why, exactly."

"Those jets fly too fast and confuse my inner clock. I don't sleep a wink for a week after I've flown that far."

I thought back to the slowing of Ruby's kitchen clock and it made perfect sense. Even from beyond, Ruby still had her sense of humor.

Evangeline's curly hair was pulled back into a ponytail, revealing broad silver loop earrings like the ones Linda Ronstadt wore when she used to perform barefoot on stage. One loop was decorated with a broken piece of unwrapped gum stuck to the inside. She wore hip-hugger jeans, a navy turtleneck sweater, and Nike shoes, but none of these were as entertaining as her jewelry.

"Aw, you didn't have to dress up for me," I said, chuckling, and reached over to pluck off the gum.

"I wondered where that went," she said. "Gum always comes unwrapped in my purse. I threw my earrings in there when I stopped for the night in Brownfield. Everybody's been smiling at me all day. Guess I know why now."

I hugged Evangeline and felt her stiffen slightly. "Glad you're home."

She shook her head and looked past me at Ruby and Walt's house. "This place is so sad without them. Don't know how you can stand living here."

"It sometimes feels like they never left."

Evangeline grimaced. "What a weird thing to say. Well, that sounds like something you'd come out with."

"You'd have to live here to understand."

Evangeline shrugged her shoulders. "Well, I don't."

"Maybe you will, someday."

Hope tinged my voice, but Evangeline acted as if she hadn't heard. I helped her unload the Volkswagen, coaxing a gigantic duffel bag out of the backseat while she gingerly lifted out a precious seedling.

"And did you have a good ride up here, Betty?" she asked, smiling.

"*Who* is weird around here?" I wanted to know.

"Everyone knows that plants react to their environment and respond accordingly. They are sensitive to every thought we have and respond to every word we say. Positive energy attracts positive energy. Negative thought attracts negative results."

"The opposite of a magnet," I said. "There we have it. Your energy attracted Itasca's gene pool at conception."

"Very funny," she said, glaring. "My trees are serious business. Talking to them isn't crazy. I'll have you know that I am considered to be the Anthony Robbins of the *Rosaceae* world. I can motivate any fruit tree to grow bigger and better."

"I was just kidding. I'm the one who inherited her gene pool, if anyone. Who else do you know dresses her dinner salad vegetables in edible evening wear? Who else makes a living decorating refrigerated eggs?"

Evangeline hadn't cracked even the tiniest of smiles, so I pressed further. "Okay, this one should do it. No one but me has ever taught a course at the Fireside branch of the University of San Saba that comes under the following description: Trash Embellishment 425—how to spruce up neighborhood trash collection day and earn cash by finger painting business advertisements on cans and bags. Don't let your trash just sit at the curb, put it to work!"

Evangeline still wasn't amused. "Well, you are *different*."

"Have you forgotten how to laugh? Don't they laugh in Oregon?"

"In Oregon, people laugh when someone is funny. You are not funny. Back home, when the comedians aren't funny, people go out for a cup of Starbucks and read about gardening or architecture in the Barnes & Noble. They don't laugh, however, if someone isn't funny."

"Oh," I said.

Evangeline put her hands on her hips. "When are we going to get the tombstone selection over with, so I can go back home?"

"Evangeline, *this* is your home."

"Not anymore. I'll never be able to forgive you, Juliet, for having hidden something so important from me for all those years."

"It was an innocent mistake."

"Your mistake took years off my life."

"Oh, you are such a Gloria Swanson."

I opened the outside door to our old bedroom and held the door wide open for my sister as she came up the steps from the yard. Her face was as red as any beet I'd ever not eaten.

"No, Juliet. I'm not just being dramatic. If I had known the truth at the time, I could have dealt with it. I could have moved on."

"I was a kid. I did what I thought was right."

"Well, you were dead wrong!"

"Let's talk through what happened. We can work this out."

"I'm too mad at you to talk."

"You were fine when you got here."

"No, I wasn't." Evangeline glared.

"Then why did you come?"

"For Walt and Ruby. Let's go pick out those headstones tomorrow morning and I'll head right back home."

"What about Christmas?" I asked, crestfallen.

"Christmas is in the eye of the beholder. To me, it's got nothing to do with eating Christmas cookies in the shapes of fat Elvises like you bake for your store."

"Fine. Suit yourself, Evangeline."

I set her duffel bag down on the four-poster bed in our and Itasca's old bedroom. I'd about had a gullet full of my sister's attitude. I told her flat out, "You act like a heifer being loaded for auction, stomping and bellowing."

"If I do, you've made me that way. All these years you knew the truth and didn't tell your own sister."

"I was trying to protect you, Evangeline. I love you."

"Oh, right," she replied sarcastically.

I walked out of Evangeline's bedroom and into Ruby's previously aromatic kitchen. I could no longer smell the fried chicken and realized that the clock was working normally. Ruby had left us alone to work through years of mistrust.

That night we read magazines at the dinner table as we ate our bowls of tortilla soup. We avoided looking at one another and pretended total absorption in articles on How to Beat Chiggers at Their Own Games and Shellacking Walnuts and Pecans for Fun and Profit in an Antishellacking Age.

When it was time to go to bed, Evangeline and I barely said good-night before heading off to our bedrooms. I don't know why I bothered to lie down and even try to rest. Sleep had never come easily to me whenever I was worried about something, not even as a child. I was forever rehearsing in my mind that I should have done this or could have done that. A life of mistakes is one of regret. I knew that I had done my best. I also realized that I had miscalculated some.

You see, when Evangeline was little, I tried to spare her a lot by not telling her the things I thought would hurt her. Later on, those things struck back like a rattler underneath a log. If you stepped over it, not seeing where you were going, or what was waiting in hiding for you, you were bound to suffer. The absence of our parents has done more damage than I can explain. I have heard that hole in our hearts referred to as a primal loss. I guess that was true because it made apes out of us.

I got up for good about four, percolated a pot of Folgers on Ruby's stove, and sat at the kitchen table. Unable to remain idle for long, I began work on a new project. I decoupaged a cigar box and turned it into a fashionable purse to sell at my store. That got me to thinking about Ruby and the time I'd found her in the washhouse smoking Walt's cigars. Then I thought about Ruby's Thunderbird and how it had been in the garage for a solid month without me starting it even once.

When it was time for Evangeline and me to strike out for the Monkmouse Monument Company to order the headstones, I pulled back the garage door, started up the Thunderbird, and backed it out.

"What on earth are you doing?" said Evangeline, standing on the steps outside the bedroom door with her arms folded across her sweat shirt.

"Taking the T-bird out for a spin, that's what."

"Well," she said, glaring. "It isn't right."

"Ruby's dead and this car will be too, if we don't drive it."

Evangeline opened her mouth and then closed it again.

I smiled, although it took some effort, and patted the leather seats. "Hop in here, Rabbit!"

She got in the passenger side and sullenly shut the door. I decided right then and there we needed the company of a third person. When we reached Fireside, I drove straight to Densesky's and persuaded Selma to go for a drive with us.

Selma might have been over the hill, but that would have been news to her. She sure didn't know it or act like it, except for a slight hearing and vision problem. I don't know whether she was more excited to see Evangeline or the Thunderbird when we emerged from the store.

"Is there a blue moon tonight or what?" said Selma loudly, giving Evangeline a huge hug. "Why have you stayed away so long, girl?" she asked as she tied a pink scarf over her blonde tower of hair. Next, she popped mirrored sunglasses onto her powdered nose and slid into the backseat.

"Work, I guess," said Evangeline.

"Well, you've got to stop that nonsense and move back to Fireside where you belong," said Selma as she sat up extra straight and squinted at herself in the rearview mirror. Unable to see herself well, she pulled a compact out of her purse and dabbed on pearlized lipstick. She pressed her lips together and blotted them on a tissue.

"Have you found yourself a man, honey?" Selma asked Evangeline.

"I've been seeing Eric Caro for a while."

"Name sounds like a drummer in a rock band," said Selma. "How long's a while?"

"Fifteen years," said Evangeline.

"And you still haven't landed him? What's wrong with both you girls? Neither of you have ever married. My word, by the time I was your age, I'd already married and buried my first husband. Not long after that came Mr. Wonderful!"

"Tell us how he became known as Mr. Wonderful, Selma," I said.

"Well, he would impersonate Mr. Jimmy Durante just to entertain me. Every Saturday night, he'd wash my back and sing his old show tunes. Each time I fixed him dinner, he'd make out like it was the best meal he'd ever tasted."

"Quick, Selma," I said. "Tell us what you fed him on Valentine's day of 1970."

"Oh, that's an easy one," she said. "He loved liver and onions, so that night I cooked him his favorite dish with a mess of green beans and mashed potatoes on the side. I made him a chocolate heart-shaped Valentine's cake and spelled out *U R 2 good 2 B true!* on the top in red icing. He loved it!"

"What did you have for Groundhog Day of 1972?" asked Evangeline, getting into the spirit. I stole a sideways peek at my sister and realized she was smiling. Oh happy day!

"Wait just a second, it will come to me," said Selma, pulling her imitation leopard coat more tightly around her. "Can you turn up the heat, Juliet? I can't think. My brain's getting cold!"

"Sure," I said, pushing the controls to the right.

"That's better. Now let me see, what *did* I have for dinner that night? Oh, now I remember. I didn't eat due to a stomach virus."

"Spare us," said Evangeline.

"You asked."

"Selma, what do you do with your leisure time these days?" asked Evangeline.

"Well, sometimes I go over to the Methodist church and say the prayer of confession. You know the one. I have a lot to confess, so that takes up most of my time. Some days Norman and I go to the Fireside Movie Palace and watch reruns of *Bigfoot,* the *Pink Panther,* or some such nonsense. I try to be a good person, mostly, and that takes a lot outta me. When you get to be my age, many people you loved have gone on ahead, so I spend a lot of time alone."

"You've got us," said Evangeline, helpfully.

"That's right," said Selma, "I do."

I raised my eyebrow, but said nothing to Evangeline's *us* comment. Soon, we'd arrived at the Monkmouse Monument Company and walked around outside looking at slabs of cut granite.

"How about that one?" said Evangeline, pointing to a double heart-shaped headstone.

"I think that fits them, the way they were with one another," I said, grateful that we'd agreed so easily. After we'd paid David Monkmouse for the tombstone, I told Evangeline and Selma that we needed to swing by the House of Cranbourne to drop off the cigar box purse I'd just designed to see if it created any interest among shoppers. "I can make twenty more that look just like this one, with a twist."

Evangeline just rolled her eyes, but Selma was raring to go. "We can go over to our house afterward, listen to some music, and eat macaroons. I've been missing Tom Jones lately. Nobody can punctuate good music like him. Those hips have got a life all their own! I saw him in Vegas twenty years ago and have been a changed woman since. C'mon to my house, girls."

"How about it, Evangeline?" I asked, as I pulled Ruby's Thunderbird to a stop in front of my store. She didn't have time to answer. No sooner had we gotten out of the car than Hadley, William Bartlett, and his cousin Jacob piled out of the store to get a good look at the vintage car.

"Oh man! She's a honey! I can't believe the old girl is still running," said William. He slapped attic dust off his knees and patted the car's front fender. "Baby, there's something right in this world, after all."

"I haven't heard you use that many words at one time in your whole life," I said.

"Me either," said Jacob, settling his Fireside Autoplex gimme cap over his black hair. He and William looked too kin to be just cousins. Dressed in typical Fireside blue-jean fashion, they were reasonably well-groomed, and yet they had a puppyish quality that amounted to sort of a "feed me" look. That hungry look appealed to me as I liked to feed folks in the same way Ruby had.

I had also never forgotten the day that William had stood up for us on the playground when Nathan Wilcot bullied Evangeline. That had taken both courage and compassion, admirable characteristics in my book.

But it had always been Willy Billy's manners that had attracted me the most. We'd never had a date but that he hadn't tripped over himself to open my car door. I'd liked that in a man. Jacob, on the other hand, was crusty like the end on a loaf of bread where all the good stuff is. If William was Clark Gable with regular-sized ears, like Hadley thought, then Jacob was Errol Flynn of the hardware store variety. He wouldn't have ever dared open Evangeline's door though. She liked to do it herself.

They all visited while I went inside my store to tag the new cigar purse creation and set it in the display window by the Santa Claus I'd had for years. When I looked up through the window, I saw Jacob showing Evangeline a thing or two underneath the Thunderbird's hood. Evangeline had never cared much about cars, but she was paying close attention now. I quickly hurried outside to join them.

"Well," said Selma, smiling underneath her pink scarf and shades. "It's all been arranged."

"What has?" I asked, afraid to hear the answer.

"The boys are coming over to hear my Tom Jones collection. *All* of it."

"Oh?" I said feeling trapped. Selma's invitation cast frost on the picture now that the guys were involved. "I think Evangeline might want to get back home." I reached out to pat Selma's arm. "We'd better not. Maybe next time."

"What's the hurry? Got to go home and paint your toenails?" Even through her big sunglasses, I could see Selma winking. "Well, honey, your excuses don't work in my book. I've already asked her, and she said she'd just love to come to our house."

"Sure enough?" I said, glaring at my sister. Evangeline knew fully well how I'd felt about Willy Billy since graduation. She just wanted to stick the knife in a little deeper and twist it.

"I've got the keys, Squirrel," said Evangeline. "Get in the car. I'm in charge now."

I noticed smiles on both those men's faces that had no right to be there. That fact only made me madder.

"Don't talk to me, Willy Billy! Just don't say a word," I said as I climbed inside the Thunderbird. William and Jacob sat in the back with Selma sandwiched in the middle like cream cheese between two big halves of a bagel.

"Well, Evangeline. You gonna drive this thing or not?" I said.

"I'm gonna show you how driving's *done*, Juliet. I'll show you how a *real* woman drives, not how a turtle like you does."

Evangeline left rubber all the way to Selma's and Norman's place, two blocks away. No teenager had ever beaten that record in Fireside, and I doubted they ever would. Just before we got out of the car, the radio came on by itself playing Elvis's rendition of "Shake, Rattle and Roll." Not Christmas music exactly, but it was Ruby's way of letting us know that she was watching what was going on in her Thunderbird and was giving it her stamp of approval.

My last thought before we pushed through Selma's front door was, if Evangeline can forgive Selma for what she and Walt did to fool us, then why couldn't she forgive me?

Twenty-Nine

When Evangeline pulled the Thunderbird to a stop in front of Selma's and Norman's house, I prayed to get beamed up by Scotty on *Star Trek.* I didn't know how I could get through a couple of hours with the man I'd avoided for so many years, not to mention the barbs that my own sister was hell-bent on sending my way.

I needn't have worried; we had "Selma power" at work. She instructed the men to carry the coffee table to the edge of the room and then roll back the rug, exposing polished hardwood floors. Selma lifted out an album from her collection and put it on the stereo. Then she leaned back against the stereo, folded her arms across her chest, and said, "Norman's still at work, but in honor of Ruby, Walt, and the Gemburree sisters, ya'll dance!"

Let me just say this: Jacob made a dive for Evangeline, and the two of them danced to "Chills and Fever" and every other song Tom Jones ever recorded just as if they'd done that all their lives. Sometimes they fast danced, and other times you could not have slipped a feather between them. I was horrified. Evangeline, for her part, was a wild dancer, shaking, shimmying, and bopping, even if the music hadn't called for it. Furthermore, she had always thrown herself 100 percent into whatever she did.

And William? He walked straight over to Selma and danced her feet off. First there was "She's a Lady," then "Delilah," and "I'll Never Fall in Love Again." I plopped down on the sofa and pretended to joyfully read *People* magazine.

Selma eventually asked me to go to her kitchen and get some A&W Root Beer for everyone and pour it into frosted mugs I pulled from her freezer.

Well, I did that all right and also poured a can of mixed nuts into a carnival dish and took the whole kit and caboodle into the living room where William and Selma laughed and cut up. Then I put macaroons on a plate, not sure about whether they'd mix all that well with root beer, but it was what Selma had offered.

While it was true that Selma was on the cutting edge of old age, she was still the life of any party. No wonder she had been so beloved by so many youngsters in Fireside. When "I (Who Have Nothing)" began to play, I was nearly reduced to tears. In that room, amid a party, I felt lonelier than I ever had in my life. Suddenly it seemed as if everything and everyone worth having had passed me by like a float in a parade. All the while, I had been on the sidelines just waving it on by. My life had felt so full, but now I knew it was simply busy. There was a huge difference between the two.

I put my jacket back on and slipped outside to sit on Selma's porch. One lone redbird came to perch in the pecan tree just outside Selma's. I'd always connected cardinals with Ruby on account of the porcelain figurine collection that my dad had given her, one by one, on every Mother's Day until he'd died. When I was a toddler, I'd had the habit of kissing each bird on its beak before setting it down on the shelf nearest the dining area floor. Ruby would tweet each time and egg me on to kiss one more bird. Like a cardinal, Ruby was colorful and a fierce protector of her young.

I heard the front door open and turned to see William emerging from Selma's dance-hall living room, flushed from exertion. Ignoring him, I turned back around to watch the cardinal.

"Oh, he's a handsome one," said William. "That's what I moved back to Fireside for, Juliet. I wanted to see real beauty again."

"Didn't they have redbirds back in Atlanta, or wherever it was you lived?"

"That's not what I'm talking about," he said, dropping down beside me on the step.

"You get winded dancing? Selma is hard to keep up with, no matter where she is," I said, changing the subject.

"No, I never get tired when I dance with a beautiful woman. Norman's a lucky man. I came outside to talk to you, Juliet."

"Oh."

"I just wanted to say I was sorry for what happened back in high school. And I'm sorry I bought your building out from under you. I didn't know you wanted it."

"All of it is spilled milk, I guess."

"True. But I'm better about cleaning up my messes than I used to be."

"It's an art that's learned over time."

"If I weren't an architect by trade, guess I'd have made a good janitor at the high school," he said, grinning slyly.

"A week of that would make you humble."

"You're right." He stood up, brushed off the seat of his pants and smiled, sadly. "Guess I'd better go back inside. Want to come?"

"Later, thanks." I could hear strains of "(It Looks Like) I'll Never Fall in Love Again" coming from the house as William slipped back inside. My heart felt about like that granite headstone we'd just chosen for Walt and Ruby. I didn't know why I had to be so all-fired stubborn sometimes. Seemed like when I got my mind made up on something, I had a hard time changing it, even when I *knew* I was wrong. Well, that about summarized my problems with William. I couldn't seem to let go of the pain and move on.

There was one thing I could feel hopeful about, however. Evangeline was in there dancing up a storm with Jacob, and just maybe she would stay through Christmas.

The next day was my Saturday afternoon broadcast at station KOFF, which I still looked forward to, even after all these years.

After we got home from Selma's and Norman's, I told Evangeline, "Why don't you come on down to the station and play the fiddle like old times?"

"I stay in practice, but don't perform like I used to. You know that."

"It would be a good way to pay tribute to Ruby, though. Wouldn't it? You could play an Elvis tune and dedicate it to her memory."

Evangeline's eyes misted over for a second, and then she smiled. "I could, couldn't I?"

"Bet you a nickel that she, Sapphire, and Pearl will all be playing along in heaven."

"Hope I can do 'em justice," she said.

I realized that Evangeline's voice was picking up a little of the old Fireside twang. She'd taken on an Oregon flair after having lived there for so many years. Just hearing a little hint of a Central Texas accent gave me the hope that the Evangeline I'd always loved was still somewhere deep inside of her.

On Saturday afternoon, Evangeline and I drove to station KOFF like the car was on fire. We were excited to no end about the broadcast. She had brought along Ruby's fiddle, and I had the small stack of copy, some of which I'd written, and some of which had been contributed by locals.

In the entryway of the old station was a photograph of Miss Alma Webster and her little dog. They'd both been long gone and buried, but were still remembered by all old enough to have known them. There were also pictures of Ruby, Sapphire, and Pearl in the middle of a broadcast performance that had been taken a year or more after Ruby's head injury. Then there was one of Evangeline and myself that had been snapped during the first year we were on the air. We were smiling at Walt who was standing outside of the studio's glass window in the hall watching us perform. Although he wasn't in the photograph, we remembered what he was wearing that day and how he held his head.

"You think he's still herding cattle up in heaven with an old pickup?" asked Evangeline.

"Yes," I said. "But I'm willing to bet that it has a horn that works and that the tires aren't bald."

"I hope you're right," she said.

It was then I realized that she was starting to mellow. Her voice had lost its sharpness, and she seemed peaceful. We went on into the studio and got situated.

I leaned into the microphone and started the show the same way I often did. "Welcome to Fireside, Texas—where no strangers are known! We are the home of the free and the brave and everlasting polite persons. We never take the last cookie. No one here eats beets, but we thank the hostess for them anyway.

"Now for local news: Our very own William Bartlett, world-renowned architect, has returned to Fireside to take up residence in his family estate located next door to the library. Why don't we give him a real Fireside welcome? Ladies, bake some pies and set them on his porch. I'm hoping there'll be fifty or more by sundown tomorrow. Do not let the sun go down without making him feel appreciated.

"Now for world news. We don't think there is much going on in the world outside of Fireside, so let's just skip that. If you do hear of anything, please contact me at station KOFF.

"Now for a special treat, we've got Evangeline Cranbourne (also known as Rabbit) on the fiddle about to play "Orange Blossom Special" for all you listeners out there in Fireside and beyond."

I turned and smiled at my sister and said, "Hit it, Rabbit!"

Evangeline rolled her eyes and started to play. I felt about half jealous. Still to this day, I couldn't play a note on any instrument, and she just did it so naturally.

It was then that Selma pressed her face against the studio glass. I opened the door for her and realized that she had brought her harmonica. No sooner had Evangeline finished "Orange Blossom Special" than Selma launched into playing "Turkey in the Straw." Selma proved to be a flat-out terrible harmonica player, a fact that I hadn't realized until now. Finally, we'd found something she couldn't do well.

After Selma's contribution to the afternoon's entertainment was over, I quickly started the items-for-sale portion of the afternoon program. Selma had it in her mind to play another piece, but I talked as fast as the words could come.

"Lester McGraw has a used combine for sale. Said he is accepting bids this afternoon and that the first three don't count. Sadie Hopkins has four manikins she'd like to part with, but is offering them free. She just wants a good home for them and hopes no one will mind their au naturel condition."

Selma looked perturbed, but silently slid her harmonica back into her purse.

"I'd like to thank Selma Davis for her contribution to today's program. Nobody does anything like Selma!"

Selma smiled as though I'd just given her the loveliest gift imaginable. I was half ashamed that I hadn't been able to ask her to play more music on her harmonica. She meant the world to Evangeline and me. The truth was, our KOFF listeners were very vocal, and the switchboard would be lighting up with gentle suggestions to cease and desist with any more harmonica pieces played by Selma.

But Selma looked happy and was picking up her purse and harmonica to leave. I gave her a hug and mouthed "good-bye."

By noon of the following day, there were forty-seven "welcome" pies sitting on William's front porch.

"Your listeners are very responsive," said William as he called me at the House of Cranbourne to thank me.

"Yes, they are tried and true," I said, laughing. "Weekly, we try their patience, and yet they are true-blue loyal to us."

"Just wondering," he said, "what I am gonna do with all this bounty?"

"Well, if you can't eat them all, you can donate them to charity. We can auction them all off for the Fireside Children's Christmas Fund tomorrow at the station. Just three days till Santa, and it is my opinion that every child in Fireside should have a gift to open. What do you think?"

"It's a wonderful idea. Why don't you come over and bring some of that fancy see-through wrapping paper you carry in your store and some ribbon? We'll make them look like a million dollars, if they don't already. I'll make you some dinner."

It was as though I could feel Ruby's hand on the back of my neck, making me nod, though William couldn't see me.

"Okay," I said, and could swear on Ruby's grave that my mind went blank when I tried to think of a way out. I just couldn't think of any handy excuses because, you see, I had absolutely nothing to do in the evening but work or play my father's old, worn-out records.

I felt as though I'd just let go of my end of the rope in a tug-of-war contest.

"Okay? You said *okay*?" asked William in apparent disbelief. "I could pick you up at seven."

"No thanks. I'll drive myself."

"All right, then, see you here at my house. You know where I live?"

"William, this is Fireside. *Everybody* knows where you live."

William said, "I remember that you liked to stargaze as a girl. Didn't you, Juliet? Do I remember that right?"

Memories of long summer evenings spent in the front yard with Ruby and Walt came to mind and brought tears of longing to my eyes. "Yes, I did."

"I've got a new toy—an Orion Sky telescope that makes a December sky look like a bucket of pearls. After we get through wrapping all those pies, we could sky watch."

"That would be wonderful," I said.

As I drove to the ranch after work, I found myself hoping and praying that Evangeline would be there so I could tell her about my invitation.

She spent most of her days tending her peach tree and talking to Jacob on the telephone. In my opinion, the seedling was losing ground in favor of a man who loved hardware, read Steinbeck, and put a lot of hip action into the electric slide. He had also sent her a vase of red roses and a note that was like chocolate for her spirit.

Next thing I knew, Evangeline sent Eric Caro a Dear John e-mail, which was unnecessary in my book since he hadn't wanted an exclusive relationship anyway. In just a few days' time, Jacob had helped Evangeline catapult out of a dead-end relationship and move on with her life.

When I walked into the house, Evangeline was there all right, but she'd whipped herself up into a frothy egg-white mess because a tiny twig had broken off her tree somehow. The seedling had been placed on the kitchen counter in the way of all meal preparations. Sure, it could have been me. It could have been that a cup towel had brushed too close or even that Walt was trying to tell Evangeline that she'd placed far too much importance on something that was fragile and not even edible.

"Juliet, did you do this to get even with me?" she said, pointing at the broken branch. Her face was the color of heirloom tomatoes, and tears had begun to trickle down her cheeks like condensation from all that heat. In essence, Evangeline was a boiling teakettle.

"No, Rabbit. I wouldn't harm your plant, at least not on purpose. Why would I want to get even with you?"

"Because I've been going out lately and you just sit home most evenings."

"No, of course, I'm not mad at you. I'm glad you are having a good time with Jacob."

"Then what happened to my poor seedling? What?"

"Maybe it's a sign."

"A sign? It must be written in a foreign language like Bantu, because I sure can't read what it says."

"A sign that it's time to move on from *plant world* and from being mad at me for so long. The last time we got along well, Gerald Ford was president."

"It's the natural consequence of your decisions, Juliet. If you'd told me the truth way back then, we might get along better."

"You've got to decide to get over it. *Move on!* You are stuck in an eight-year-old's mind." My own words took my breath away because I had been stuck too. I was unable to move on in my own life, so how could I expect my sister to move on in hers?

We were both still stuck to the past like burned caramelized sugar left in the bottom of the dish after the flan had been eaten. No one else would want it but us. I now know that if you lose your parents when you are young, you perpetually whip up fabulous upside-down cakes, chess pies, and all the sweet things in life for strangers, but you rarely eat them yourself. You hoard raw, bitter cranberries of memories and pick at them one at a time because that is all you think will come your way. You savor that which cannot be savored or understood by anyone else.

Thirty

I prepared for my date with William the way Ruby had taught me to when I was a teenager. First, I soaked myself into the prune stage in a tub of lavender-scented bubbles. Then I dusted myself in talcum powder with a similar mission as a crop duster would over cotton. I wanted to eradicate any threat of unpleasantness. Next, I applied deodorant and washed my face in Noxzema. Finally, I applied makeup in an attempt to look *naturally* improved so that William would not think I was overly excited about seeing him.

My overall appearance would have been a vast disappointment to Selma. No ornate hairdo teased into oblivion. No pearlized lipstick. My fingernails weren't even painted because I never could do that well, not without getting more polish on my skin than my nails. I wore black slacks, a black angora sweater, and a red-and-black vest. I put the strand of pearls I'd inherited from Ruby around my neck, but hid them from view. They did not go with my outfit, but I desperately needed to feel as though Ruby were with me.

William's home, which has been in his family since 1880, is milk white with long Corinthian columns that reach up toward heaven. Looking at it, you would not know it had been through three fires—two in the kitchen and one in the master bedroom—and that its front porch had served as the best place to watch the Fireside parade on a Saturday morning in August every year. The front yard has two huge pecan trees, a mimosa tree, and a haw tree that looks like a bush. On both sides are redbud trees that bloom every March in time for Easter. Now, at Christmas, the holly berries are at peak blush while the trees stand naked as jaybirds.

When I arrived, the clock on my Avalanche said straight-up seven o'clock, which gratified me since I cannot stand to be a hair late. The first thing I noticed coming up the walk to William's front porch was the soft glow of candlelight from his dining room window.

"My word," I said softly, as I gathered up the cellophane wrapping paper and ribbons for the pies. I felt as awkward as a squirrel in a hen house as I tried to juggle my armload full and knock. Quick as lightning, William opened the door. He wore starched-to-high-heaven blue jeans, a blue-plaid shirt, a red sweater vest, and his big old, goofy grin.

"Did you just burn our dinner?" I asked, teasing.

"That would be hard to do in a microwave," he said. "But if I set my mind to it, I'm sure I could."

The first thing I noticed when we walked into the dining room was that he'd brought out the family heirloom china for the occasion. I felt both touched by that fact and a little afraid, since it probably hadn't been used in twenty years. Did that man's hands wash porcelain? I wondered about it briefly and decided probably not.

"I thought we'd eat first and then wrap all the pies, except one, that coconut cream one over there," he said pointing to the card tables that had been erected along the side of the room to hold all those pies. "I thought we'd eat that one later tonight after we stargaze."

"All right," I said.

William pulled out a ladder-back chair for me and then began carrying in steaming dishes from the kitchen. Right away, I recognized the menu from Wilma's Close to Home Cooking Café. There were fried, stuffed pork chops with cranberry relish, green beans and pearl onions, and a casserole that had butternut squash, sour cream, poultry seasoning, and butter galore. All those dishes had the reputation for melting in your mouth and then sticking to your buttocks.

"You did all this for me?" I asked after we'd finished eating dinner and wrapping pies. As he nodded, I said, "Why?"

He didn't say a word, but just pulled me by the hand to the crow's nest on the roof overlooking the street. His Orion Sky Quest telescope was poised to show us the universe.

"Seeing how it's the Christmas season, let's look for the North Star."

"Thunder, it's cold out here," I said through chattering teeth. That was when William walked up behind me, wrapped his arms over mine, and steadied my hands on the telescope.

"See it?" he asked.

I leaned into the telescope and said, "No, I can't. Don't know why I can't. Just can't get her in focus."

"Look closer. Tune out the distractions and focus. You might completely miss what you're looking for, if you don't."

Suddenly, the North Star shined largely in the lens as though I wasn't meant to see it until precisely that moment. "Yes, there she is," I said.

"She's a pearl of a girl, isn't she?"

"Oh my, she certainly is."

For a brief moment, I thought he meant to kiss my cheek, but he hugged me and said, "And so are you, Juliet."

It was at that moment that Jacob and Evangeline roared down the street in his truck and lurched to a stop in front of William's home. Even from where we stood on William's roof and in the veil of nightfall, I just knew that a glint of mischievousness was in Evangeline's eyes. In the glow of streetlights, I could see my sister waving two DVDs and a monstrously large bag of popcorn in our direction.

"We've come to help you children pass the time," she called. "Right, Jacob?"

"Darned tootin'," he replied, adjusting his baseball cap.

When William let them in the front door, Evangeline said, "Still not much to do in this town after all these years. You've got to either make your own fun in Fireside, or have someone make it for you."

We all wandered into the living room and turned on the television set and DVD player. I looked at the movie's title and said, "*Jaws,* really?"

"Really," said Evangeline. "It was either that or *Attack of the Killer Tomatoes.* That's all Jacob has at home."

"Oh."

William and I sat down on the sofa first, and then Jacob and Evangeline inserted themselves in between us. My job was to act as keeper of the popcorn until it was requested again by someone, usually Evangeline. Just as the shark ate the first swimmer, whom I thought for an instant might be myself, I had a jerk reflex and threw the bag of popcorn into the air. Within an instant, popcorn decorated much of William's living room. Everyone erupted in laughter.

"I am so sorry," I said as I retrieved the empty bag and started cleaning. William got right down on his hands and knees and helped me pick up hard kernels and fluffy white, salted clouds from the sofa and heirloom carpet. We met behind the couch, finding the last white bits, and he whispered, "This is my favorite part of the evening."

"Right," I replied, embarrassed.

"No, I mean it," he said and kissed my forehead.

"Thanks for a great evening. Sorry about all this," I said, cocking my head toward the pair on the sofa. "I didn't know they were coming."

"That doesn't bother me. This kind of evening, all of it, is why I moved back to Fireside. I've known everyone in this room my entire life. You can't experience anything quite so comfortable and cozy among the strangers where I used to live. The chemistry just wasn't the same."

"It would be perfect if Selma were here," I said.

"Next time, maybe."

Late that night, Evangeline and I sat around Ruby's table, eating the last two slices of westerner cake with a spiced peach placed on top of each.

"It's still just as good as the first slice was the other day," said Evangeline, smiling.

"Why, thank you," I replied, pleased that she was not angry with me for once.

"Christmas will be here shortly," she said.

"You're not leaving, are you?" I asked.

"No, Juliet, I think I'll stick around for the holidays."

"Well, good then. I've got to do the broadcast tomorrow and auction off all those pies, but after that, let's start work on a Christmas feast. We can invite Jacob, William, Selma and Norman to share it with us."

"Turkey or fat baking hen?" she asked.

"You call it. Heads or tails?"

"Oh no. I know how you play that game, Juliet. You always win."

"Let's just do what Ruby did—bake a big hen really slow. I'll make her cornbread stuffing. You make some fruitcake. We'll both set the table and do the dishes."

"Fine, except let's have the boys do the dishes. Walt always helped Ruby clean up."

"Not much of the Cranbourne family left except in our memories."

"Guess we have to make our own family with friends. Mama is the only one who could be alive. Heaven only knows where she might be spending this Christmas."

"Do you still miss her?" I asked.

"I don't remember much about her anymore. There's just this great big hole inside where someone I can't quite recall used to be," Evangeline said.

"My recollection of her is about the same way you'd remember a movie you saw eons ago."

"If I had known what had happened with Mama in New York that time Walt saw her, I'd be over it by now."

"Evangeline, I knew, and I'm still not over it. Some things you don't just get over. You make a choice to go on, in spite of everything."

A tear slipped down my sister's face. She looked away and said, "So I'll make a fruitcake. Anything else?"

"I'll put my thinking cap on and let you know in the morning."

That night after I went to bed and leaned back against a row of lavender-scented down pillows in Ruby and Walt's old bed, I was sure I smelled something sweet that was strangely familiar. It was the scent of Ruby's icebox cookies baking in the oven. You know the kind, the ones that have all those chopped nuts and candied watermelon rind in them.

I got out of bed to see whether or not Evangeline had a hard time sleeping and had started baking early for Christmas. The kitchen was dark, except for the light above the stove. There was nothing baking that I could see, but the scent was so real that I was made hungry for all those little stained-glass icebox cookies Ruby had made a thousand times.

I didn't at first know what to make of things, and then I realized what Ruby was trying to say. The evening had tasted sweet to her spirit—all of it from the time we'd spent at William's to the conversation between Evangeline and myself. Ruby meant to reward us for good behavior. Even as old as we were, we were still her girls.

Thirty-One

The following afternoon, I leaned into the microphone at station KOFF and said, "Welcome to Fireside, Texas, land of a jillion pies. A local resident received a bonanza of pies and wants to donate them to the Fireside Children's Christmas Fund. Evangeline has posted pictures of each and every one to our KOFF website. Please submit your bids and be generous folks, Christmas is nearly here. Every child needs to be remembered by Santa. You can help make that happen.

"Speaking of pies, I want to talk to you about one of my favorite activities, which is eating. In order to eat, you have to either spend time in the kitchen or find someone else who will.

"Here's a little piece I wrote, called Autumn."

Autumn comes so late in Fireside, that it sometimes arrives in December. When autumn apples don scarlet and great pumpkins blush orange, I shiver in delicious anticipation of days to come. Thousands of blackbirds migrate beyond the limits of my vision, yet I see their purpose and am sad for them. I love to nest at home on the ranch when the days shed long-held heat and reach for reflection.

I live for fall and winter so that I might enjoy the comfort of my favorite knitted sweater and light a fire of live oak in my grandmother Ruby's wood stove. I long for the scent of juniper berry venison roast, cheese grits, green bean and onion casserole, and gingerbread baking in the oven—all while I read recipes by the cheerful glow of my favorite hot apple pie candle. With these simple indulgences, autumn smells, looks, and feels as good as my favorite memories of it.

I pause to thank God for this day in all its abundance and then decide to play some old Glenn Miller records on the phonograph. Next, I put on the Queen's Mill flour-sack apron that my sister, Evangeline, made for my twentieth birthday so long ago. Now it is too faded to be worn in front of company, but too comfortable and meaningful to throw away. Then I pull out my favorite jade-green cooking pot and get to work. I feel as though I'm making more than a meal; I am creating a future, something that will make people happy.

My listeners have been asking me to share my recipe for grits since the Fireside casserole cook-off years ago. Here we go…

Juliet's Fireside Grits

12 ounces Velveeta cheese, cut into small chunks
8 cups cooked grits
1 ½ teaspoons garlic salt
4 jumbo eggs
1 cup milk
2 sticks butter, melted
4 ounce can of mild diced green chilies (optional)
6 ounce can of fried onions, or crushed cornflakes for topping

Cook grits and then add cheese and garlic salt right away. Add butter and stir until melted. Whisk eggs with milk and add to grits mixture. Add chilies (optional). Stir well. Pour into large buttered baking dish, sprinkle onions or crushed cornflakes over top. Bake under a foil tent at 350 degrees for one hour. Serves twelve people.

"Hope you enjoyed today's recipe and that it feeds your spirit as well as your body. Now, Fireside listeners, as you prepare for Christmas, go online and put a bid in on a pie or two. You're building more than Christmas for needy tots, you're building memories and helping to change their destinies."

The switchboard started lighting up just as soon as I finished reading my essay. Some listeners had suggestions for improvement, some loved it, and others just wanted me to give them my tortilla soup recipe too. Give some folks an inch and they will take a mile! It was a typical day until we tallied up the results of the pie silent auction. We made over $5,000 for those children who otherwise would have been without Christmas presents.

That night before we retired for the evening, Evangeline sat at the kitchen table chopping onions to go in a variety of dishes the following day. I pulled the ironing board out of the closet and set it up in the kitchen so we could talk while we worked. I had soaked the white tablecloth and napkins in starch earlier, and now that they were beginning to dry, ironed them the way Itasca had taught me so long ago.

"Know what?" said Evangeline, wiping onion tears away from her eyes.

"What?" I said, careful not to iron my hand instead of the damask cloth.

"I thought I heard Walt talking inside my head today."

"That doesn't surprise me. What did he have on his mind?"

"When I was making fruitcake this afternoon, he distinctly said I needed to add more pecans. Then when I did, he said that I'd done a good job and that it was time for me to come back home to live on the ranch. Then right away I asked him why? You know what he said?"

"What?" I asked.

"Something that's just about the kind of thing Walt would say. He said, and I quote, "Cause the bull's in the pen and the heifer's in the barn.'"

"You've got to be kidding me!" I held my hand over my mouth and tried not to laugh.

"Don't you get it?" she said. "They only end up in the barnyard when they have been *led* there by someone else."

"Are you thinking that Walt and Ruby led you home?"

"I *know* they did."

"How?"

"Because I wasn't going to come to Fireside, but kept seeing things that reminded me of you and them. You know how redbirds remind us of Ruby? I saw pictures of cardinals in advertisements, on billboards, and as ornaments on many Christmas trees in department stores. Then one afternoon, I was pulling into the grocery store parking lot and saw the back of a man who was wearing khakis and boots the way Walt did. You don't ever see men dressed that way in Portland, Oregon. They wear blue jeans and flannel shirts and tennis shoes, but never Western khakis. Anyway, I followed him into the grocery store and from aisle to aisle. I almost caught up to him by the popcorn section and that was when he vanished."

"Just like that?" I said, setting the iron on its plate and looking at my sister.

"In an instant, just like a light had been turned off. Poof! He was gone and my heart went with him. Oh, Juliet, I'd give every penny I have to hug Walt and Ruby one more time."

"I know. I know."

"Anyway, I felt like I had to come back home, but didn't really want to. I was afraid it would be like peeling a scab off a wound. On the other hand, it was as if Walt had given me an order, and I didn't want to, you know, get *grounded*," she said and laughed.

"No matter how old we get, we're still *their* girls, aren't we?" I said.

"That's right."

The next morning we awoke at 6:00 a.m. to the sound of the Kyle Sisters singing "Christmas Time in Texas," brought to us by station KOFF and the Fireside Inn, *where anyone's holiday wedding plans can be filled with magic, even at the last minute with Mona's handy marriage kits. In case you want one, they also have New Year's Eve "Party in a Bag" kits, complete with instant eggnog, noisemakers, canned party tuna, a box of Velveeta cheese, Ro-Tel tomatoes, and Texas-shaped chips.*

It was my job to stoke the fire in the wood stove, throw in some kindling, and heat up the place. This was quickly accomplished whenever I was cold and desperate in the morning. Mostly, however, the fact that I could move at all that early was due to my own creation—Aurora Coffee, which was composed of Cajun chicory and Kenyan coffee beans. Whenever Hadley sold some of my coffee at the store, she always said, "Honey, this coffee is strong enough to throw you over its back and carry you *wherever* you want to go."

My coffee maker has a timer, so it comes on before I stick my foot out from under the covers, and a computer chip that whistles "Reveille." While I do not ever drink volumes of coffee, I believe that a morning without at least one cup is simply not worth getting out of bed for. What no coffee? Then just head on back to bed and pull the covers up over your head.

Next, I went into the living room and pulled Evangeline's gift out from behind the couch. I had hand-crocheted a decorative warmer for her prized potted tree. In contrasting red yarn, I had stitched the seedling's given name, Betty, around the circumference. In addition to this fine gift, I'd gone way overboard and crocheted a matching green winter hat for Evangeline with her name stitched across it as well. In my opinion, that hat on Evangeline's head along with her plant presented another photo opportunity with which to decorate the walls at the station.

I rolled my sister out of bed, bribing her with a cup of coffee and a slice of banana bread. "Time's a wastin'," I said. "We've got miles of food to cook before dinner time."

Eventually, Evangeline made it to the Christmas tree and we shared our gifts. She exclaimed over the ones I'd made for her and Betty. I snapped a fine picture of them.

Evangeline gave me a pair of blue suede shoes I'd had a fit over at Densesky's, *the store where any woman could dress like a queen for under fifty dollars.* I'm talking fancy shoes, dress, hose, and a tiara. (Notice, I don't say queen of *what.)*

Just as soon as we'd picked up the bits of wrapping paper and ribbon off the living room floor, I jumped into motion. I had much to do to get ready for our Christmas guests, and not all of it was in the kitchen. You might think that a woman my age should be way past primping in front of the mirror, but not me. I had just finished stuffing the hen with cornbread dressing and sliding it back into the oven when I realized I could finally get cleaned up before our guests arrived.

I drew my bath water and reached into the bathroom linen and supply closet for a fresh bar of Dove soap. Well, at first I flat couldn't find any, and then my hands rested upon an old plastic tub of something. I pulled it out into the light and read Dippity-do Styling Gel. I unscrewed the encrusted jar and peered into its green gooey contents. One whiff made me feel like a teenager again. I don't know what came over me, but I put some of that ancient goo on my hair and stood smiling like an idiot into the mirror until it dried into delicious crusts of curls. I felt not a day over sixteen.

I tucked the tub of Dippity-do back inside the linen closet and sighed with contentment. I luxuriated in primping until Evangeline pounded on the door, just like old times.

"Did you die in there?" she called. "I think I can smell the rot from here."

"That's my perfume," I called. "You're just jealous."

"Am not!"

"Are too!"

"Well, anyhow, you've been in there so long that the cornbread stuffing is smoking."

The word *smoking* has the power to get the lead out of a cook's drawers rather quickly. I dressed frantically and returned to the kitchen to see a smiling Evangeline and no smoke coming from Ruby's oven.

"I thought you said there was smoke?"

"I just wanted to see how fast you could move," said Evangeline, wickedly. "By the way, you are wearing your blouse inside out."

I looked down and, sure enough, rough seams and hanging threads decorated my front. I was a seamstress's nightmare.

"Thanks loads," I said.

By the time I'd poured fresh cream into the pitcher and set it on Ruby's lace-covered table, our guests had arrived. Selma came in our front door wearing red Spandex pants and a big sweater with crocheted poinsettias across her chest. She carried a decoupaged cigar purse with Marilyn Monroe's smoldering picture across its broadside that she'd bought from my store.

"I'll have you know I dressed myself, thank you very much," said a smiling Norman. Norman wore khaki clothes, and had an unlit cigar hanging from his mouth like a pacifier.

"You're styling," said Evangeline.

"Darned tootin'," replied Selma. "If it's in style, I either know about it or started the trend myself."

"Where are the boys?" said Evangeline.

"Checking out the old Aeromotor windmill. Seeing what makes it work, I guess." Selma sniffed the air. "This house smells so goooood. It's just like old times. What are we having, girls?"

"Chicken and dressing, Evangeline's fruitcake, and every side dish known to man," I said.

"Did you make that strawberry Jell-O with Cool Whip I love so much?"

"I did."

"Last time I had that was on Tuesday, July fourth, twelve years ago at the Fireside Community Picnic. That's way too long between bites."

Just then William and Jacob pushed through the front door wearing matching plaid shirts and jeans. Jacob carried a Christmas cactus, and William held a cake pan.

"Well, glad you cute little twin boys finally came in outta the cold," said Selma.

"Why are you dressed alike?" Evangeline asked.

"It was an accident," said William. "That's what you get when you shop a sale at Densesky's and Selma's not at work to warn you that your own first cousin just bought the exact same shirt a month ago."

"Well, I'm too durned old to work all the time," said Selma. "Besides, I'm living proof that you can have a life beyond work."

"You and Norman still shake a leg in your spare time?" I asked.

"Norman's still got a lot of kick left in his dance step."

"What kind of dancing do you do?" I asked.

"Well, we used to do the electric slide, but I think it went out of style. Now we're kind of interested in learning to tango."

I noticed that William was shifting the cake pan around while we were talking. "You want me to take that?" I asked.

"Please," he said, beaming. "Made it myself."

"Oh?" I said as I lifted the cake cover and peered in at the naked, lopsided white cake.

"It's a mashed potato cake. Got the recipe off the Internet."

"Oh boy!" I said. "Looks too good to have been made out of mashed potatoes."

"Thank you…I think," he said.

"What kind of potatoes did you use? Red, Yukon Gold, Russet?"

"Instant," he replied, smiling.

"Wow! How creative!"

Then Jacob handed Evangeline his little Christmas cactus in a gold basket with red balls hanging from its succulent arms. "It's just perfect," she said. "You are so thoughtful, Jacob!"

Evangeline smiled and then scooted back into the kitchen where she turned on Walt's old radio to station KOFF. It was Millie Townsend's Christmas Tribute featuring carols on the guitar.

"Come on in and have a seat," my sister called. "We've got a Christmas dinner that will put shine on your cheeks and zip in your step!"

After we'd all sat down around the table, I asked, "Will you return thanks, William?"

"Sure," he replied, bowing his head and simultaneously reaching for my hand on his right and Selma's on his left. "Our heavenly Father, we are grateful for the birth of your Son, Jesus Christ, and for this beautiful gathering among friends at a bountiful table. We are thankful for our lovely chefs, Juliet and Evangeline. We know that to whom much is given, much is expected, and there is an abundance of talent at this table. Help us to remember to always be in service to others in the example set for us by Selma and Ruby. We know, too, that we don't always realize how much our loved ones meant to us until we've lost them. If we are lucky enough to have a second chance, let us not fail to recognize it. Let us *not* fail. In the name of the Father, the Son, and the Holy Spirit. Amen."

Thirty-Two

Not only had I enjoyed spending Christmas with Evangeline, William, and Jacob, but being with Selma and Norman had also given so much meaning to the day. They had been such constant stars on our horizons for so long. Despite a little mischief worked on her appearance by time and gravity, she was essentially the same now as she had been back during our youth. Norman still adored her as much as he ever had.

Just having her around my table during Christmas lunch had comforted me. She was so worthy of appreciation and admiration, and we heaped it upon her continually. She couldn't take Ruby's place, but she made us feel better somehow.

Now it was January, and it seemed like ever since Christmas Day, I'd been hungry for the color green. Ruby used to wear a lot of it, and in particular preferred a certain shade of jade. When it came to skirt lengths, motherhood, and their views on liver and onions, Ruby and Selma had been direct opposites.

There were other aspects of them that were the same, however. They both loved to dance and had a way of grabbing hold of fun moments and making the most of them. The way they celebrated life made them sisters of a common cause.

A whole truckload of good memories cascaded right through me whenever I looked at jade green. There was the one of Ruby smiling as she pinned up the hem of my new green-lace formal. Another of Ruby hugging me as we stood next to the branches of the Christmas tree covered in jade-green bows and ornaments and candy canes galore, waiting for Walt to snap our picture with her Brownie camera. And finally of Ruby passing me the jade-green bowl filled with Cling peaches from the orchard behind the house, swimming in syrup.

All those memories of green were just too precious to be left unobserved, so I made the resolution to redecorate my House of Cranbourne store using Ruby's trademark shade of jade. Faux-finished jade on the walls, oriental jade Formica countertops, and mopable jade paint on the cement floor, except for in the bathroom where I would install jade linoleum. With all that delicious green around me, it was bound to become a productive year, brushed into being by broad strokes of good luck.

By the third week of January, everything in the House of Cranbourne exuded all that was green. My reverie ended when Evangeline came into the store with a package in her hand and said, "Good gravy, Juliet! Did you spill a bottle of sheep dip in here?"

"Sheep dip?" I cried. "This is a decorator's dream!"

"Well, all I can say is that you won't have any trouble with heartworms while you're working in this store," she said, handing me a package from the US Postal Service.

I took the package from her and said, "What is this?"

Evangeline shrugged her shoulders and said, "I am smart, but I do not have x-ray vision."

"It looks suspicious."

"What, you think it is a letter bomb from Uncle Sam?"

"No, and I'm sure it's not a late Christmas present from the president either."

"Just open it, Juliet."

I read the label and was startled when I realized that it was made out to Ruby and Walt. How strange! I opened the bubble-wrapped mailer and pulled out a letter of apology from the postal service saying that the package had been lost in the Fireside Post Office since 1967 and found again during a renovation. It had fallen down between a damaged counter and the wall and had been sealed over during a repair that year.

Inside was a small white box stamped with the US Army insignia, addressed once again to our grandparents and secured with brown packing tape. Evangeline's head was pressed against mine as we opened it to find our father's last effects: his dog tags, wallet, and a Timex watch. Most important of all, there was a letter from our daddy. It read:

May 30, 1967
Dear Juliet and Evangeline,

If you girls get this letter, then that means I've gone on ahead for good. Know that I didn't want to leave you—I just had to do my duty for this country.

I have a few words to say about what I want you both to do with your time out there on the ranch. Help your grandparents as much as possible, but have fun too. Watch Captain Kangaroo and Gunsmoke—you can learn a lot about being civilized from them. When you get sad, try and count doodlebugs, or go looking in the backyard for marbles. I know I must have lost at least one blue-eyed beauty when I played there as a kid. No telling what others you might find. Most of all, don't you girls fight. You're like oil and water, but I love you both best.

I know you must be missing your mother. I don't know what to tell you about her being gone. It's just her nature, I guess, but she has broken all our hearts. For your own sakes, forgive her and move on. You've always got to forgive people before you can get over the hurt yourselves. Remember that.

When I get to heaven, I'll try to build us a country house so we can be together as a family. I'll make us a huge porch swing and be waiting for you with a great big hug when it's your time to join me. Don't try to get there early. I'll wait. There's plenty of time, later.

Most important of all—remember that I love you, always.
—Daddy

Just then, a breeze came from nowhere and wafted throughout my jade-colored store, lifting our father's letter from our hands, twirling it about, and then settling it right back down on our open palms again.

"That's Ruby's work," I said.

"I know," replied Evangeline, softly. "I can smell her Noxzema. Can't you just feel her around us, Juliet? I can."

"But what's she trying to say?"

Then it came to me just as if the words had been strung together by someone other than myself so that even *I* couldn't get it wrong. "She wants us to try and get along. We should forgive our mother and each other. Love is eternal. We are still loved from beyond by those who have gone before us."

"You mean you think that Ruby and Walt and Daddy can hear what I've been saying to you, Juliet?"

"You bet," I said, smiling wickedly.

"Thunder!" she said, red-faced.

"That's exactly what Ruby would have said."

I thought about the information I'd kept from Evangeline regarding the whereabouts of our mother and the fact that she'd been seen by Walt just a year or two after she'd left us for good. For so long, I'd thought I'd been protecting my sister from the pain of the awful truth, but I'd been wrong.

I looked at Evangeline and decided it was now or never. "I just want to say I'm sorry for not having told you what I knew about Mama when we were kids."

"You were easy to blame," she replied, her eyes filling with tears. "I was just mad in general over having lost the both of them. When I found out that you'd kept something back, I felt cheated. I'm sorry too. I realize now that you weren't trying to hurt me."

Evangeline placed her hand on my forearm and looked at me with tears spilling down her cheeks. "You know that I love you, don't you, Squirrel?"

"Yes, Rabbit. I believe I do."

I hugged Evangeline and glanced around at the newly painted jade-green walls.

Breaking the seriousness of the moment, I said, "Sheep dip? You think this place looks like sheep dip?"

"Well," she said, thoughtfully. "I guess we could say that this jade color has the power to drive out bad spirits and maybe even heartworms." She smiled and cocked her head. "Yeah, it's just like sheep dip."

"I guess we can chalk up clearing the air between us to Daddy's letter."

"And Ruby's presence," she said.

The next morning, Evangeline and I had just polished off a batch of waffles topped with strawberries and whipped cream when the receptionist called from Monkmouse Monuments to say that Ruby and Walt's twin-hearts headstone had been placed on their graves the previous afternoon.

"I think we need to do something to mark this occasion for them," I said as I hung up the receiver and returned to the table.

"Like what?" said Evangeline as she took a sip of coffee.

"Let's round up Selma and the guys and have a little ceremony. We could carry Ruby's old Elvis albums to the station, have Ethel play an hour of his gospel music while we're at the cemetery, and listen to it on the old transistor radio. What do you say?" I looked at her with expectation, excited I'd thought it up. "I mean, I guess it'd work as long as I can find them."

"They're in the attic," she said. "Walt had me get them out of his sight just as soon as Ruby died. They made him more depressed just looking at them. C'mon, I'll show you where they are."

We went into the garage and pulled down the attic stairs. Let me just say that had it been during the heat of summer, I would have been on the lookout for snakes, even up there. But as it was, there were other surprises.

First, we came across the blue ribbon that Ruby had won for her Beefmaster tomatoes at the Maitlin County Fair. It was the same year as her head injury and Itasca's death. The ribbon was framed next to a photograph of a smiling Ruby in her sunflower party dress, straw hat, and white gloves. She shook hands with Horton Hall, star of the Supersonic Garden Fertilizer TV ads, just as she finished filming a commercial. It was a gig she'd won by entering his contest.

Next, Elvis's gospel albums were found carefully enclosed in huge Ziploc bags. Sandwiched in between the albums were a few letters written by Walt and Ruby, and two signed by Elvis.

"Love letters," said Evangeline. "I never knew they were there. What a treasure."

"Look at this one from Elvis," I said, handing her one yellowed page. I reached for a wooden box that rested near the albums and love letters, thinking that there might be more letters inside. What I found though, were Walt's treasures: an iron pull-toy shaped like a horse, a coin bank that looked like an Egyptian crow, a pocket watch with Ruby's picture inside, and a bill of sale for one Thunderbird car.

"My word," I said, my heart pounding. "I can't believe it!"

"Believe what?"

"Ruby's Thunderbird was sold to Walt from a dealership in Austin. Elvis never gave that car to Ruby, she only *thought* he did."

"You mean that Walt was the real Elvis?"

"Yes, and I'll bet that Ruby eventually figured it out. It was just the two of us who were fooled." Then I thought about the packages he'd sent us pretending our mother had, just hoping to make us feel better. "Walt loved playing Santa Claus when we needed to believe in magic the most."

"What about the day when Elvis called and invited her to lunch?"

"I'll bet that Walt had a friend who impersonated Elvis."

Evangeline smiled sadly. "Maybe we didn't know what it felt like to grow up in a normal family, but we did know how it felt to be really loved. And Ruby…well, she was queen of Walt's universe."

The next day, we drove Ruby's Thunderbird to station KOFF, dropped off Elvis's records, and then headed to the Fireside Cemetery. We had arranged with Selma and the guys to meet them there at two o'clock. We had rounded up a thermos of steaming coffee and the transistor radio from the cellar. I had replaced the transistor's batteries and had wiped it clean.

By the time we reached the cemetery, Selma was shivering in her faux bobcat fur coat and pulling on her matching hat. It was a trick to get her tower of blonde hair underneath it, but she managed. The guys were hopping up and down to keep warm on this frosty late January morning.

"Did you girls take the scenic route?" inquired Selma.

"We're only three minutes late," I said.

"Three minutes might as well be three years in this cold."

I poured steaming cups of coffee into House of Cranbourne mugs and passed them around. Evangeline pulled out a love letter that Walt had written to Ruby during their dating years and read it aloud:

Dear Ruby,

I have missed you while you've been traveling with Pearl and Sapphire. I hope the train ride wasn't too rough, although I know you'd enjoy yourself, regardless.

Last night, I looked for the North Star because I knew you would too, just as we'd planned. The sky was too durned overcast, and I just couldn't see any stars. Well, that about covers the way I've been feeling since you've been gone, anyway. Without you, Ruby darling, I have no starlight and no direction. I am lost as a spotted pup in a cave.

When you return to Fireside, I'll be waiting. I know now what's important in this life, and I don't want to miss out. When you step off that train from Memphis, I'll have something to ask you. If you say yes, I'll spend the rest of my life dancing with you.

Love,

Walt

William raised his cup of coffee into the air and said, "I'd like to make a toast."

"Oh boy," said Jacob. "It's nap time."

William ignored his cousin and continued. "Here's to Walt and Ruby and to the transcendent love they shared. I have no doubt that they are slow dancing in heaven as I speak."

"Or that Elvis is singing for them," said Evangeline. "I can say that now because I finally believe that Elvis is really dead and not in Hawaii on vacation like I thought."

"I'll bet that once again they look as they did when we were kids. Like Gregory Peck and Jane Powell at their best," I said.

William said, "All right, let's get back to our toast." Then he looked directly into my eyes and continued. "It is important that we *pay attention* and not miss out on what's really essential in this life when we have the chance. Today, we look to Walt and Ruby as our shining example of all that is right and good in a marriage. The universe that was their relationship was ever expanding and brilliantly dynamic, like a supernova at the moment of explosion. Their love for one another, Juliet and Evangeline, was as captivating and beautiful as the Omega Nebula. What a privilege to have known them. How much we learned by simply having shared the same space at the same time. I am reminded of Walt's love of the Big Dipper and—"

Selma interrupted, "Honey, can I put my coffee mug down now? My arm's getting numb from holding this toasting pose. You sure do talk more than you did as a boy."

"Willy Billy, get on with it," said Jacob, grumbling.

"My audience is turning on me," said William sheepishly. "All right then, having said all that, we don't have to look to the cosmos to find that which is sublime."

"Even at home by the fireside, the human heart can outshine any star in the universe," I added.

"Well said!" William lifted his coffee cup into a semisalute as we looked at Walt and Ruby's twin-heart headstone. "To Walt and Ruby and the love they shared on earth. May it be even more wonderful in heaven."

"To Walt and Ruby!"

Acknowledgments

I would like to thank my good friend Linda Amey, author of many works, including the Blair Emerson Series, for her unending support and wisdom and for giving me a good push whenever I faltered.

I want to recognize my high school teacher, Bill Voron, who taught our class much about creative writing and literature and who possessed the patience of Job.

My brilliant and much-appreciated friends Karen and Jim Duban, thank you for your thoughtful guidance.

Thanks to my amazing mother, Carolyn Gipson, for having taught me to savor a good book and for countless sacrifices that made my life possible. I thank my children—Dustin and his wife, Ashley; Lauren; Elizabeth and her husband, Tim; Patricia and her husband, Mark—who are the best gifts I have ever received and who bring so much joy to a world that seems in perpetual chaos.

Special thanks to my younger sister, Kit, who used to outlast me on the swing set, outsmart me in hide-and-go-seek, and today can wrestle rattlers, build barns (with her husband, Al), and decorate cakes with the best of them; and to my witty brothers, Colin and Mike (now gone from us), whose endless knock-knock jokes and masquerades as Batman and Zorro as children helped create wonderful memories that are a healing salve upon the sometimes harsher days of adulthood.

I thank my sister-in-law Ruthie and her husband, Bob; sister-in-law Suzy; and mother-in-law, Billie Sue, for their loving prayers, insight, and support.

My sweet grandmother, Marie, who entertained me by spinning fabulous bedtime stories, ignited my imagination. My cherished father, Jules, gave me my love for foreign language and family history. And thanks go to his parents: Max, who loved to stargaze and would let us, as wild-eyed youngsters, comb his hair until we tired, and Opal, who whipped up miles of sweet butternut squash, fried chicken, and golden westerner cakes drizzled with powdered sugar icing still etched in my memory, and who was an expert (like Ruby) in the art of making all of us feel loved.

CPSIA information can be obtained
at www.ICGtesting.com
Printed in the USA
LVHW041700061120
670968LV00006B/950

9 781733 279130